COP KILLER

COP KILLER
THE STORY OF A CRIME

Maj Sjöwall · Per Wahlöö

Translated from the Swedish by Thomas Teal

VINTAGE BOOKS
A Division of Random House
New York

*Library of Congress Cataloging in Publication
Data*
Sjöwall, Maj, 1935–
  Cop killer.

  Translation of Polismördaren.
  I. Wahlöö, Per, 1926–   joint author.
  II. Title.
[PZ4.S61953Co 1978] [PT9876.29.J63]
839.7'3'74 77–16363
ISBN 0–394–72444–5

COP KILLER

1.

She reached the bus stop well ahead of the bus, which would not be along for half an hour yet. Thirty minutes of a person's life is not an especially long time. Besides, she was used to waiting and was always early. She thought about what she would make for dinner, and a little about what she looked like—her usual idle thoughts.

By the time the bus came, she would no longer have any thoughts at all. She had only twenty-seven minutes left to live.

It was a pretty day, clear and gusty, with a touch of early autumn chill in the wind, but her hair was too well processed to be affected by the weather.

What did she look like?

Standing there by the side of the road this way, she might have been in her forties, a rather tall, sturdy woman with straight legs and broad hips and a little secret fat that she was very much afraid might show. She dressed mostly according to fashion, often at the expense of comfort, and on this blustery fall day she was wearing a bright green 1930s coat, nylon stockings, and thin brown patent leather boots with platform soles. She was carrying a small square handbag with a large brass clasp slung over her left shoulder. This too was brown, as were her suede gloves. Her blond hair had been well sprayed, and she was carefully made up.

She didn't notice him until he stopped. He leaned over and threw open the passenger door.

"Want a lift?" he said.

"Yes," she said, a little flurried. "Sure. I didn't think . . ."

"What didn't you think?"

"Well, I didn't expect to get a ride. I was going to take the bus."

"I knew you'd be here," he said. "And it's not out of my way, as it happens. Jump in, now, look alive."

Look alive. How many seconds did it take her to climb in and sit down beside the driver? Look alive. He drove fast, and they were quickly out of town.

She was sitting with her handbag in her lap, slightly tense, flustered perhaps, or at least somewhat surprised. Whether happily or unhappily it was impossible to say. She didn't know herself.

She looked at him from the side, but the man's attention seemed wholly concentrated on the driving.

He swung off the main road to the right, but then turned again almost immediately. The same procedure was repeated, and the road grew steadily worse. It was questionable whether it could be called a road any more or not.

"What are you going to do?" she said, with a frightened little giggle.

"You'll find out."

"Where?"

"Here," he said and braked to a stop.

Ahead of him he could see his own wheeltracks in the moss. They were not many hours old.

"Over there," he said with a nod. "Behind the woodpile. That's a good place."

"Are you kidding?"

"I never kid about things like that."

He seemed hurt or upset by the question.

2

"But my coat," she said.

"Leave it here."

"But . . ."

"There's a blanket."

He climbed out, walked around, and held the door for her.

She accepted his help and took off the coat. Folded it neatly and placed it on the seat beside her handbag.

"There."

He seemed calm and collected, but he didn't take her hand as he walked slowly toward the woodpile. She followed along behind.

It was warm and sunny behind the woodpile and sheltered from the wind. The air was filled with the buzzing of flies and the fresh smell of greenery. It was still almost summer, and this summer had been the warmest in the weather bureau's history.

It wasn't actually an ordinary woodpile but rather a stack of beech logs, cut in sections and piled about six feet high.

"Take off your blouse."

"Yes," she said shyly.

He waited patiently while she undid the buttons.

Then he helped her off with the blouse, gingerly, without touching her body.

She was left standing with the garment in one hand, not knowing what to do with it.

He took it from her and placed it carefully over the edge of the pile of logs. An earwig zigzagged across the fabric.

She stood before him in her skirt, her breasts heavy in the skin-colored bra, her eyes on the ground, her back against the even surface of sawed timber.

The moment had come to act, and he did so with

3

such speed and suddenness that she never had time to grasp what was happening. Her reactions had never been especially quick.

He grabbed the waistband at her navel with both hands and ripped open her skirt and her pantyhose in a single violent motion. He was strong, and the fabric gave instantly, with a rasping snarl like the sound of old canvas being torn. The skirt fell to her calves, and he jerked her pantyhose and panties down to her knees, then pulled up the left cup of her bra so that her breast flopped down, loose and heavy.

Only then did she raise her head and look into his eyes. Eyes that were filled with disgust, loathing, and savage delight.

The idea of screaming never had time to take shape in her mind. For that matter, it would have been pointless. The place had been chosen with care.

He raised his arms straight out and up, closed his powerful suntanned fingers around her throat, and strangled her.

The back of her head was pressed against the pile of logs, and she thought: My hair.

That was her last thought.

He held his grip on her throat a little longer than necessary.

Then he let go with his right hand and, holding her body upright with his left, he struck her as hard as he could in the groin with his right fist.

She fell to the ground and lay among the muskmadder and last year's leaves. She was essentially naked.

A rattling sound came from her throat. He knew this was normal and that she was already dead.

Death is never very pretty. In addition, she had never been pretty during her lifetime, not even when she was young.

4

Lying there in the forest undergrowth, she was, at best, pathetic.

He waited a minute or so until his breathing had returned to normal and his heart had stopped racing.

And then he was himself again, calm and rational.

Beyond the pile of logs was a dense windfall from the big autumn storm of 1968, and beyond that, a dense planting of spruce trees about the height of a man.

He lifted her under the arms and was disgusted by the feel of the sticky, damp stubble in her armpits against the palms of his hands.

It took some time to drag her through the almost impassable terrain of sprawling tree trunks and uptorn roots, but he saw no need to hurry. Several yards into the spruce thicket there was a marshy depression filled with muddy yellow water. He shoved her into it and tramped her limp body down into the ooze. But first he looked at her for a moment. She was still tanned from the sunny summer, but the skin on her left breast was pale and flecked with light-brown spots. As pale as death, one might say.

He walked back to get the green coat and wondered for a moment what he should do with her handbag. Then he took the blouse from the timber pile, wrapped it around the purse, and carried everything back to the muddy pool. The color of the coat was rather striking, so he fetched a suitable stick and pushed the coat, the blouse, and the handbag as deep as he could down into the mud.

He spent the next quarter of an hour collecting spruce branches and chunks of moss. He covered the pool so thoroughly that no casual passerby would ever notice the mudhole existed.

He studied the result for a few minutes and made several corrections before he was satisfied.

Then he shrugged his shoulders and went back to where he was parked. He took a clean cotton rag from the floor and cleaned off his rubber boots. When he was done, he threw the rag on the ground. It lay there wet and muddy and clearly visible, but it didn't matter. A cotton rag can be anywhere. It proves nothing and can't be linked to anything in particular.

Then he turned the car around and drove away.

As he drove, it occurred to him that everything had gone well, and that she had got precisely what she deserved.

2.

A car stood parked outside an apartment house on Råsundavägen in Solna. It was a black Chrysler with white fenders and the word POLICE in big, white, block letters on the doors, hood, and trunk. Someone who had wanted to describe the vehicle's occupants even more exactly had used tape on the black-on-white license plate to cover the lower loop of the B in the first three letters, BIG.

The headlights and interior lights were turned off, but the glow from the streetlights glistened dully on shiny uniform buttons and white shoulder belts in the front seat.

Even though it was only 8:30 on a pretty, starlit, not especially chilly October evening, the long street was from time to time utterly deserted. There were lights in the windows of the apartment houses on either side, and from some of them came the cold blue glow of a TV screen.

An occasional passerby glanced curiously at the police car but lost interest quickly when its presence did not seem to be connected with any noticeable activity. The only thing to be seen was two ordinary policemen sitting lazily in their cruiser.

The men inside the car would not have objected to a little activity either. They had been sitting there over an hour, and all that time their attention had been fixed on a doorway across the street and on a lighted window on the first floor to the right of the doorway. But they knew how to wait. They had had lots of experience.

It might have occurred to anyone taking a closer look that these two men didn't really look like ordinary police constables. There was nothing wrong with their uniforms, which were entirely regulation and included shoulder belts and night sticks and pistols in holsters. What was wrong was that the driver, a corpulent man with a jovial mien and alert eyes, and his companion, thinner and slouching a bit, with one shoulder against the side window, both looked to be about fifty years old. As a rule, patrol cars are manned by young men in good physical condition, and where exceptions to this rule occur, the older man is usually paired with a younger companion.

A patrol car crew whose combined ages exceeded 100 years, as in this case, had to be regarded as a unique phenomenon. But there was an explanation.

The men in the black-and-white Chrysler were merely masquerading as patrolmen. And concealed behind this clever disguise were none other than the chief of the National Homicide Squad, Martin Beck, and his closest colleague, Lennart Kollberg.

The disguise had been Kollberg's idea, and was based on his knowledge of the man they were out to try and capture. The man's name was Lindberg, known as The Breadman, and he was a thief. Burglary was his specialty, but he also committed an occasional armed robbery and had even tried his hand at fraud, with less fortunate results. He had spent many years of his life behind bars but was a free man at the moment, having completed his most recent sentence. A freedom that would be short-lived if Martin Beck and Kollberg were successful.

Three weeks earlier, The Breadman had stepped into a jewelry store in downtown Uppsala, drawn a revolver, and forced the owner to hand over gems, watches, and cash to a combined value of nearly 200,000 crowns. Up to this point, that was all comparatively well and good, and The Breadman could have taken his haul and vanished, except for the fact that a sales clerk suddenly appeared from the inner reaches of the store, and The Breadman panicked and let fly a bullet that struck the woman in the forehead and killed her on the spot. The Breadman managed to make his escape, and two hours later, when the Stockholm police went to look for him at his girlfriend's apartment at Midsommarkransen, they found him in bed. His fiancée maintained that he had a cold and had not left the house in twenty-four hours, and a search produced nothing in the form of rings, jewels, watches, or money. The Breadman was taken in for questioning and confronted with the owner of the store, who was reluctant to make a positive identification because the robber had worn a mask. But the police felt no such reluctance. In the first place, they could assume that The Breadman was broke after his long stay in prison, in addition to which an informer had told them that The Breadman had mentioned a job he was planning "in another city," and in the second place, there was a witness who, two days before the crime, had seen The Breadman strolling down the street where the jewelry store was located, presumably to reconnoiter. The Breadman denied ever having been in Uppsala and finally had to be released for lack of evidence.

For three weeks now, the police had had The Breadman under constant surveillance, convinced that sooner or later he would visit the place where he had hidden the loot from the holdup. But The Breadman seemed to realize he was being shadowed. On a couple of occasions he had even waved to the plainclothesmen who were watching him, and his single purpose seemed to be to keep them occupied. He clearly had no money. At least he spent none, since his girlfriend had a job and provided him with food and shelter over and above the routine assistance he picked up at the social welfare office once a week.

In the end, Martin Beck decided to attend to the matter himself, and Kollberg hit on the brilliant idea of dressing themselves up as patrolmen. Since The Breadman could spot the most plainly clothed plainclothesman at a great distance but had always taken a contemptuous and nonchalant attitude toward uniformed personnel, the uniform, in this case, ought to be the best disguise. Such was Kollberg's reasoning, and Martin Beck, with some reservations, agreed with him.

Neither one of them had hoped for any immediate result of this new tactic, and they were pleasantly surprised when The Breadman jumped into a taxi as soon as he realized he was no longer being watched and had himself brought to this address on Råsundavägen. The very fact that he had taken a cab seemed to indicate a certain purposefulness, and they were convinced that something was up. If they could collar him with the

9

stolen goods and maybe even the murder weapon in his possession, that would definitely link him to the crime, and the case would be closed as far as they were concerned.

The Breadman had now been in the building for an hour and a half. They had had a glimpse of him in the window to the right of the doorway an hour earlier, but nothing had happened since then.

Kollberg was starting to get hungry. He was often hungry, and he often talked about losing weight. Every now and then he would go on some new diet, but he generally gave up pretty quickly. He was at least forty pounds overweight, but he worked out regularly and was in good physical condition. When occasion demanded, he was astonishingly quick and lithe for the size of his body and his age, which was nearly fifty.

"It's a hell of a long time since I had anything in my belly," Kollberg said.

Martin Beck didn't answer. He wasn't hungry, but he had a sudden longing for a cigarette. He had pretty much stopped smoking two years before, after a serious gunshot wound in the chest.

"A man my size really needs a little more than one hard-boiled egg a day," Kollberg went on.

If you didn't eat so much you wouldn't be that size and you wouldn't need to eat so much, Martin Beck thought, but he said nothing. Kollberg was his best friend, and it was a touchy subject. He didn't want to hurt his feelings and he knew Kollberg was in an especially bad mood whenever he was hungry. He also knew that Kollberg had urged his wife to keep him on a reducing diet that consisted exclusively of hard-boiled eggs. The diet was not a great success, however, since breakfast was the only meal he ate at home. He ate his other meals out, or at the police canteen, and they did not consist of hard-boiled eggs—Martin Beck could vouch for that.

Kollberg nodded in the direction of a brightly lit pastry shop half a block away.

"I don't suppose you'd . . ."

Martin Beck opened the door on the curb side and put out one foot.

"Sure. What do you want? Danish?"

"Yes, and a *mazarin*," Kollberg said.

Martin Beck came back with a bag of pastry, and they sat quietly and watched the building where The Breadman was while Kollberg ate, dribbling crumbs all over his jump suit. When he was done eating, he pushed the seat back one more notch and loosened his shoulder belt.

"What have you got in that holster?" Martin Beck asked.

Kollberg unbuttoned the holster and handed him the weapon. It was a toy pistol of Italian manufacture, well-made and massive and almost as heavy as Martin Beck's own Walther, but incapable of firing anything but caps.

"Nice," said Martin Beck. "Wish I'd had one like that when I was a kid."

It was common knowledge on the force that Lennart Kollberg refused to carry arms. Most people were under the impression that his refusal was based on some kind of pacifist principles and that he wanted to set a good example, since he was the police department's most enthusiastic advocate of eliminating weapons altogether under normal circumstances.

And all of that was true, but it was only half the truth. Martin Beck was one of the few people who knew of the primary reason for Kollberg's stand.

Lennart Kollberg had once shot and killed a man. It had happened more than twenty years before, but Kollberg had never been able to forget, and it was a good many years now since he had carried a weapon, even on critical and dangerous assignments.

The incident took place in August 1952, while Kollberg was attached to the second Söder precinct in Stockholm. Late one evening, there was an alarm from Långholm Prison, where three armed men had attempted to free a prisoner and had shot and wounded one of the guards. By the time the emergency squad with Kollberg reached the prison, the men had smashed their car into a railing up on Väster Bridge while trying to get away, and one of the men had been captured. The other two had managed to escape by running into Långholm Park on the other side of the bridge abutment. Both of them were thought to be armed, and since Kollberg was considered a good shot, he was included in the group that was sent into the park to try and surround the men.

With his pistol in hand, he had climbed down toward the water and then followed the shore away from the glow of the lights up on the bridge, listening and peering into the darkness. After a while, he stopped on a smooth granite outcropping that projected out into the bay and bent over and dipped one hand in the water, which felt warm and soft. When he straightened up again, a shot rang out, and he felt the bullet graze the sleeve of his coat before it hit the water several yards behind him. The man who fired it had been somewhere in the darkness among the bushes on the slope above him. Kollberg immediately threw himself flat on his face and squirmed into the protective vegetation along the shore. Then he started to crawl up toward a boulder that loomed over the spot where he thought the shot had come from. And sure enough, when he reached the huge rock he could see the man outlined against the light, open water of the bay. He was only fifty or sixty feet away. He was turned halfway toward Kollberg, holding his pistol ready in his raised hand and moving his head slowly from side to side. Beside him was the steep slope down into Riddar Bay.

Kollberg aimed carefully for the man's right hand. Just as his finger squeezed off the shot, someone suddenly appeared behind his target and threw himself toward the man's arm and Kollberg's bullet and then just as suddenly vanished again down the hillside.

Kollberg did not immediately realize what had happened. The man started running, and Kollberg shot again and this time hit him in the knee. Then he walked over and looked down the hill.

Down at the edge of the water lay the man he had killed. A young policeman from his own precinct. They had often been on duty together and always got along unusually well.

The story was hushed up, and Kollberg's name was never even mentioned in connection with it. Officially, the young policeman died of an accidental bullet wound, a wild shot from nowhere, while pursuing a dangerous criminal. Kollberg's chief gave him a little lecture in which he warned him against brooding and self-reproach and closed by pointing out that Charles XII himself had once shot to death his head groom and close friend through carelessness and inadvertence and that consequently it was the sort of accident that could happen to the best of men. And that was supposed to be the end of it. But Kollberg never really recovered from the shock, and for many years now, as a result, he always carried a cap pistol whenever he needed to appear to be armed.

Neither Kollberg nor Martin Beck thought about any of this as they sat in the squad car waiting for The Breadman to show himself.

Kollberg yawned and squirmed in his seat. It was uncomfortable sitting behind the wheel, and the uniform he had on was too tight. He couldn't remember the last time he'd worn one, but it was definitely a long time ago. He had borrowed the one he was wearing, and even though it was small, it was not nearly as tight as his own old uniform would have been, which was hanging on a hook in a closet at home.

He glanced at Martin Beck, who had sunk deeper into the seat and was staring out through the windshield.

Neither one of them said anything. They had known each other for a long time; they had been together on the job and off for many years and had no need to talk just for the sake of talking. They had spent innumerable evenings this same way—in a car on some dark street, waiting.

Since he became chief of the National Homicide Squad, Martin Beck did not actually need to do much trailing and surveillance—he had a staff to attend to that. But he often did it anyway, even though that kind of assignment was usually deadly dull. He didn't want to lose touch with this side of the job simply because he'd been made chief and had to spend more and more of his time dealing with all the troublesome demands made by a growing bureaucracy. Even if the one did not, unfortunately, preclude the other, he preferred sitting and yawning in a squad car with Kollberg to sitting and trying not to yawn in a meeting with the National Police Commissioner.

Martin Beck liked neither the bureaucracy, the meetings, nor the National Chief. But he liked Kollberg very much and had a hard time picturing this job without him. For a long time now, Kollberg had been expressing an occasional desire to leave the police force, but recently he had seemed more and more determined to carry out this impulse. Martin Beck wanted neither to encourage nor discourage him. He knew that Kollberg's feeling of solidarity with the police force had come to be virtually nonexistent and that his conscience bothered him more and more. He also knew it would be very hard for him to get a satisfying and roughly equivalent job. In a time of high unemployment, when young people in particular, but even university graduates and well-trained professionals of every description, were going without work, the prospects for a fifty-year-old former policeman were not especially bright. For purely selfish reasons, he wanted Kollberg to stay on, of course, but Martin Beck was not a particularly selfish person, and the thought of trying to influence Kollberg's decision had never crossed his mind.

Kollberg yawned again.

"Lack of oxygen," he said and rolled down the window. "We were lucky to have been patrolmen back in the days when cops still used their feet to walk on and not just to kick people with. You can get claustrophobia sitting in here like this."

Martin Beck nodded. He too disliked the feeling of being shut in.

Both Martin Beck and Kollberg had begun their careers as policemen in Stockholm in the mid-Forties. Martin Beck had worn down the pavements in Norrmalm, and Kollberg had trudged the narrow alleyways of the Old City. They hadn't known one another in those days, but their memories from that time were by and large the same.

It got to be 9:30. The pastry shop closed, and the

lights started going out in many of the windows down the street. The lights were still on in the apartment where The Breadman was visiting.

Suddenly the door opened across the street, and The Breadman stepped out onto the sidewalk. He had his hands in the pockets of his coat and a cigarette in the corner of his mouth.

Kollberg put his hands on the steering wheel and Martin Beck sat up in his seat.

The Breadman stood quietly outside the doorway, calmly smoking his cigarette.

"He doesn't have any bag with him," Kollberg said.

"He might have it in his pockets," Martin Beck said. "Or else he's sold it. We'll have to check on who he was visiting."

Several minutes passed. Nothing happened. The Breadman gazed up at the starry sky and seemed to be enjoying the evening air.

"He's waiting for a taxi," said Martin Beck.

"Seems to be taking a hell of a long time," Kollberg said.

The Breadman took a final drag on his cigarette and flicked it out into the street. Then he turned up his coat collar, stuck his hands back into his pockets, and started across the street toward the police car.

"He's coming over here," Martin Beck said. "Damn. What do we do? Take him in?"

"Yes," Kollberg said.

The Breadman walked slowly over to the car, leaned down, looked at Kollberg through the side window and started to laugh. Then he walked around behind the trunk and up onto the sidewalk. He opened the door to the front seat where Martin Beck was sitting, leaned over, and burst into a roar of laughter.

Martin Beck and Kollberg sat quietly and let him

laugh, for the simple reason that they didn't know what else to do.

The Breadman finally recovered somewhat from his paroxysms.

"Well, now," he said, "have you finally been demoted? Or is this some kind of a costume party?"

Martin Beck sighed and climbed out of the car. He opened the door to the back seat.

"In you go, Lindberg," he said. "We'll give you a lift to Västberga."

"Good enough," said The Breadman good-naturedly. "That's closer to home."

On the way in to Södra police station, The Breadman told them he'd been visiting his brother in Råsunda, which was quickly confirmed by a squad car despatched to the spot. There were no weapons, money, or stolen goods in the apartment. The Breadman himself was carrying twenty-seven crowns.

At a quarter to twelve they had to release him, and Martin Beck and Kollberg could start to think about going home.

"I never would have thought you guys had such a sense of humor," said The Breadman before he left. "First this bit with the costumes—now that was fun. But the part I liked best was writing PIG on the back of your car. I couldn't have done better myself."

They themselves were only moderately amused, but his hearty laughter reached them from a long way down the stairs. He sounded almost like The Laughing Policeman.

In point of fact, it didn't matter much. They would catch him soon enough. The Breadman was the type who always gets caught.

And for their own part, they would soon have quite other things to think about.

3.

The airport was a national disgrace and lived up to its reputation. The actual flight from Arlanda Airport in Stockholm had taken only fifty minutes, but now the plane had been circling over the southernmost part of the country for an hour and a half.

"Fog," was the laconic explanation.

And that was exactly what might have been expected, for the airfield had been built—once the inhabitants were displaced—in one of the foggiest spots in Sweden. And as if that weren't enough, it lay in the middle of a well-known migratory bird route and at a very uncomfortable distance from the city.

In addition, it had destroyed a natural wilderness that should have been protected by law. The damage was extensive and irreparable and constituted an act of gross ecological malfeasance, typical of the anti-humanitarian cynicism that had become increasingly characteristic of what the government called A More Compassionate Society. This expression, in turn, represented a cynicism so boundless that the common man had difficulty grasping it.

The pilot finally grew tired and brought the plane down fog or no fog, and a handful of pale, sweating passengers filed sparsely into the terminal building.

Inside, the very color scheme—gray and saffron yellow—seemed to underline the odor of incompetence and corruption.

Martin Beck had several unpleasant hours to look back upon. He had always loathed flying, and the new machines didn't make it any better. The jet had been a DC-9. It had begun by climbing precipitously to an altitude that was incomprehensible to the average earthbound human being. Then it had raced across the countryside at an abstract speed, only to conclude in a monotonous holding pattern. The liquid in the paper mugs was said to be coffee and produced immediate nausea. The air in the cabin was noxious and sticky, and his few fellow passengers were harried technocrats and businessmen who glanced constantly at their watches and shuffled nervously through the papers in their attaché cases.

The arrivals hall could not even be called uncomfortable. It was monstrous, a design catastrophe that would make a dusty bus station miles from anywhere seem lively and convivial by comparison. There was a hot dog stand that served an inedible, nutrition-free parody of food, a newsstand with a display of condoms and smutty magazines, some empty conveyor belts for luggage, and a number of chairs that might have been designed during the heyday of the Spanish Inquisition. Add a dozen yawning policemen and bored customs officials, all of them undoubtedly there against their will, and one taxicab, whose driver had fallen asleep with the latest issue of a pornographic magazine spread across the steering wheel.

Martin Beck waited an unreasonably long time for his small suitcase, picked it off the belt and stepped out into the autumn fog.

A passenger stepped into the cab, and it drove off.

No one inside the arrivals hall had said anything or indicated in any way that they recognized him. They had seemed apathetic, almost as if they had lost the power of speech, or, in any case, lost all interest in using it.

The chief of the National Homicide Squad had arrived, but no one seemed to appreciate the importance of that event. Not even the greenest of cub reporters could be bothered to drag themselves out here to enrich their lives with card games, overboiled wieners, and petrochemical soft drinks. Anyway, the so-called celebrities never showed up here.

There were two orange buses standing in front of the terminal. Plastic signs showed their destinations: Lund and Malmö. The drivers were smoking in silence.

The night was mild, and the air was humid. Misty halos surrounded the electric lights.

The buses drove off, one of them empty, the other with a single passenger. The other travelers hurried toward the long-term parking area.

Martin Beck's palms were still sweaty. He went back inside and searched out a men's room. The flushing mechanism was broken. There was a half-eaten hot dog and an empty vodka bottle in the urinal. Strands of hair clung to the greasy ring of dirt in the sink. The paper towel dispenser was empty.

This was Sturup Airport, Malmö. So new it still wasn't complete.

He doubted there was any point in completing it. In a way, it was perfect already—epitomized the fiasco.

Martin Beck dried his hands with his handkerchief. He went back outside and stood in the darkness for a moment feeling lonely.

He hadn't exactly expected the police band lined up in the arrivals hall, or the local chief of police out on horseback to receive him.

But perhaps he had expected something more than nothing at all.

He dug for change in his pocket and considered

searching for a pay phone that did not have the cord to its receiver cut or its coin slot stuffed with chewing gum.

Lights cut through the fog. A black-and-white patrol car came sneaking along the ramp and swung in toward the door of the huge saffron-yellow box.

It was moving slowly, and when it drew even with the solitary traveler it came to a stop. The side window was rolled down, and a red-haired person with skimpy police sideburns stared at him coldly.

Martin Beck said nothing.

After a minute or so the man raised his hand and beckoned to him with his finger. Martin Beck walked over to the car.

"What are you hanging around here for?"

"Waiting for transport."

"Waiting for transport! You don't say!"

"Perhaps you can help me."

The patrolman looked dumbfounded.

"Help you? What do you mean?"

"I've been delayed. I thought maybe I could use your radio."

"Who do you think you are?"

Without taking his eyes off Martin Beck, he threw several remarks back over his shoulder.

"Did you hear that? He says he thought maybe he could use our radio. I guess he thinks we're some kind of pimp service or something. Did you hear him?"

"I heard," said the other policeman wearily.

"Can you identify yourself?" said the first policeman.

Martin Beck put his hand to his back pocket, but changed his mind. He let his arm drop.

"Yes," he said. "But I'd really rather not."

He turned on his heel and walked back to his bag.

"Did you hear that?" the policeman said. "He says he'd rather not. He thinks he's pretty tough. Do you think he's tough?"

The sarcasm was so heavy that the words fell to the ground like bricks.

"Oh, forget it," said the man who was driving. "Let's not have any more trouble tonight, okay?"

The redhead stared hard at Martin Beck, for a long time. Then there was a mumbled conversation, and the car began to roll away. Sixty feet off it stopped again so the policemen could observe him in the rear-view mirror.

Martin Beck looked in a different direction and sighed heavily.

As he stood there at this moment, he could have been taken for anyone at all.

During the last year he had managed to get rid of some of his police mannerisms. He no longer invariably clasped his hands behind his back, for example, and he could now stand in one place for a short time without rocking back and forth on the balls of his feet.

Although he had put on a little weight, he was still, at fifty-one, a tall, fit, well-built man, with a slight stoop. He also dressed more comfortably than he had, though there was no labored youthfulness in his choice of clothes—sandals, Levi's, turtleneck, and a blue Dacron jacket. On the other hand, it might be considered unconventional for a detective superintendent of police.

For the two patrolmen in the squad car it was obviously difficult to swallow. They were still pondering the situation when a tomato-colored Opel Ascona swung up in front of the terminal building and braked to a stop. A man climbed out and walked around the car.

"Allwright?" he said.

"Beck."

"People generally get a chuckle out of that."

"A chuckle?"

"You know, they laugh at the way I say Allwright."

"I see."

Laughter did not come quite that easily to Martin Beck.

"And you'll have to admit it is a silly name for a policeman. Herrgott Allwright. So I usually introduce myself that way, like it was a question. Allwright? It sort of flusters people."

He stowed the suitcase in the trunk of his car.

"I'm late," he said. "No one knew where the plane was going to come down. I took a chance it would be Copenhagen, as usual. So I was already in Limhamn when I got the word it had landed here. Sorry."

He peered inquiringly at Martin Beck, as if trying to determine whether his exalted guest was out of sorts.

Martin Beck shrugged his shoulders.

"It doesn't matter," he said. "I'm not in any hurry."

Allwright threw a glance at the patrol car, which remained in position with its engine idling.

"This isn't my district," he said with a grin. "They're from Malmö. We'd better go before we get arrested."

The man obviously had a ready laugh, which, moreover, was soft and infectious.

But still Martin Beck wouldn't smile. Partly because there wasn't all that much to smile at, and partly because he was trying to form an opinion of the other man—sketch out a sort of preliminary description.

Allwright was a short, bow-legged man—short, that is, for the police department. With his green rubber boots, his grayish-brown twill suit, and the sun-bleached safari hat on the back of his head, he looked like a farmer, or, at any rate, like a man with his own territory. His face was sunburned and weatherbitten, and there were laugh lines around the corners of his lively brown eyes. And yet he was representative of a certain category of rural policeman. A type of man who didn't fit in with the new conformist style and was therefore on his way to dying out, but was not yet completely extinct.

He was probably older than Martin Beck, but he had the advantage of working in calmer and healthier surroundings, which is not to say that they were calm and healthy, by any means.

"I've been here almost twenty-five years. But this is a first for me. The National Homicide Squad, from Stockholm, on a case like this."

Allwright shook his head.

"I'm sure everything will work out fine," said Martin Beck. "Or else . . ."

He finished the sentence silently to himself: Or else it won't work out at all.

"Exactly," Allwright said. "You people from National Homicide understand this kind of case."

Martin Beck wondered if that was the polite plural, or if he were really referring to both of them. Lennart Kollberg was on his way from Stockholm by car and could be expected the next day. He had been Martin Beck's right-hand man for many years.

"The story's going to leak out pretty soon," Allwright said. "I saw a couple of characters in town today—reporters, I think."

He shook his head again.

"We're not used to this sort of thing. All this attention."

"Someone has disappeared," said Martin Beck. "There's nothing so unusual about that."

24

"No, but that's not the crux of the matter. Not at all. Do you want to hear about it?"

"Not right now, thanks. If you won't take it amiss."

"I never take anything amiss. Not my style."

He laughed again, but stopped himself and added, soberly, "But then I'm not in charge of the investigation."

"Maybe she'll turn up. That's usually the way."

Allwright shook his head for the third time.

"I don't think so," he said. "In case my opinion makes any difference. Anyway, it's an open and shut case. Everyone says so. They're probably right. All this nonsense with the . . . I mean, excuse me, but calling in National Homicide and all that is just because of the unusual circumstances."

"Who says so?"

"The chief. The boss."

"The Chief of Police in Trelleborg?"

"That's the man. But you're right, let's let it go for now. This is the new airport road we're on. And now we're coming out on the expressway from Malmö to Ystad. Also brand new. You see the lights off to the right?"

"Yes."

"That's Svedala. Still part of Malmö Police District. It's one hell of a district for sheer size."

They had emerged from the fog belt, which was apparently confined to the immediate vicinity of the airport. The sky was full of stars. Martin Beck had rolled down the side window and was breathing in the smells from outside. Gasoline and diesel oil, but also a fertile mixture of humus and manure. It seemed heavy and saturated. Nourishing. Allwright drove only a few hundred yards along the expressway. Then he turned off to the right, and the country air grew richer.

There was one special smell.

"Stalks and beet pulp," Allwright said. "Reminds me of when I was a kid."

On the expressway there had been passenger cars and enormous trailer trucks thundering along in a steady stream, but here they seemed to be alone. The night lay dark and velvety on the rolling plain.

It was clear that Allwright had driven this same stretch of highway hundreds of times before and literally knew every curve. He held a steady speed and hardly even needed to look at the road.

He lit a cigarette and offered the pack.

"No, thank you," said Martin Beck.

He had smoked no more than five cigarettes over the last two years.

"If I understood correctly, you wanted to stay at the inn," Allwright said.

"Yes, that would be fine."

"Anyway, I've arranged for a room there."

"Good."

The lights of a small town appeared ahead of them.

"We have arrived, as it were," said Allwright. "This is Anderslöv."

The streets were empty, but well lit.

"No night life here," Allwright said. "Quiet and peaceful. Nice. I've lived here all my life and never had a thing to complain about. Before now."

It looked awfully damned dead, Martin Beck thought. But maybe that's the way it was supposed to look.

Allwright slowed down and pointed to a low, yellow brick building.

"Police station," he said. "Of course it's closed at the moment. But I can open up if you like."

"Not for my sake."

"The inn's right around the corner. The garden we just drove by belongs to it. But the restaurant isn't open at this hour. If you want, we can go to my place and have a sandwich and a beer."

Martin Beck wasn't hungry. The flight down had taken away his appetite. He declined politely. And then he said:

"Is it a long way to the beach?"

The other man didn't seem to be surprised by the question. Perhaps Allwright was not a man to be easily surprised.

"No," he said. "I wouldn't say that."

"How long would it take to drive there?"

"About fifteen minutes. Tops."

"Would you mind?"

"Not a bit."

Allwright swung the car onto what looked to be the main street.

"This is the town's main attraction," he said. "The Highway. Highway with a capital H. Formerly the main road from Malmö to Ystad. When we turn off to the right, you will be south of The Highway. And then you'll really be in Skåne."

The side road was winding, but Allwright drove it with the same easy confidence. They passed farms and white churches.

Ten minutes later they could smell the sea. A few minutes more and they were at the beach.

"Do you want me to stop?"

"Yes, please."

"If you want to go wading, I've got an extra pair of rubber boots in the trunk," Allwright said, and chuckled.

"Thanks, I'd like to."

Martin Beck pulled on the boots. They were a little too tight, but he wasn't planning any lengthy excursions.

"Where are we now, exactly?"

"In Böste. Those lights to the right are Trelleborg. The lighthouse on the left is Smygehuk. Further than that you can't get."

Smygehuk was Sweden's southernmost point.

To judge by the lights and the reflection in the sky, Trelleborg must be a large city. A big brightly lit passenger ship was headed for the harbor—probably the train ferry from Sassnitz in East Germany.

The Baltic was heaving listlessly against the shore. The water disappeared down into the fine-grained sand with a soft hiss.

Martin Beck stepped on the swaying rampart of seaweed and then took a couple of steps out into the water. It felt pleasantly cool through the leg of the boot.

He bent forward, cupped his hands and filled them. Rinsed his face and drew the cold water in through his nose. It tasted fresh and salty.

The air was damp. It smelled of seaweed, fish, and tar.

Several yards away he could see nets hung up to dry and the outlines of a fishing boat.

What was it Kollberg always said?

The best part of Homicide was that it got you out of the city now and then.

Martin Beck lifted his head and listened. All he could hear was the sea.

After a while he walked back to the car. Allwright was leaning against the fender, smoking. Martin Beck nodded.

He would study the case in the morning.

He didn't expect much of it. These things were usually just routine. The same old stories over and over again, usually tragic and depressing.

The breeze from the sea was mild and cool.

A freighter plowed by along the dark horizon. Westward. He could see the green starboard lantern and some lights amidships.

He longed to be aboard.

4.

Martin Beck was wide awake as soon as he opened his eyes. The room was spartan but pleasant. There were two beds, and a window facing north. The beds were parallel, three feet apart. His suitcase lay on one of them and he on the other. On the floor was the book of which he had read half a page and two picture captions before he fell asleep. It was a book in the series "Famous Passenger Liners of the Past," and its title was *The Turboelectric Quadruplescrew Liner "Normandie."*

He looked at the clock. 7:30. Scattered sounds came from outside—automobiles and voices. Somewhere in the building a toilet flushed. Something was different. He identified it right away. He had been sleeping in pajamas, which he now only did when he was traveling.

Martin Beck got up, walked over to the window, and looked out. The weather looked fine. The sun was shining on the lawn behind the inn.

He washed and dressed quickly and went downstairs. For a moment he considered having breakfast, but he dismissed the thought. He had never liked eating in the morning, especially not as a child when his mother had forced cocoa and three sandwiches down his throat before he left home. He had often thrown up on his way to school.

Instead of breakfast, he located a one-crown piece in his pants pocket and stuffed it into the slot machine that stood to the right of the entrance. Pulled the handle, got three cherries, and pocketed his winnings. Then he left the building, walked diagonally across the cobblestone square, past the state liquor store, which wasn't open yet, rounded two corners, and found himself at the police station. The volunteer fire department was apparently housed next door, for a ladder truck had been backed up in front of the building. He practically had to crawl under the revolving ladder stage in order to get by. A man in greasy overalls was fixing something on the truck.

"Hi, how are ya?" he said cheerfully, and in defiance of all rules of Swedish formality.

Martin Beck was startled. This was clearly an unconventional town.

"Hi," he said.

The police station door was locked, and taped to the glass was a piece of cardboard on which someone had written in ballpoint pen:

> *Office Hours*
> *Weekdays 8:30 a.m.—12 noon*
> *1:00 p.m.—2:30 p.m.*
> *Thursdays also 6 p.m.—7 p.m.*
> *Closed Saturdays*

Sundays were not mentioned. Crime had probably been discontinued on Sundays, perhaps even forbidden.

30

Martin Beck stared at the sign thoughtfully. To anyone coming from Stockholm, it was hard to imagine things could ever be like this.

Maybe he ought to have some breakfast after all.

"Herrgott will be right back," said the man in overalls. "He went out with the dog ten minutes ago."

Martin Beck nodded.

"Are you the famous detective?"

It was a difficult question, and he didn't answer right away.

The man went on working with something on the fire truck.

"No offense," he said, without turning his head. "But I heard there was supposed to be some famous cop at the inn. And then I didn't recognize you."

"Yes, I guess that must be me," said Martin Beck uncertainly.

"So that means Folke's going to jail."

"What makes you think so?"

"Oh, everyone knows that."

"Really?"

"It's too bad. His smoked herring were awful damned good."

The man brought the conversation to a close by crawling in under the fire truck and disappearing.

If this was the general opinion, then clearly Allwright had not exaggerated.

Martin Beck stayed where he was, rubbing the edge of his scalp thoughtfully.

A minute or two later, Herrgott Allwright appeared on the other side of the fire truck. He had the same lion-hunter's hat on the back of his head, and was otherwise dressed in a checkered flannel shirt, uniform trousers, and light suede shoes. A large gray dog

31

strained at its leash. They edged under the ladder, and the dog rose up on its hind legs, put its front paws on Martin Beck's chest, and began to lick his face.

"Down, Timmy!" Allwright said. "Down, I said! What a dog!"

It was a heavy dog, and Martin Beck reeled back two steps.

"Down, Timmy!" Allwright said.

The dog dropped to the ground and turned around three times. Then it sat down reluctantly, looked at its master, and pricked up its ears.

"Probably the world's worst police dog. But he has an excuse. No training. No obedience. But since I'm a policeman, that does make him a police dog. In a way."

Allwright laughed, without much cause. As far as Martin Beck could see.

"When HSC was here I took him to the game."

"HSC?"

"Helsingborg Sports Club. Soccer team. You're not a soccer fan, are you?"

"Not really."

"Well, he got away from me, of course, and ran out on the field. Took the ball away from one of the Anderslöv players. Almost caused a riot. And I got chewed out by the referee. It's the most dramatic thing that's happened around here for years. Until now, of course. What was I supposed to do? Arrest the referee? From a purely legal point of view, I have no idea what the status of a soccer referee might be."

He laughed again.

"I walk out on the field and collar the ref. 'Allwright?' I say. 'Police Inspector. Come along with me, please—interfering with an officer in the performance of his duties.' It wouldn't wash. So I just stood there like an idiot."

Allwright laughed, and Martin Beck couldn't help asking him why.

"Well, I was thinking—what if Timmy had scored a goal? What would have happened then?"

Martin Beck was completely at a loss for what to say.

"Oh, hi there," Allwright said.

"Morning, Herrgott," said a sepulchral voice from underneath the fire truck.

"Say, Jöns, do you have to park that crate right in front of police headquarters?"

"You're not even open yet," said Jöns.

His voice sounded muffled.

"But I'm about to."

Allwright rattled his keys, and the dog jumped to its feet.

Allwright opened the door and threw a quick glance at Martin Beck.

"Welcome," he said, "to the Anderslöv local station house, Trelleborg Police District. This is actually the village hall. Health insurance office, police station, library. I live upstairs. It's all brand new and spic and span, as they say. Terrific jail. Got to use it twice last year. Here's my office. Come on in."

It was a pleasant room, with a desk and two easy chairs for visitors. The large windows looked out on a kind of patio. The dog lay down under the desk.

Behind the desk were shelves full of large volumes. The Swedish Statutes, mostly, but a lot of other books as well.

"They've been on the phone from Trelleborg already," Allwright said. "The Superintendent. The National Commissioner too. Seemed disappointed you were staying here."

He sat down at his desk and shook out a cigarette.

Martin Beck took a seat in one of the easy chairs.

Allwright crossed his legs and poked at his hat, which he'd put down on the desk.

"They'll be driving up today, for sure. At least the Superintendent will. Unless we drag ourselves down to Trelleborg."

"I think I'd prefer to stay here."

"Okay."

He shuffled among the papers on his desk.

"Here's the report. Want to look?"

Martin Beck thought for a moment.

"Can you give it to me verbally?" he said.

"Love to."

Martin Beck felt comfortable. He liked Allwright. Everything was going to work out fine.

"How many people do you have here?"

"Five. One secretary. Nice girl. Three patrolmen, when there aren't any vacancies. One patrol car. By the way, have you had any breakfast?"

"No."

"Want some?"

"Yes."

He was actually starting to feel a little hungry.

"Good," said Allwright. "Now how shall we do this? Let's go up to my place. Britta will come and open up at eight-thirty. If anything special happens, she'll call up and let us know. I've got coffee and tea and bread and butter and cheese and marmalade and eggs. I don't know what all. You want coffee?"

"I'd rather have tea."

"I drink tea myself. So I'll take the report with me, and we'll go on upstairs. Okay?"

The apartment upstairs was pleasant and full of character, neatly arranged, but not for family life. It was immediately apparent that whoever lived there was a bachelor, with a bachelor's habits, and had been for some time, perhaps his whole life. There were two hunting rifles and an old police saber hanging on the wall. Allwright's service pistol, a Walther 7.65, lay disassembled on a piece of oilcloth on what was presumably the dining room table.

Guns were clearly one of his hobbies.

"I like to shoot," he said.

He laughed.

"But not at people," he added. "I never have shot a person. In fact, I've never even aimed at anyone. For that matter, I never carry it on me. I've got a revolver, too, a competition model. But that's locked in the vault downstairs."

"Are you good?"

"Oh, you know. Win once in a while. That is to say, rarely. I've got the badge, of course."

That could mean only one thing. The gold badge. Which only elite shots ever won.

For his own part, Martin Beck shot like a rake. There had never been any question of a gold badge. Or any other kind. On the other hand, he had aimed at people, and shot at them, too. But never killed anyone. There was always a silver lining.

"I could clear off the table," said Allwright without any particular enthusiasm. "I mostly just eat in the kitchen."

"So do I," said Martin Beck.

"Are you a bachelor too?"

"More or less."

"I see."

Allwright didn't seem interested.

Martin Beck was divorced and had two grown children—a daughter who was twenty-two and a son eighteen.

"More or less" meant that for the past year he'd had

35

a woman living with him pretty regularly. Her name was Rhea Nielsen, and he was probably in love with her. Having her around had changed his home—for the better, it seemed to him.

But that was no concern of Allwright's, who seemed to be utterly indifferent to how the chief of the National Homicide Squad had arranged his private life.

The kitchen was practical and efficient, with all the modern conveniences. Allwright put a pot of water on the burner, took four eggs from the refrigerator, and made tea in the coffeepot—that is, he heated water in it and put the teabags in the cups. An effective method, though not one to satisfy the connoisseur.

With a feeling that he ought to be doing something useful, Martin Beck put two pieces of sliced bread in the electric toaster.

"They make some really good bread around here," Allwright said. "But I usually just buy Co-op. I like the Co-op."

Martin Beck did not like the Co-op, but he didn't say so.

"It's so close," Allwright said. "Everything's close around here. I've got an idea that Anderslöv has the highest commercial concentration in Sweden. Or pretty near anyway."

They ate. Washed the dishes. Went back to the living room.

Allwright took the folded report out of his back pocket.

"Papers," he said. "I'm sick of paper. This has gotten to be a paper job—nothing but applications and licenses and copies and crap. In the old days, being a policeman here was dangerous. Twice a year, at beet season. There'd be all sorts of people here. Some of them used to drink and fight like you wouldn't believe. And sometimes you'd have to go in and break it up. And that meant being quick with your fists, if you wanted to save your looks. It was tough, but it was fun too, in a way. Now it's different. Automated, mechanical."

He paused.

"But that isn't what I was going to talk about. For that matter, I don't need the report. The facts are pretty damned simple. The woman in question is named Sigbrit Mård. She's thirty-eight years old and works in a pastry shop in Trelleborg. Divorced, no children, lives alone in a little house in Domme. That's out on the road toward Malmö."

Allwright looked at Martin Beck. His expression was grim, but still full of humor.

"Toward Malmö," he repeated. "That is to say, west of here on Highway 101."

"You don't have much faith in my sense of direction," said Martin Beck.

"You wouldn't be the first person to get lost on the Skåne Plains," Allwright said. "Speaking of which . . ."

"Yes?"

"Well, the last time I was in Stockholm—and I hope to heaven it was the last time—I was looking for the National Police Administration and wandered into Communist Party Headquarters instead. Ran into the head of the Party himself on the stairs and wondered what the hell he was doing at the NPA. But he was very nice. Took me where I wanted to go. Walked his bicycle the whole way."

Martin Beck laughed.

Allwright took the opportunity of joining in.

"But that wasn't all. The next day I thought I'd go up and say hello to your Commissioner. The old one, the one who used to be in Malmö. I don't know the new one, thank God. So I went to the City Hall, and some sort of guard tried to give me a tour of the Blue Gallery. When I finally managed to tell him what I wanted, he sent me over to Scheelegatan and I wandered into the courthouse. The guard wanted to know which room my case was coming up in and what I was on trial for. By the time I finally got to the police building on Agnegatan, Lüning had gone for the day. So that took care of that. I took the night train home. Had a wonderful time all the way. South. Three hundred and fifty miles. What a difference."

He looked thoughtful.

"Stockholm," he said. "What a miserable city. But then, of course, you like it."

"Lived there all my life," said Martin Beck.

"Malmö's better," Allwright said. "Though not much. I wouldn't want to work there, unless they made me Commissioner or something. But let's not even talk about Stockholm."

He laughed loudly.

"Sigbrit Mård," said Martin Beck.

"Sigbrit had the day off that day. And she'd left her car to be fixed, so she took the bus to Anderslöv. Ran some errands. Went to the bank and the post office. And then disappeared. She didn't take the bus. The driver knows her, and he knows she wasn't on board. No one's seen her since. That was the seventeenth of October. It was about one o'clock when she left the post office. Her car, a VW, is still at the garage. There's nothing there. I went over it myself. And we took some samples and sent them to the lab in Helsingborg. All negative. Not a clue, as it were."

"Do you know her? Personally?"

"Yes, sure. Until this back-to-nature kick got started, I knew every soul in the district. It's not so easy any more. People live in old abandoned houses and dilapidated outbuildings. They don't register in the township, and when you drive out there, often as not they've already moved. And someone else has moved in. The only thing left is the goat and the macrobiotic vegetable garden."

"But Sigbrit Mård is different?"

"Yes, indeed. She's one of the ordinary types. She's lived here for twenty years. She comes from Trelleborg, originally. She seems like a stable sort of person. Always held her jobs, and like that. Highly normal. Maybe a little frustrated."

He lit a cigarette, after inspecting it thoughtfully.

"But then that's normal in this country," he went on. "For example, I smoke too much. That's probably frustration too."

"So she could simply have run away."

Allwright bent down and scratched the dog behind the ears.

"Yes," he said finally. "That's a possibility. But I don't believe it. This isn't the sort of place you can run away from just like that, without anyone's noticing. And people don't leave their homes completely intact. I went over the house with the detectives from Trelleborg. Everything was still there, all her papers and personal property. Jewelry and all that sort of thing. The coffeepot and her cup were still on the table. It all looked as if she'd gone out for a while and expected to be right back."

"Then what *do* you believe?"

This time Allwright's answer was even longer in coming. He held his cigarette in his left hand and let the dog chew playfully on his right. Every trace of laughter was gone from his face.

"I believe she's dead," he said.

And that was all he said on the subject.

From a distance came the sound of heavy traffic thundering along the highway.

Allwright looked up.

"Most of the big trucks still take this road from Malmö to Ystad," he said. "Even though the new Route 11 is a lot faster. Truck drivers are creatures of habit."

"And this business with Bengtsson?" said Martin Beck.

"You ought to know more about him than I do."

"Maybe. Maybe not. We got him for a sex murder almost ten years ago. After a lot of ifs and buts. He was an odd man. But what happened to him afterward, I don't know."

"I know," Allwright said. "Everyone in town here knows. They declared him sane, and he spent seven and a half years in prison. Eventually he moved down here and bought a little house. He had some money, apparently, because he also got hold of a boat and an old station wagon. He makes a living smoking fish. Catches some of it himself and buys some of it from people who do a little fishing on the side—non-union. It's not popular with the professional fishermen, but it's not actually illegal, either. At least not as far as I can see. Then he drives around and sells smoked herring and fresh eggs, mostly to a few steady customers. The people around here have accepted Folke as a decent person. He's never done anyone any harm. Doesn't talk much and keeps mostly to himself. Retiring type. The times I've run into him, it always seems as if he wanted to apologize for simply existing. But . . ."

"Yes?"

"But everybody knows he's a murderer. Tried and convicted. It was apparently a pretty ugly murder, too. Some harmless foreign woman."

"Roseanna McGraw was her name. And it really was revolting. Sick. But he was sexually provoked. The way he saw it. And we had to provoke him again in order to catch him. Myself, I can't imagine how he ever passed the psychiatric examination."

"Oh, come on," said Allwright, laugh lines spreading around his eyes like a spider web. "I've been in Stockholm too. The cram course in legal psychiatry. In fifty percent of the cases the doctors are crazier than the patients."

"As far as I could gather, Folke Bengtsson was definitely disturbed. A combination of sadism, puritanism, and misogyny. Does he know Sigbrit Mård?"

"Know?" said Allwright. "His house isn't two hundred yards from hers. They're each other's closest neighbors. She's one of his regular customers. But that's not the worst of it."

"Really?"

"The key point is that he was in the post office at the same time she was. There are witnesses who saw them talking to each other. He had his car parked in the square. He was standing behind her in line and left the place about five minutes after she did."

There was a moment's silence.

"You know Folke Bengtsson," Allwright said.

"Yes."

"And would he be capable . . . ?"

"Yes," said Martin Beck.

5.

"To be perfectly honest, and I always am, Sigbrit's dead, and things look pretty damned bad for Folke," Allwright said. "I don't believe in coincidence."

"You said something about her husband?"

"Yes, that's right. He's a ship's captain, but he drinks too much. Six years ago he got some mysterious liver disease, and they sent him home from Ecuador. They didn't fire him, but the doctors wouldn't give him a clean bill of health, so he couldn't ship out again. He came out here to live, and went on drinking, and then pretty soon they separated. Now he lives in Malmö."

"Do you have any contact with him?"

"Yes. Unfortunately. Close physical contact, you might say. If you wanted to put it nicely. The fact is, she was the one who wanted the divorce. He was against it. Dead against it. But she got her way. They'd been married for a long time, but he'd been away at sea mostly. Came home once a year or so, and apparently that worked fine. But then when they tried to live together all the time, it was a complete disaster."

"And now?"

"Now every time he gets really liquored up he comes out here to 'talk it over.' But there's nothing to talk about, and he usually winds up giving her a real alarming."

"A what?"

Allwright laughed.

"An alarming," he said. "Local dialect. What do you

call it in Stockholm? He warms her hide for her. 'Domestic disturbance' in police talk. What a lousy expression—'domestic disturbance.' Anyway, I've had to go out there twice. The first time, I talked some sense into him. But the second time wasn't so easy. I had to hit him and bring him in to our fancy jail. Sigbrit looked pretty miserable that time. Big black eyes, and some ugly marks on her throat."

Allwright poked at his lion-hunting hat.

"I know Bertil Mård. He goes on binges, but I don't think he's as bad as he seems. And I think he loves Sigbrit. And so, of course, he's jealous. Though I don't think he has any real cause. I don't know anything about her sex life, supposing she has one. And if she does have one I ought to know about it. Around here, everybody pretty much knows everything about everybody. But I probably know most."

"What does Mård say himself?"

"They questioned him in Malmö. He has a sort of alibi for the seventeenth. Claims he was in Copenhagen that day. Rode over on the train ferry, the *Malmöhus,* but . . ."

"Do you know who questioned him?"

"Yes. A Chief Inspector Månsson."

Martin Beck had known Per Månsson for years and had great confidence in him. He cleared his throat.

"In other words, things don't look so good for Mård either."

Allwright scratched the dog for a while before answering.

"No," he said. "But he's in a hell of a lot better shape than Folke Bengtsson."

"If, in fact, anything has happened."

"She's disappeared. That's enough for me. No one

43

who knows her can think of any reasonable explanation."

"What does she look like, by the way?"

"What she looks like right now is something I'd rather not think about," said Allwright.

"Aren't you jumping to a conclusion?"

"Sure I am. But I'm only telling you what I think. Normally she looks like this."

He put his hand in his back pocket and took out two photographs—a passport photo and a folded color enlargement.

He glanced at the pictures before handing them over.

"They're both good," he commented. "I'd say she was of normal appearance. She looks the way most people look. Pretty attractive, of course."

Martin Beck studied them for a long time. He doubted that Allwright was capable of seeing them with his eyes, which, of course, for that matter, was a technical impossibility.

Sigbrit Mård was not pretty attractive. She was a rather homely and ungainly woman. But she undoubtedly did her best to improve her looks, which often produces unfortunate results. Her features were irregular, narrow, and sharp, and her face was hopelessly careworn. Unlike most such pictures these days, the passport photo had not been taken with a Polaroid or in an automatic booth. It was a typical studio portrait. She had taken great pains with her make-up and her hairdo, and the photographer had no doubt given her a whole page of proofs to choose among. The other one was an amateur photograph, but not a machine-made copy. It had been enlarged and retouched by hand, a full-length portrait. She was standing on a pier, and in the background was a white passenger liner with two funnels. She was gazing up at the sun unnaturally, holding a pose that she presumably thought did her justice. She was wearing a thin green sleeveless blouse and a blue pleated skirt. She was barelegged and had a large orange and yellow summer handbag over her right shoulder. On her feet she was wearing sandals with platform soles. She was holding her right foot slightly forward, the heel off the ground.

"That one's recent," Allwright said. "Taken last summer."

"Who took it?"

"A girlfriend. They went on a trip together."

"To Rügen apparently. That's the train ferry *Sassnitz* in the background, isn't it?"

Allwright seemed vastly impressed.

"Now how the hell did you know that?" he said. "I've even had duty in passport control when they were shorthanded, and I can't tell those boats apart. But you're right. That is the *Sassnitz,* and they made an excursion to Rügen. You can go have a look at the chalk cliffs and stare at the Communists and that sort of thing. They're very ordinary looking. A lot of people are disappointed. The one-day cruise only costs a few crowns."

"Where did you get this picture?"

"I took it out of her house when we went through it. She had it taped up on the wall. I guess she thought it was pretty good."

He put his head on one side and peered at the photograph.

"By golly, it is pretty good. That's just what she looks like. Nice gal."

"Haven't you ever been married?" Martin Beck asked suddenly.

Allwright was delighted.

"Are you going to start questioning me?" he said, laughing. "Now that's what I call thorough."

"Sorry," said Martin Beck. "Dumb thing to say. An irrelevant question."

This was a lie. The question was not irrelevant.

"But I don't mind answering it. I went with a gal from down in Abbekås one time. We were engaged. But I'll be damned, she was like a flesh-eating plant. After three months I'd had plenty, and after six months she still hadn't had enough. Since then I've stuck to dogs. Take it from someone who knows. A man doesn't need a wife. Once you get used to it, it's a huge relief. I feel it every morning when I wake up. She's made life miserable for three men. Of course, she's a grandmother several times over by now."

He sat silently for a moment.

"It does seem a little sad not having any children," he said then. "At times. But other times I feel just the opposite. Even if conditions are pretty good right here, still there's something wrong with society as a whole. I wouldn't have wanted to try and raise kids here. The question is whether it can be done at all."

Martin Beck was silent. His own contribution to child-rearing had consisted mostly of keeping his mouth shut and letting his children grow up more or less naturally. The result had been only a partial success. He had a daughter who had become a fine, independent human being, and who seemed to like him. On the other hand, he had a son he had never understood. To be perfectly frank, he didn't like him much, and the boy, who was just eighteen, had never treated him with anything but mistrust, deception, and, in recent years, open contempt.

The boy's name was Rolf. Most of their attempts at

46

conversation ended with the line, "Jesus Christ, Dad, there's just no point in talking to you, you never get what I mean anyway." Or: "If I were fifty years older, maybe we'd have a chance, but this isn't the nineteenth century any more, you know." Or: "If only you weren't a fucking cop!"

Allwright had been busy with the dog. Now he looked up.

"May I ask *you* a question?" he said with a little smile.

"Sure."

"Why did you want to know if I'd ever been married?"

"It was just a stupid question."

For the second time since they met, the other man looked completely serious. And a little hurt.

"That's not true. I know it's not true. And I think I know why you asked."

"Why?"

"Because you think I don't understand women?"

Martin Beck put down the photographs. Since meeting Rhea, he found he had much less trouble being honest.

"Okay," he said. "You're right."

"Good," said Allwright, lighting a new cigarette absentmindedly. "Good enough. Thanks. You may very well be right. I'm a man who's had no women in his private life. Outside of my mother, of course, and the fishergirl from Abbekås. And I've always regarded women as regular people, essentially no different from me and men in general. So if there are any subtle differences, then it's possible they've passed me by. Since I know I'm ignorant on the subject, I've read a number of books and articles and things on women's lib, but most of it is nonsense. And the part that isn't nonsense

47

is so obvious a Hottentot could understand it. Equal pay for equal work, for example, and sex discrimination."

"Why a Hottentot?"

Allwright laughed so loud the dog jumped up and started licking his face.

"There was a guy on the town council who claimed the Hottentots were the only culture that in two thousand years never managed to invent the wheel. Bullshit, of course. I hardly have to tell you which party *he* represented."

Martin Beck didn't want to know. Nor did he want to know what political persuasion Allwright represented. Whenever people started talking politics he always went as silent as a clam.

And he was still sitting there in clamlike silence when, thirty seconds later, the phone rang.

Allwright picked up the receiver.

"Allwright?" he said.

Whoever it was apparently made some amusing remark.

"Yes, I am, sort of."

And then, with a certain hesitation:

"Yes, he's sitting right here."

Martin Beck took the receiver.

"Beck."

"Hi, this is Ragnarsson. We've made about a hundred calls trying to locate you. What's up?"

One of the drawbacks to being chief of the National Homicide Squad was that the large newspapers had people who kept an eye on where you went and why. In order to do that, they needed paid informers inside the police department, which was irritating, but couldn't be helped. The National Police Commissioner was especially irritated, but he was also scared to death that it would get out. Nothing was ever supposed to get out.

Ragnarsson was a newspaperman, one of the better and more decent ones, which by no means meant that his paper was one of the better and more decent papers.

"Are you still there?" Ragnarsson said.

"Someone has disappeared," said Martin Beck.

"Disappeared? People disappear every day, and they don't call you in. What's more, I heard Kollberg is on his way down there. There's something fishy about all this."

"Maybe. Maybe not."

"We're sending down a couple of men. You might as well be prepared. That's all I wanted to tell you. I didn't want to do anything behind your back, you know that. You can trust me. So long."

"So long."

Martin Beck rubbed the edge of his scalp. He trusted Ragnarsson, but not his reporters, and least of all his newspaper.

Allwright was looking thoughtful.

"Newsman?"

"Yes."

"From Stockholm?"

"Yes."

"That busts it open then."

"Definitely."

"We've got local correspondents here too. They know all about it. But they're obliging. A kind of loyalty. The *Trelleborg Allehanda* is fine. But then there are the Malmö papers. *Kvällsposten,* that's the worst. And now we'll have *Aftonbladet* and *Expressen.*"

"Yes, I'm afraid so."

"Balls!"

Balls was a mild, everyday expression in Skåne.

Farther north, it sounded very bad.

Maybe Allwright didn't know that. Or else maybe he didn't care.

Martin Beck liked Allwright very much.

A sort of obvious, natural friendship. Things were going to work out fine.

"What do we do now?"

"Up to you," said Martin Beck. "You're the expert."

"Anderslöv district. Yes, I ought to be. Shall I give you an orientation? By car? But let's not take the patrol car. Mine's better."

"The tomato-colored one?"

"Right. Everyone knows it, of course. But I feel more comfortable in it. Shall we go?"

"Whatever you say."

They talked about three things in the car.

The first was something Allwright hadn't mentioned before, for some reason.

"There's the post office over there, and now we're coming to the bus stop. The last time Sigbrit was seen she was standing right about here."

He slowed down and stopped.

"We've got a witness who saw something else too."

"What?"

"Folke Bengtsson. He came driving along in his station wagon, and when he passed Sigbrit he slowed down and stopped. Seems natural enough. He'd picked up his car and was headed home. They knew each other, lived next door. He knows she's waiting for the bus, and he gives her a lift."

"What sort of a witness?"

Allwright drummed his fingers on the wheel.

"An older woman from town here. Her name is Signe Persson. When she heard Sigbrit had disappeared, she came in and told us she'd been walking down the other side of the street and noticed Sigbrit, and just then

50

Bengtsson drove up from the other direction. He put on his brakes and stopped. Now it happens Britta was alone at the station when she came in, so she told her she ought to come back and talk to me. And she came back the next day, and I talked to her. She told me pretty much the same story. That she'd seen Sigbrit and that Folke stopped his car. So then I asked her if she had actually seen the car stop and Sigbrit get into it."

"And what did she say?"

"She said she didn't want to turn around and look because she didn't want to seem nosy. Which is a silly answer, since this old lady is probably the nosiest woman in the county. But when I coaxed her a little she did say she turned her head right afterward, and neither Sigbrit nor the car were anywhere to be seen. So we chatted a little about one thing and another, and after a while she said she wasn't sure. Said she didn't want to talk about people behind their backs. But then the next day she ran into one of my men at the Co-op and stated definitely that she'd seen Bengtsson stop and that Sigbrit got into the car. If she sticks to that, then Folke Bengtsson is definitely linked to the disappearance."

"What does Bengtsson say?"

"Don't know. I haven't talked to him. Two detectives from Trelleborg were out there, but he wasn't home. Then they decided to call you in and more or less ordered me not to do anything. Didn't want me to anticipate events, as it were. Bide my time and wait for the experts. I haven't even written up a report about my talk with Signe Persson. Do you think that sounds slipshod?"

Martin Beck didn't answer.

"I think it's pretty slipshod," said Allwright with a little laugh. "But I'm a little wary of Signe Persson.

She was mixed up in the worst case I ever had. Must be five years ago. She claimed a neighbor lady had poisoned her cat. Made a formal complaint, so we had to investigate. Then the other old lady made a complaint against Signe Persson, because the cat had killed her budgie. We dug up the cat and sent it to Helsingborg. They couldn't find any poison. So then Signe claimed the other woman had bought two cigars at the cigar store and boiled them. She'd read in some magazine that if you boil cigars long enough you get nicotine crystals, which are deadly poisonous and don't leave any trace. The neighbor lady actually had bought two cigars, but she said they were just to offer guests and her brother had smoked them. I asked her how the cat had managed to kill the budgie, since it was always in its cage. And she claimed Signe got the damned cat to scare the budgie to death, because the bird could talk and had uttered some dreadful truths. Signe said it was quite true that the budgie had called her a whore on no fewer than five occasions. There was a police cadet here at the time who was a real go-getter, and he investigated this theory about the cigars and decided it was theoretically possible, and that if the victim was an habitual smoker then poisoning couldn't be proved. So when Signe Persson came in for the tenth or twelfth time I asked her if her cat had been a heavy smoker. After that she wouldn't even say hello to me for several years. We closed the case, and the cadet stayed home boiling cigars until they canned him. Then he settled down in Eslöv and became an inventor."

"What did he invent?"

"The only thing I heard about was that he applied for a patent for a potty with a luminous rim and for a nicotine detector that meowed if you dipped it in poisoned cabbage soup. That didn't work out, so he tried to rebuild it into a mechanical cat that ran on batteries."

Allwright looked at his watch.

"So that was point of interest number one. The bus stop. Plus the story of our witness Signe Persson and of a man who had his life ruined by a cigar-smoking cat. I must say, the thought of a case where Signe figures as the key witness does not make me happy. We'd better move on. The bus will be here pretty soon."

He put the car in gear and looked in the rear-view mirror.

"We've got someone behind us," he said. "A green Fiat with two men in it. They've been sitting back there ever since we stopped. Shall we show them around a little?"

"Okay by me."

"Interesting to be shadowed," Allwright said. "New experience for me."

He was driving at less than twenty miles an hour, but the other car made no attempt to pass.

"Those buildings up there to the right, that's Domme. That's where Sigbrit Mård and Folke Bengtsson live. Do you want to drive up?"

"Not right now. Has anyone done a proper crime lab job up there?"

"At Sigbrit's? No, I can't say we have. We were there and had a look around, and I took that picture off the wall above her bed. And I suppose we left some fingerprints here and there."

"If she were dead . . ."

Martin Beck stopped himself. It was a fairly stupid question.

"And if I had killed her, what would I do with the body? I've thought about that myself. But there are just

53

too many possibilities. Lots of marl pits and tumble-down old houses. And shacks and sheds. A long coast-line on the Baltic, empty summer cottages. Woods and windfalls and thickets and ditches and every other damned thing."

"Woods?"

"Yes, up by Börringe Lake. The police used to have a pistol match up there every year in a clearing on the east shore. Since the storm in sixty-eight, it's such a mess up there you couldn't get in with a tank. It'll take a hundred years to get rid of the windfalls. Besides . . . By the way, there's a map in the glove compartment."

Martin Beck took out the map and unfolded it.

"We're in Alstad now, on Highway 101 heading for Malmö. You can get your bearings from that."

"Are you planning to drive this slowly all the way?"

"No. Jesus! Pure absentmindedness. Just wanted to be sure we didn't lose those hotshots behind us."

Allwright swung off to the right. The green car fol-lowed.

"Now we've left the Anderslöv police district," he said. "But we'll be right back in it."

"What were you going to say a minute ago? Be-sides . . . what?"

"Oh yes. Besides, it's the general belief that Sigbrit Mård was picked up by someone in a car. There's even a witness who says so. If you look at the map you'll see there are three main roads through the district. The old Highway, which we just left; Highway 10, which follows the coast from Trelleborg to Ystad and then goes on all the way to Simrishamn; and, in addition, a section of the new European Highway 14, which connects with the ferry from Poland in Ystad and then runs on through Malmö and God knows where all. And on top of that we've got a network of back roads that probably doesn't have its equal anyplace else in the country."

"So I see," said Martin Beck.

True to form, he was beginning to get carsick.

It did not, however, prevent him from studying the landscape they were traveling through. He had never been in this part of the country before and didn't know much more about it than what he remembered from old Edvard Persson movies. The plains of Skåne have a soft, rolling beauty. This was more than a populous rural idyll, it was a singular piece of countryside with a kind of inherent harmony.

He suddenly remembered a disconnected sentence from the general chorus of complaints about conditions in the country. "Sweden's a rotten country, but it's a very pretty rotten country." Someone had said that or written it, but he couldn't remember who.

Allwright went on talking.

"The Anderslöv district is sort of unusual. When we're not pushing paper, we're mostly concerned with traffic. For example, we put fifty thousand miles a year on the patrol car. We've got about a thousand people in town and maybe ten thousand in the whole district. But we've got over fifteen miles of beach, and in the summer the population grows to over thirty thousand. So you can imagine how many buildings are standing empty at this time of year. Now so far I'm talking about people we know, and pretty much know where we can find them. But I'd estimate there's another five to six thousand people we don't have any check on at all, people who live in old houses or campers and then move away and other people take their place."

Martin Beck turned to look at an unusually pretty whitewashed church. Allwright followed his gaze.

"Dalköpinge," he said. "If you're interested in picturesque churches, I can supply at least thirty of them. In the whole district, of course."

They came to the coast road and turned east. The sea was calm and grayish-blue. Freighters stood along the horizon.

"What I mean is, if Sigbrit's dead, there are several hundred places she might be. And if someone gave her a ride, Folke or someone else, then there's a pretty good chance she's not in this district at all. In that case, the possibilities are in the thousands."

He looked out over the coastal landscape and said, "Magnificent, isn't it?"

He was clearly a man who was proud of his home.

And not without reason, Martin Beck thought.

They passed Smygehuk.

The green Fiat was following them faithfully.

"Smygehamn," Allwright said. "In my day it was called East Torp."

The villages lay close together. Beddinge Beach. Skateholm. Fishing villages, partially converted to seaside resorts, but still pretty. No high rise and no fancy hotels.

"Skateholm," Allwright said. "This is where my territory ends. Now we're coming into the Ystad police district. I'll take you to Abbekås. This is Dybeck. Swampy and miserable. Worst part of the whole coast. Maybe she's out there in the mud. Okay, this is Abbekås."

Allwright drove slowly through the village.

"Yes, this is where she lived," he said. "The woman who got me to give up women. Do you want to have a look at the harbor?"

Martin Beck didn't bother to answer.

56

There was a little harbor with some benches for telling fish stories and a few old men in Vega caps. Three fishing boats. Stacks of herring boxes, and some nets hung up to dry.

They got out and sat down on separate bollards. Gulls screamed above the breakwater.

The green Fiat had stopped sixty feet away. The two men stayed in the front seat.

"Do you know them?" said Martin Beck.

"No," said Allwright. "They're just boys. If they want anything, they can come over here and talk. Must be awful damned dull just sitting there staring."

Martin Beck said nothing. He got older and older himself, while the reporters got younger and younger. Their relations grew worse and worse every year. Besides, the police weren't popular any more, assuming they ever had been. Personally, Martin Beck didn't feel he had to be ashamed of his job, but he knew a lot of men who were, and still more who really ought to be.

"What was all that about me and women?" Allwright asked.

"It occurred to me that we know very little about Sigbrit Mård. We know what she looks like and where she works, and we know she has never made trouble. We know she's divorced and doesn't have any children. And that's about all. Have you considered the fact that she's at an age when a lot of women feel frustrated, especially if they don't have any children or family or any special interests? When they're approaching menopause and starting to feel old? They feel like their lives have gone wrong, their sex lives in particular, and they often do dumb things. They're attracted to younger men, they get involved in stupid affairs. And they often get taken, financially or emotionally."

"Thanks for the lecture," Allwright said.

57

He picked up a board from the ground and threw it in the water. The dog splashed in immediately to retrieve it.

"Terrific," Allwright said. "Now he'll make an even worse mess in the back seat. And so you think maybe Sigbrit had a secret sex life or something."

"I think it's possible. I mean we have to look into her private life. As much as we can. I mean maybe, after all, there is a chance, just maybe, that she's simply run off with some man who's seven or eight years younger. Just run away from everything in order to be happy for a while. Even if it's only two weeks or a couple of months."

"Get herself good and laid," Allwright said.

"Or get a chance to talk to someone she thinks she can relate to."

Allwright put his head on one side and grinned.

"That's one theory," he said. "But I don't believe it."

"Because it doesn't fit."

"Right. It doesn't fit at all. Do you have a plan? Or is that a presumptuous question?"

"I'm planning to wait until Lennart gets here. And then I think it's time for an informal chat with Folke Bengtsson and Bertil Mård."

"I'd be happy to come along."

"I don't doubt it."

Allwright laughed. Then he stood up, walked over to the green car, and rapped on the side window. The driver, a young man with a red beard, rolled it down and looked out at him questioningly.

"We're going back to Anderslöv now," Allwright said. "I'll be driving through Källstorp to pick up some eggs from my brother. But you can save your paper some money if you take the road through Skivarp."

The Fiat followed them and supervised the egg pickup.

"They clearly don't trust the police," Allwright said.

Otherwise nothing much happened that day, which was Friday, November 2.

Martin Beck made his obligatory visit to Trelleborg and met the Commissioner and the Superintendent who was head of the criminal division. He envied the police chief his office, because it had a view of the harbor.

No one had anything to say about the case.

Sigbrit Mård had been missing for seventeen days, and all anyone knew was what was gossip in Anderslöv.

On the other hand, gossip is often well founded.

Where there's smoke, there's fire.

That evening, he got a call from Kollberg, who said he hated driving and was planning to spend the night in Växjö.

"And how are things in Anderstorp?" he said.

"The name is Anderslöv."

"Oh yes."

"And it's very pleasant here, but the reporters are after us already."

"Put your uniform on, you'll get more respect."

"None of your wisecracks!" said Martin Beck.

Then he called Rhea, but there was no answer.

He tried again an hour later and once more just before he went to bed.

This time she was home.

"I've been trying to get you all evening," he said.

"Really?"

"What have you been up to?"

"None of your business," she said cheerfully. "How's it going?"

"I don't know for sure. There's a woman who's disappeared."

"People can't disappear. You ought to know that, you're a detective."

"I think I love you."

"I know you do," she said happily. "I went to the movies, and then I went to Butler's for something to eat."

"Good night."

"Was that all you wanted?"

"No, but it can wait."

"Sleep well, darling," she said, and hung up.

Martin Beck hummed as he brushed his teeth. If anyone had been there to hear it, it would probably have sounded odd.

The next day was a holiday. All Saints' Day. He could always spoil it for someone. Månsson in Malmö, for example.

6.

"I've met a lot of gorillas in my day," Per Månsson said. "But Bertil Mård is one of the worst."

They were sitting on Månsson's balcony overlooking Regementsgatan, enjoying a lovely day.

Martin Beck had taken the bus to Malmö, mostly for the fun of it and so he could say that he had actually traveled the stretch that Sigbrit Mård apparently had not.

He had also tried to question the bus driver, to no

60

avail, since the man was a substitute and had not been driving on the day in question.

Månsson was a large, leisurely man, who took life easy and was seldom guilty of an overstatement. But now he said:

"The man struck me as a bully."

"Lots of sea captains get a little funny," said Martin Beck. "They're often very lonely men, and if they're the overbearing type they tend to get tough and autocratic. They turn into gorillas, as you said. The only person they'll talk to is their chief."

"Their chief?"

"The Chief Engineer."

"Oh."

"A lot of them drink too much and tyrannize their crews. Or else they pretend they don't even exist. Won't even speak to their mates."

"You know a lot about ships."

"Yes, it's my hobby. I had a case once on a ship. Murder. In the Indian Ocean. On a freighter. One of the most interesting cases I ever had."

"Well, I know the skipper of the *Malmöhus*. He's a decent fellow."

"Passenger ships are usually a different matter. The owners put on a different kind of officer. After all, the captains have to socialize with the passengers. On the big ships, they have a captain's table."

"What's that?"

"The captain's own table in the dining room. For entertaining prominent first-class passengers."

"I see."

"But Mård sailed on tramp steamers. And there's a certain difference."

"Yes, he was pretty damned arrogant," Månsson said. "Yelled at me and cursed his old lady. Nasty son

of a bitch. He thought he was something special. Rude
and arrogant. I'm pretty easygoing, but I damned near
lost my temper. That takes some doing."

"How does he make a living?"

"He's got a beer shop in Limhamn. You know the
story. He drank his liver to pieces in Ecuador or Ven-
ezuela. They had him in the hospital out there for a
while. Then the shipping company flew him home. They
wouldn't give him a clean bill of health, so he couldn't
ship out again. He moved home to his wife in Anderslöv, but that didn't work out at all. He boozed it up
and beat her. She wanted out. He didn't. But she got
her divorce, no sweat."

"Allwright says he's got an alibi for the seventeenth."

"Yes, sort of. He took the train ferry over to Copenhagen to tie one on. But it's a rotten alibi. Seems to me.
Claims he sat in the forward saloon. The ferry sails at
a quarter to twelve these days—it used to sail at noon.
He says he was alone in the saloon, and the waiter was
hung over. And there was one crewman standing in
there playing the slot machine. I often take that boat
myself. The waiter, whose name is Sture, is always
hung over, with bags under his eyes. And that same
crewman is generally standing there stuffing one-crown
pieces in the slot machine."

Månsson took a noisy sip of his drink. He always
drank the same thing, a mixture of gin and grapefruit
soda. It is a Finland-Swedish specialty, called a Gripenberger after some obscure officer and nobleman.

The weather was nice in Malmö. The city seemed
almost inhabitable.

"I think you ought to talk to Bertil Mård yourself,"
Månsson said.

Martin Beck nodded.

"The witness on the ferry identified him," Månsson

62

said. "He's got the kind of looks you don't forget. The only trouble is that all those things happen every day. The ferry leaves here at the same hour, usually with the same passengers. You can't count on the crew remembering someone a couple of weeks later, and you can't be sure they'd have the right day. Talk to him yourself and see what you think."

"But you have already questioned him?"

"Yes, and I wasn't specially convinced."

"Does he have a car?"

"Yes. He lives on the West Side, a stone's throw from here if you've got a hell of a good arm. Mäster Johansgatan Twenty-Three. Takes him half an hour to drive to Anderslöv. Roughly."

"What makes you point that out?"

"Well, he seems to have made the trip now and then."

Martin Beck let the question drop.

It was November 3, a Saturday, and still almost summer. It was also a holiday—All Saints' Day—but Martin Beck was planning to disturb Captain Mård's tranquillity in spite of it. The chances were he wasn't a religious man.

There had been no word from Kollberg. Perhaps he had found Växjö fascinating and decided to stay over for a day. But in what way fascinating? Perhaps someone had seduced him with illegal fresh crayfish. Of course, frozen crayfish were now available, but Kollberg was not easily deceived. Least of all in the matter of crayfish.

Rhea had called that morning and cheered him up. As always. In one year she had changed his life and given him more satisfaction than twenty years of marriage to a person he had actually loved once, a person who had presented him with two children and many a joyful moment. Just count them. For that matter, "presented" was a lousy word. They had been in it together, hadn't they? Well maybe so, but he had never had that feeling.

With Rhea Nielsen, everything was different. They had a free and open relationship, of course. Perhaps a little too free and open, it seemed to him every once in a while. But first and foremost, there was a sense of community that stretched far beyond his love for this curiously perfect woman. Together with her, he had begun to mix with people in a manner that had never been possible for him before. Her building in Stockholm was quite different from the ordinary average apartment house. You might almost call it a commune, though with none of the negative connotations—often warranted but just as often imaginary—of that discredited term. People in communes smoked pot and screwed around like rabbits. The rest of the time they talked a lot of bullshit and ate macrobiotic food, and none of them worked and they all lived on welfare. The commune members considered themselves the victims of an evil social system. They often took LSD and thought they could fly, or drove a stiletto into their best friend's belly for the enrichment of the experience, or else they killed themselves.

It wasn't so very long since he had thought that way himself, at least in part and at times. And certainly there was a grain of truth there, or rather a whole wheatfield.

Martin Beck's position gave him the doubtful pleasure of reading confidential reports. Most of them were political, and he threw them directly into the Out basket for secret papers, to be passed on to the next bureaucrat with a clearance. But he usually read the ones that seemed to have some connection with his own job.

Suicide, for example, was a subject that had begun to interest him more and more. And secret memoranda on the subject cropped up with increasing regularity. The point of departure was always the same: Sweden led the world by a margin that seemed to grow larger from one report to the next, but, as with so many other things, the National Commissioner had decreed that nothing must get out. On the other hand, the explanation varied. Other countries cheated on their statistics. For a long time it had been popular to single out the Catholic countries, but then the Archbishop and some religious bigwigs within the police department had begun to complain, so then countries with a socialist form of government had had to take their place. But Swedish intelligence had immediately made difficulties, on the grounds that they could no longer use priests as spies. Since the secret activities of the Security Police fell into the category of things that always, inevitably, got out, a sigh of relief was heaved at National Police Administration Headquarters. Rumor had it that the National Commissioner himself had expressed certain misgivings at the suggestion that Swedish priests, some of whom were outright card-carrying Reds, would be able to spy on Swedish Communists or bring so formidable an opponent as the Soviet Union to its knees.

But as usual, all of this was unconfirmed rumor. Out must nothing get, as they sometimes put it—for a joke, or at least for the sake of putting it some different way. But the faithful would tolerate no deviation. "Nothing must get out" was the proper expression.

And that was that.

The gist of the latest suicide manifesto was as follows: Since most people neither shoot themselves nor jump off Väster Bridge but get good and drunk instead and then swallow a bottle of sleeping pills, they could

65

be written off as cases of accidental poisoning and completely eliminated from the statistics, which would thus suddenly become amazingly auspicious.

Martin Beck thought about these things a lot.

Månsson poured some more grapefruit soda in his Gripenberger.

He had not spoken for some time, and to judge by his clothing he wasn't planning to go anywhere.

He was wearing a nightshirt, flannel pants, and terry-cloth slippers, plus a bathrobe that seemed to be part of the ensemble.

"The wife will be here in a little while," he said. "Usually shows up toward three o'clock."

Månsson had apparently gone back to his life as five-sevenths bachelor, in that he spent five days of the week alone and the weekends with his wife.

They had separate apartments.

"It's a good system," he said. "It's true, I did have a girlfriend in Copenhagen for a year or so. And she was terrific, but it got to be too much of a good thing. I'm not as young as I used to be."

Martin Beck thought for a moment about what the other man had said.

True, Månsson was older than he was, but not by more than a couple of years.

"But she was damned good for me as long as it lasted. Her name was Nadja. I don't know if you ever met her."

"No," Martin Beck said.

He suddenly wanted to change the subject.

"By the way, how's Benny Skacke doing?"

"Not bad. He's an inspector now, and married to his physiotherapist. They had a little girl last spring. She was born on a Sunday, a little ahead of schedule, and he was in Minnesberg playing soccer when it happened. He claims all the important things in his life happen while he's playing soccer. God knows what he means."

Martin Beck knew quite well what Skacke was referring to, but he didn't say anything.

"In any case, he's a good policeman," Månsson said. "And there's getting to be a shortage of those. Unfortunately, I get the feeling he's not happy here. He can't get used to this city, somehow. He's been here almost five years, but I think he's still homesick for Stockholm."

"Of all godforsaken places," he added philosophically and emptied his glass.

Then he looked demonstratively at his watch.

"I guess I'd better be going now," said Martin Beck.

"Yes," Månsson said. "I was about to say that was a good idea if you wanted to catch Mård sober. But that's not the real reason."

"Oh?"

"No. If you stay another fifteen minutes you'll meet my wife. And in that case, I'd have to get dressed. She's sort of conventional, and she'd never stand for the idea of my sitting around with prominent police chiefs in this getup. Shall I call you a cab?"

"I'd rather walk."

He'd been in Malmö many times before, and he knew his way around, at least in the inner city.

Besides, it was a pretty day, and he wanted to organize his thoughts before he talked to Bertil Mård.

He was conscious of the fact that Månsson had furnished him with a presupposition.

This was clearly going to be a case where presuppositions played an important part.

Presuppositions were never good. Letting them affect your judgment was as dangerous as ignoring them. You always had to remember that a supposition could be right even if it was preconceived.

Martin Beck was eager to form his own opinion of Mård. He knew they would soon be face to face.

The beer shop was closed for the holiday, and Månsson had gone to the trouble of assigning a police recruit to watch the house on Mäster Johansgatan and had instructed him to give the alarm if Mård left home.

7.

The police recruit would have been a great success on TV doing a parody of someone trying not to look as if he were watching a house. In addition, the house was very small, and the buildings on either side had been torn down. He was standing across the street with his hands behind his back, gazing out into empty space but casting continuous sidelong glances at the door behind which the object of his attentions was supposed to lurk.

Martin Beck stopped some distance off and watched. A minute or so went by and then the recruit walked slowly across the street and inspected the door in detail. And poked at the nameplate. Then he ambled back to his post with studied nonchalance and then spun around to be sure nothing improper had occurred behind his back. Like so many other policemen out on confidential or delicate assignments, he was wearing black shoes, dark blue socks, the pants to his uniform, a light blue shirt, and a dark blue tie. To this he had added a yellow stocking cap, a leather jacket with big

68

shiny buttons and red and yellow embroidery on the sleeves, and, around his neck, a scarf in colors that even Martin Beck recognized as being those of the Malmö Soccer Club—white and sky blue. His jacket bulged on the right side as if he had a pint of liquor in his pocket.

When Martin Beck walked up to him he jumped as if bitten by a snake and immediately raised his hand to the nonexistent peak of his cap and delivered his report.

"No one has left the building, Inspector."

Martin Beck stood silently for a moment in his amazement at being recognized. Then he reached out and took a corner of the scarf between thumb and forefinger.

"Did your mother knit this for you?"

"No, sir," said the young man, blushing. "She didn't. It was my little sister's boyfriend. His name is Enok Jansson, sir, and he's a terrific knitter, although he actually works at the post office and everything. He can even knit while he's watching TV."

"What if Mård's gone out the back way?"

The recruit blushed still harder.

"What?" he said. "But that's impossible."

"It is?"

"Well, sir, I can't stand in front of the house and behind it at the same time, after all. It can't be done. You . . . Sir, you're not going to report me for this?"

Martin Beck shook his head. He crossed the street, wondering where the police force managed to find all these odd young men.

"It's the right house, anyway," the boy said, following him. "I went over three times to check it out. It says Mård on the door."

"And it didn't change?"

"No, sir. Shall I go in with you? I mean, I have a

gun and everything if we need it. And I've got my radio stuffed in my shirt—so no one could see it, I mean."

"Goodbye," said Martin Beck, putting his finger on the bell.

Bertil Mård opened the door almost before the bell had had a chance to ring.

He too was wearing the pants to a uniform, black ones, plus an undershirt and wooden clogs. The stink of last night's liquor surrounded him like a wall, but it was mixed with the odor of aftershave, and in one of his huge hands he was holding a bottle of Florida Water and an open straight razor, which he waved in the direction of the recruit.

"Who the hell is this goddam clown," he yelled, "who's been standing here staring at the house for two hours?"

"That's insulting an officer of the law," the recruit said cockily.

"I lay eyes on you one more time, you little plainclothes bastard, and I'll cut your ears off," Mård bellowed.

"And that's threatening an officer . . ."

"Not at all," said Martin Beck, closing the door behind him. "Not at all . . ."

"What do you mean, 'not at all'?" Mård said. "What the hell is this all about?"

"Take it easy for a minute."

"I won't take it easy. I want to be left alone. And I don't want any damn kids in costumes spying on me. What's more, I'm in the habit of getting what I want. And who the hell are you? The head fucking cop himself?"

"Exactly," said Martin Beck.

He took a couple of steps past Mård and glanced

around the room. It smelled as if fifty people had slept there, and hardly as if they had been human. There were old quilts with grease spots and ragged stuffing nailed up in front of the windows, and they let in a very sparse light. But it was possible to turn up the corners and peer out. Against one wall was a bed that had obviously not been made for weeks, maybe months. Other than that, the furnishings consisted of four chairs, a table, and a large wardrobe. On the table was a glass and two bottles of 120-proof smuggled Russian vodka with blue labels, one of them empty and one of them half full. There was a very large pile of dirty laundry in one corner, and through the rear door he could see out into the kitchen, where the mess was indescribable, and on into the bathroom, where an electric bulb was burning and where Mård had apparently just been shaving.

"I've been in one hundred and eight countries," Mård said. "And I've never seen such a load of shit. The cops are after you. The health insurance is after you. Or the tax collector or the temperance board or the welfare office or whatever the fuck it's called. Or the power company or the customs or the national registration or the public health. Even the fucking post office, and I don't want any mail."

Martin Beck took a closer look at Mård. He was a big man, a good six two, with a fighting weight of at least 275 pounds. He had black hair and dark brown, brutal eyes.

"Tell me, Mård, how do you know it's exactly one hundred and eight countries?" Martin Beck asked.

"Don't call me Mård. I don't want everyone treating me like an old buddy. Call me 'mister' at least, or 'sir.' How I know? Because I keep track of course. The one hundred and eighth country was Upper Volta. I flew there from Casablanca. The one hundred and seventh was South Yemen. But I swear this one takes the fucking cake. I've been in the hospital in North Korea and Honduras, and in Macao and the Dominican Republic, and in Pakistan, and in Ecuador. But I've never seen one any worse than the one right here in Malmö last summer. I was crammed into a ward that must have been built in 1890. There were twenty-nine of us in there, and seventeen had just come out of surgery. And then the fucking social workers come along and wonder what we're bitching about. We're supposed to keep our mouths shut—after all, it's free. Free! When the tax collector's on your tail like a wolf. Can you explain to me how the fucking government stays in power? I've been in a lot of places where they hang people for things like that."

Mård looked around.

"It's a mess in here," he said. "I'm no good at cleaning. Don't know how."

He picked up the empty vodka bottle and carried it out to the kitchen.

"There," he said. "That's better. Now I want to ask you a question. What the fuck is going on here? Why is that idiot out there scratching on my door while I shave? I always shave twice a day, six in the morning and three in the afternoon. And I always shave myself. And I like a straight razor. It gives a better shave."

Martin Beck was silent.

"I asked a question," Mård said. "And I didn't get an answer. Who are you, for example? And what the fuck are you doing in my home?"

"My name is Martin Beck, and I'm a policeman. A Detective Chief Inspector, to be exact, and head of something called the National Homicide Squad."

"When were you born?"

"September twenty-fifth, nineteen twenty-two."

"All right. It's fun to *ask* the fucking questions for a change. What do you want?"

"Your wife's been missing since the seventeenth of October."

"And?"

"We wonder where she is."

"Fine. But I have already said, for Christ's sake, that I don't know. And on the seventeenth I was sitting on the train ferry *Malmöhus* having a few drinks. Okay, getting drunk. She's the only decent boat in the city. A man can't exist in this country, so I mostly sit on the Copenhagen boats and drink."

"You operate some sort of restaurant, don't you, Captain Mård?"

"Yes. I've got a couple of women who run it for me. And, by God, the place is clean and the brass is polished or else I'd kick 'em in the harbor. I go the rounds there every so often. And they never know when I'm coming."

"I see."

"You mumbled something about homicide."

"Yes, it's a possibility. It looks like someone abducted her. And you've got a poor alibi."

"I've got a damn good alibi. I was on the *Malmöhus*. But there's a sex maniac next door to her. If he's done anything to Sigbrit, I'll strangle her with my own hands."

Martin Beck looked at Mård's hands. They were formidable hands. He could probably strangle a bear.

"You said 'her.' You would strangle 'her.'"

"That isn't what I meant. I love Sigbrit."

Suddenly Martin Beck understood a great deal. Bertil Mård was a dangerous man, with an unpredictable temper. For many years now, he'd been used to giving

73

orders and doing very little himself. He was probably a very good seaman and was having a hard time adjusting to life ashore. He had to be considered capable of anything, including, presumably, the worst.

"The tragedy of my life was being born in the goddam city of Trelleborg," Mård said. "With a citizenship I never wanted. In a country I've never been able to stand for more than a month at a time, or two at the most. Even at that, everything was fine until I got sick. But I liked Sigbrit, and I'd come home to see her almost every year. We had it good together. And then I'd be off again. And then this damned thing. My liver gave out, and finally they wouldn't pass me on the physical."

He stood there silently for a minute.

"Go away now," he said suddenly. "Otherwise I'll get mad and break your jaw."

"Okay," said Martin Beck. "If I come back it will probably be to take you in."

"Go to hell," Mård said.

"What's your wife like? What sort of person is she?"

"That's none of your business. Out."

Martin Beck took a step toward the door.

"Goodbye, Captain Mård," he said.

"Wait," said Mård suddenly.

He put down the Florida Water and folded up the razor.

"I changed my mind," he said. "Why, I don't know."

He sat down and poured himself a glass of vodka.

"Do you drink?"

"Yes," said Martin Beck. "But not right now, and definitely not lukewarm vodka with no mixer."

"I wouldn't drink it this way either," Mård said. "Not if I had a steward or a mess boy to come running with lime and crushed ice as soon as I cleared my throat.

74

Sometimes I wonder if I shouldn't sell the beer shop and get out of here and ship out from Panama or Liberia."

Martin Beck sat down at the table.

"The only trouble is I'd never get my own command. At the very most, I'd get to be first mate to someone just like me. And I couldn't stand that. I'd strangle the son of a bitch."

Martin Beck still didn't say anything.

"But at least I could drink myself to death on the open sea. I want Sigbrit and I want a ship. And now I haven't got either one. And around here, I can't even drink myself to death without every fucking busybody in sight sticking his nose in."

He looked around the room.

"Do you think I want to live like this?" he said. "Do you think I like living in all this shit?"

He slammed his hand on the table so hard his glass nearly overturned.

"No, I know what you think," he roared. "You think I did something to Sigbrit. But I didn't. Can't you get that through your heads? Goddam cops, you're all the same, all over the world. Policemen are beach pigs, and all they're good for is to come on board and take a little booze and cigarettes for not giving you any trouble. I remember one son of a bitch in Millwall when I worked that route. A regular 'bobby.' He'd be standing there like a statue every time we berthed, and he'd salute and say 'Yes, sir,' and 'Glad to see you, Captain,' and by the time he'd leave he'd have such a load of tobacco and bottles he could hardly get down the gangplank. And it's the same thing here."

"I don't want any of your liquor and tobacco."

"Then what the fuck do you want?"

75

"I want to know what's happened to your ex-wife. That's why I'm asking you what she's like. What sort of person."

"Fine. She's fine. What do you want me to say? I love her. But you're out to get me. That cop in Anderslöv told you I beat her up a few times. Did you know he punched me out one time? I never would have thought he had the guts. I've only lost one fight in my whole life, and that was four against one. In Antwerp. But he was right, and I was wrong and I knew it."

Martin Beck looked at Mård thoughtfully.

It was possible the man was trying to present himself in some sort of better light.

"You were married for a long time," said Martin Beck.

"Yes. Sigbrit was only eighteen when we got hitched. Two months later I shipped out. And after that I was always at sea, but I'd come home for a month or two every year, and we had it good together."

"Sexually?"

"Yes. She liked me. She used to say it was like being run over by a train."

"And what about the rest of the year?"

"She said she was faithful, and I never had any cause to think otherwise. But I always thought it was kind of funny the way she was so damned horny for just one month and then went without completely for eleven. But she said there wasn't any trick to that. Just don't think about it."

"What about you?"

"Well, of course, I'd go to a whorehouse whenever we got to port."

"In a hundred and eight countries?"

"No, I never counted the whorehouses, but I guess there were quite a few. I can give you some addresses if you want. But in some countries there aren't any whores. I remember one. Romania. I was stuck in Constanta for three months with some old tub, and there wasn't a whore in town. I took the train to Bucharest. There weren't any there either. I've never seen anything like it."

"So what did you do?"

"Went to Piraeus. Thousands of them. I drank and fucked and didn't get out of bed for two weeks. Yes, by God ..."

Mård stared into his glass but didn't drink.

"And now what you're thinking is that seamen do nothing but run to the cat house in every port, and that just shows one thing."

"What?"

"That you don't know much about seamen. I sailed with the same chief for seven years. He had a wife in Bergkvara. And I'll take an oath he never touched a woman all those seven years. I think that's pretty damned good. That's the kind of man to be. And I knew a lot of others."

"What did you tell her when you got home?"

"Sigbrit? Well naturally I told her I'd been faithful as hell, just waiting and waiting for my vacation. So all I had to do was be sure not to come home with crabs and the clap and teeth marks all over my body. Thank God for penicillin. But I told Sigbrit I never looked at another woman. I swore it up and down. And I wouldn't admit it now, either, except that it's too late. It doesn't matter any more."

"Because Sigbrit's dead, you mean?"

If Martin Beck had expected the other man to break down, he was mistaken. Mård took a swallow of his drink, with a very steady hand.

"You're just trying to draw me into some sort of

trap," he said calmly. "But it won't work. In the first place, I was on that train ferry, and in the second place, I don't think Sigbrit is dead."

"What do you think?"

"I don't know. But I do know certain things you never thought of."

"For example?"

"Sigbrit's some kind of snob. She thought it was terrific being the wife of a sea captain and having that nice house. And that worked fine on her own salary plus mine. Plus which, I always had a little money of my own. So then we separated, okay, but I didn't figure she ought to get any money for kicking me out, so I didn't give her any alimony or anything like that. So after the divorce I guess it was pretty hard times."

"Why did you split up?"

"I couldn't stand sitting around in that fucking jerkwater town without anything to do. So I just drank and yelled at her to shine my shoes and clean the house, and I beat her up a lot, and she got sick of it. I can see why. I was sorry as hell after. And now I can sit here all day and be sorry. I can also be sorry I drank two bottles of booze every day for fifteen years. *Skoal!*"

Mård downed his drink. It consisted of about ten ounces of 120-proof alcohol, and he poured it down like water, without so much as a sigh.

"I'd like to know something," said Martin Beck.

"What's that?"

"Have you had sexual relations with her since the divorce?"

"Sure. I've driven out and laid her a number of times. But it's been a while now. A year and a half, at least."

"What did she have to say about it then?"

"She still thought it was like being run over by an express train. Terrific. Her cunt just got bigger and wetter the older she got. I was still hoping we'd be able to patch things up, but now it's too late."

"Why?"

"Lots of reasons. Because I'm sick, for one thing. But also because there wasn't really anything to patch up. A marriage built mostly on lies and cheating, what was it worth? Even if I was the only one who lied. And still I really do love Sigbrit."

Martin Beck thought for a moment.

"Captain Mård," he said, "from what you've said yourself, you seem to have considerable experience with women."

"Yes, I guess you might put it that way. Good whores know one thing. They know how to fuck. What of it?"

"Was, or is, your wife an especially exciting woman sexually?"

"You bet your ass she is. It wasn't just for laughs I sat around in Anderslöv for at least a month every goddam year."

Martin Beck was uncertain. The longer the conversation went on, the less he knew what he ought to believe. He wasn't even certain that he still disliked Mård.

"This business of one hundred and eight countries," he said. "I'm impressed you can really remember . . ."

Mård stuck his hand in his back pocket and pulled something out. It was a little notebook bound in leather, almost as thick as a hymnal.

"I keep track of things, like I said. Look there."

He flipped through the pages, which seemed to be partly filled with notes. The paper was lined, and the lines were very close together.

"Here," Mård said. "Here's the whole list. Starts with Sweden, Finland, Poland, Denmark, and ends with Ras Al Kaima, Malta, South Yemen, and Upper Volta. I'd been in Malta long before that, of course, but I didn't put it on the list till it got its independence. This is a hell of a good notebook. I bought it in Singapore over twenty years ago, and I've never seen another one like it."

He put the notebook back in his pocket.

"It's sort of a log book of my life," he said. "A little book like that's all you need for a human life. A much smaller one would do for most people."

Martin Beck stood up.

And so did Mård.

He was on his feet like a shot, holding out his huge paws.

"But if anyone's done anything to Sigbrit, just let me take care of him. For that matter, no one better touch her. She belongs to me."

His dark eyes flashed.

"I'll tear him to pieces," he said. "These hands have torn people to pieces before."

Martin Beck looked at the hands.

"Maybe you should do a little thinking about what you were doing on the seventeenth, Captain Mård. That alibi of yours doesn't seem to be worth much."

"Alibi," said Mård in disgust. "For what?"

He took a couple of long strides across the room and threw open the door outside.

"Now go to hell," he said. "And quick, before I get really mad."

"Goodbye, Captain Mård," said Martin Beck politely.

When he saw the man's face in the light, he noticed that the whites of his eyes were yellow.

"Beach pig," said Mård.

And slammed the door with a bang.

Martin Beck walked up toward town for about 100 yards.

Then he turned and walked down toward the harbor. When he came to the Savoy, he went into the bar and sat down.

"Good afternoon," the bartender said.

Martin Beck nodded.

"Whisky," he said.

"Ice water on the side as usual?"

Martin Beck nodded again.

It was over four years since the last time he had been in this bar. People with good memories clearly did exist.

He sat with his drink for a long time and thought.

He really didn't know what to make of the man. He almost thought Mård had tricked him in some way, but he couldn't really imagine how.

Mård had been either recklessly honest or thoroughly cunning. In either case, he had talked a little too much about killing people.

After a while he began to think about other things. He had a number of memories of this hotel, and at least one of them was pleasant.

He ordered another whisky.

When he had finished it, he paid and left, crossed the canal, and walked up to the row of taxis in front of the railroad station. He climbed into the car at the head of the line.

"Anderslöv," he said.

By cab, the trip took exactly twenty-nine minutes.

8.

Kollberg called that evening from a place called Jät.

"I've been trying to get you all day. Where have you been?"

"In Malmö."

"At Per Månsson's?"

"For a while. Where are you?"

"I ran into an old buddy of mine in Växjö. He's got a summer house here on Lake Åsnen, with a beach and a sauna and the whole works. Would you be very disappointed if I didn't show up till tomorrow?"

"You stay there and have a sauna," said Martin Beck. "Can you still swim in Åsnen? At this time of year?"

"Well, I'm planning to give it a try after the sauna. And guess what we're going to have for dinner afterwards."

Martin Beck smiled.

"I give up," he said, not quite truthfully. "What?"

"Crayfish."

Kollberg sounded like a child on Christmas Eve.

"He sounds like a good buddy to have," said Martin Beck. "Good night. See you in the morning."

He hung up the receiver and went back to his room. He stood in the window alcove and looked down into the garden, at the lights from the dining room falling on the gravel paths and the lawn beneath him. He wasn't hungry and had no desire to go down. Allwright was at his brother's in Källstorp, and he didn't know anyone else in Anderslöv to spend the evening with. Folke Bengtsson could wait until Kollberg arrived, and anyway, he had talked enough for one day. Rhea was visiting friends in the country, she'd said, so he couldn't call her, and a walk through the village didn't sound inviting. He decided on the only alternative that seemed to remain—bed, and his book about the *Normandie*.

Kollberg didn't show up until late Sunday afternoon, with the quite acceptable explanation that the crayfish had been accompanied by more than a little aquavit, which had to be driven from the body with steam and cold water before he could get behind the wheel of his car again with a clean conscience and a bloodstream free of alcohol.

In the evening, they all fixed dinner together at Allwright's place, and, as Martin Beck had expected, Allwright and Kollberg liked one another at once.

Early Monday morning, Allwright enthusiastically resumed his role as local tour conductor, and Kollberg did not disguise his delight at their loquacious guide and at his captivating native district. Martin Beck sat in the back seat with Timmy and struggled with car sickness. He was amazed at Allwright's ability to describe the same things they had seen on their earlier excursions without actually repeating himself, and at his inexhaustible supply of anecdotes about the area and the people who lived there.

In Domme, they drove up to Folke Bengtsson's house. His station wagon was not there, and no one answered when they knocked at the door.

"He's down fishing," Allwright said. "Or driving around to his customers. He'll probably be back this evening."

They separated outside the police station, Allwright had his routine duties to attend to. Martin Beck and

Kollberg strolled leisurely down toward the highway. The air was clear and fresh, and the sun was warm.

"It's almost enough to make you envy Herrgott," Kollberg said. "What a difference from Stockholm."

"Maybe you should apply for duty in some small town," said Martin Beck.

Kollberg squinted at the sun and shook his head.

"It wouldn't work," he said. "It seems like a good idea when you look at Herrgott, but I'd go stir crazy in two weeks in a hole like this. You're the same way, so you ought to know what I mean. Besides, Gun wants to start working, or at least go on studying if she can't find a job."

Kollberg had been married to Gun for seven years. They had two children, a girl six and a boy three, and Martin Beck had always looked on their marriage as ideal. Before he himself met Rhea Nielsen, he had envied Kollberg. Gun was clever and full of vitality; she had warmth and a sense of humor and was a good companion and, as far as he could see, a marvelous mother. Moreover, she was pretty and looked younger than her thirty-five years. He could imagine Gun running courses in Spanish or jazz ballet or whatever she and the other wives in a place like Anderslöv might think up. She would undoubtedly find something to occupy her time, but, like Kollberg, she wouldn't be happy. She too was a dyed-in-the-wool Stockholmer.

A yellow distribution truck with KVÄLLSPOSTEN in red letters on the side swung away from the curb in front of the Co-op. As it drove on up the hill, a woman came out of the newspaper kiosk and put up a newsbill with the headlines.

Half the placard was taken up by the words WOMAN MURDERED on two lines, and under that, in smaller type, it said: *in Anderslöv?*

Kollberg took Martin Beck by the arm and stepped out into the street, but Martin Beck nodded toward the newspaper truck, which had now stopped outside the pharmacy across the street from the inn.

"I usually buy the paper at the tobacconist in the square," He said.

"Usually?" Kollberg said. "Have you already developed habits around here?"

"Well it's a nice store," said Martin Beck. "A country store, well stocked. They've even got toys, if you want to buy something for Bodil and Joakim."

The shop owner was standing behind the counter with the newsbill in her hand.

"So you've found Sigbrit," she said.

Martin Beck was already well known.

"Poor thing," she said.

"Don't believe everything you read in the papers," Kollberg said. "She's still only missing. There is a question mark down there, as a matter of fact, although it's pretty small."

"Well, can you beat that," the woman said. "The way the newspapers are these days, a person hardly wants to sell them. Nothing but lies and filth and misery."

They bought *Kvällsposten* and *Trelleborgs Allehanda*, and Kollberg had a look at the toy department, which really was well stocked. He found a couple of things he had never seen at NK, PUB, Åhléns, or any of the other big department stores in Stockholm, and decided to come back later and buy them for his children.

Next to Kollberg's car stood an open sportscar, parked with its rear end toward the state liquor store. It was an older model, with clean, straight lines. It looked well cared for, and the bottle-green enamel sparkled in the sun. Martin Beck, who was not usually the least bit interested in cars, stopped to look.

"A Singer," Kollberg said. "At least twenty-five years old. Nice car, but cold as hell in the winter."

Kollberg's specialty was knowing almost everything.

They went into the dining room at the inn. It was lunchtime, and several tables were occupied. They sat down at a corner table near the veranda and opened their papers.

Trelleborgs Allehanda had a brief two-column story on the front page about the disappearance of Sigbrit Mård. The text was objective and accurate and bore the impress of Allwright's temperate statements to the press. The article contained only the names of the missing woman, Allwright, and Martin Beck. Although the lead and the body of the text both reported that the National Homicide Squad had been called in on the case, the reporter had taken pains not to present his readers with any presuppositions, and the words "murdered" and "murderer" were not mentioned. The story was illustrated with the passport photo, and the caption was a request for information from anyone who might have seen the woman since the time of her disappearance.

Kvällsposten was not so restrained. The front page carried a two-column picture of a twenty-year-old Sigbrit Mård with a pony tail and big white earrings. There were additional pictures inside the paper—Sigbrit Mård's house and the house of the Roseanna murderer, the bus stop where she was last seen, an eight-year-old shot of Folke Bengtsson in a police car looking frightened, and a picture of Martin Beck with his mouth open and his hair ruffled.

The story made a great deal of the fact that Sigbrit

Mård lived next door to a sex murderer, and there was a special article recounting the Roseanna case of nine years before. There were comments from a couple of Anderslöv residents, giving their opinions of the missing woman ("a bright, pleasant girl, who always had a smile and a friendly word for everyone") and of Folke Bengtsson ("an odd one, a loner, he put people off"). Mrs. Signe Persson, "perhaps the next to the last person to see Mrs. Mård alive," gave a lively description of how she had seen her standing at the bus stop and then "presumably" climb into Bengtsson's car.

There was also a special box about Martin Beck, "the well-known detective and chief of the National Homicide Squad," but when Martin Beck reached the words "Sweden's Maigret," he threw down the newspaper in the empty chair beside him.

"Ugh," he said with emphasis and looked around for the waitress.

"You can say that again," Kollberg said. "And now we'll have *Expressen* and *Aftonbladet* and the whole lot, and they're all going to pounce on you wanting statements."

"I'm not planning to make any statements," said Martin Beck. "But eventually I suppose we'll have to hold some kind of press conference."

The waitress came, and they ordered *Skånsk* beef stew with beets and pickles.

They ate in silence. Kollberg finished first, as he always did. He wiped his mouth and looked around the room, which by now was almost empty.

Besides himself and Martin Beck, there was only one other person left—a man sitting at a table by the door to the kitchen.

There was a bottle of mineral water and a glass on

the table in front of him. The man was smoking a pipe and flipping through a newspaper, and every now and then he threw a glance at the two detectives.

Kollberg had a vague feeling that he recognized him and studied him surreptitiously.

He looked to be in his forties and had lots of dark blond hair, so long in the back that it hung down over the collar of his light-brown suede jacket. He was wearing steel-rimmed glasses and was smooth-shaven, except for his thick, curly sideburns. His face was thin, with prominent cheekbones, and the lines around his mouth were bitter, or possibly cynical. He wrinkled his brow as he scraped out his pipe into the ashtray in front of him.

He had long, sinewy fingers.

All of a sudden he lifted his head and looked straight into Kollberg's eyes. His gaze was calm and steady and very blue. Kollberg didn't have time to look away, and for a moment they stared at each other.

Martin Beck pushed away his plate and emptied his glass of beer.

As he set down the glass, the man folded his newspaper, stood up, and walked over to their table.

"I don't know if you recognize me," he said.

Martin Beck looked at the man searchingly and shook his head.

Kollberg waited.

"Åke Gunnarsson. Although now my name is Boman."

They remembered him very well. Six years earlier he had killed a man in a fight—a fellow reporter his own age named Alf Matsson. They had both been drunk. Matsson had given him plenty of provocation, and the death could almost be characterized as accidental. When Gunnarsson recovered from the immediate shock, he had acted coldly and intelligently to cover the traces of what he had done. Martin Beck had been in charge of the investigation, and, among other things, had spent a week in Budapest before picking up Gunnarsson's trail. Kollberg had also been present at the arrest, which had not seemed especially gratifying to either one of them. They had developed a certain sympathy for Gunnarsson, whom they regarded as the victim of unfortunate circumstances rather than as a cold-blooded murderer.

Gunnarsson had had a beard and short hair in those days and had been rather fat.

"Sit down," said Martin Beck, moving the newspaper off the chair.

"Thank you," the man said, and sat down.

"You've changed," Kollberg said. "Lost weight, for one thing."

"It wasn't intentional. But for that matter I've deliberately tried to alter my appearance, and I suppose I can congratulate myself on the fact that neither of you recognized me. Although maybe you wouldn't have recognized me anyway."

"Why 'Boman'?" Kollberg wondered.

"It was my mother's name before she married. It seemed the best thing to do. Now I'm used to it, and I've almost forgotten my old name. I'd be grateful if you'd forget it too."

"Okay, Boman," Kollberg said.

Martin Beck thought about the curious coincidence that had suddenly brought him and Kollberg and two people who were the cause of two of their most difficult cases together again after so many years, in a place like Anderslöv.

"What are you doing in Anderslöv?" he asked. "Do you live here?"

"No," said Åke Boman. "As a matter of fact, I'm here to try and get an interview with you. I live in Trelleborg and I work for *Trelleborgs Allehanda*. I wrote that piece on the front page that you were reading a little while ago."

"Didn't you write about cars?" Kollberg said.

"Yes, but on a provincial paper you have to do a little of everything. I was lucky to get this job. It was my parole officer who fixed it up."

The waitress came over and cleared the table.

"Shall we have some coffee?" Kollberg said.

"Okay," said Åke Boman and Martin Beck together. "Maybe you'd like a cognac?"

Åke Boman shook his head, and the waitress went out to the kitchen.

"Don't drink on the job?" said Kollberg.

"I don't drink at all," said Åke Boman. "Not since . . ."

He didn't finish the sentence, but took out a can of Capstan and started to fill his pipe.

"How long have you been working on the paper?" asked Martin Beck.

"A year and a half now. I was sentenced to six years, as you may know. Second-degree murder. I spent three years in prison and then I got an automatic reduction in sentence and a parole. Those first few months on the outside were God-awful. Almost worse than prison, and that was indescribable. I didn't know where to go. All I knew for sure was that I had to stay away from Stockholm. Partly because so many people knew me up there, and partly because the whole merry-go-round would have started again, with the booze and the bars . . . well, you know. I eventually got a job in a garage in Trelleborg and a parole officer who was marvelous. She convinced me to start writing again, and then I got this job. There's only the editor and a couple of other people in town who know . . . I've been damned lucky, as a matter of fact."

But he did not look particularly glad or happy.

They drank their coffee in silence for a while.

"Is that your Singer parked out there?" Kollberg asked.

Åke Boman beamed with pride as he answered.

"Yes, that was a piece of good luck too. It was standing in the barn on an estate up near Önnestad where I was on an assignment last summer. The man who owned it had been dead for a year, and his widow had just let it sit."

He puffed on his pipe.

"It looked pretty scruffy, but that was easily fixed. I bought it on the spot. I do a little writing on the side now and then—special articles for sportscar magazines and a short story once in a while—so I had a little money put away."

"Are you still on parole?" asked Martin Beck.

"No, not since September," said Åke Boman. "But I still see my parole officer occasionally. And her family. She has me to dinner every now and then. You know, I'm a bachelor, and she figures I can't cook for myself."

Martin Beck remembered a photograph he had seen in Boman's apartment six years before. A young, blond woman he had been planning to marry.

Åke Boman puffed on his pipe and stared thoughtfully at Martin Beck.

"The fact is, the paper sent me here to pump you about this disappearance," he said apologetically. "And here I've been sitting talking about myself the whole time."

"We don't have much to add to what you've already

printed," said Martin Beck. "You did speak to Herrgott Allwright, didn't you?"

"Yes, but the very fact that you two are here at all must mean you suspect something," said Åke Boman. "Seriously now, do you thing Folke Bengtsson has murdered her?"

"We don't think anything yet," said Martin Beck. "We haven't even talked to Bengtsson. The only thing we know for sure is that Sigbrit Mård hasn't been home since the seventeenth of October, and that no one seems to know where she is."

"You've read the evening papers," said Åke Boman.

"Yes, but they'll have to be responsible for their own speculations," Kollberg said. "You seem to work for a decent newspaper, in any case."

"We're thinking of holding a press conference by and by," said Martin Beck. "It would be pointless at the moment, because there still isn't anything to say. But if you can take it easy for a while, I'll call and let you know as soon as there's anything new. Is that okay?"

"Okay," said Åke Boman.

They both had the feeling they owed him something. What it was, and why, they didn't know.

9.

Martin Beck couldn't stop thinking about Bertil Mård's hands, and after lunch he decided to go down to Trelleborg and send a telex query on Mård to Interpol in Paris.

Most people, even most policemen, are under the impression that Interpol is a rather ineffective international agency, unwieldy and bureaucratic, primarily a facade, behind which there is essentially nothing to be found.

The case of Bertil Mård gave the lie to all such notions.

Martin Beck had not been able to think up any clever questions. He merely asked if Mård had ever been booked anywhere, and if so, what for.

He had his answer within six hours, a fairly detailed answer at that.

They sat in Allwright's apartment that same evening and pondered the document, not without a certain astonishment.

They were having sandwiches and beer.

At Allwright's, they still had a chance of being left more or less in peace, since the police station was, as usual, closed at this time of day.

An automatic answering device referred all telephone calls to the police in Trelleborg, where switchboard duty was no longer much of a pleasure.

The inn was full of reporters.

For safety's sake, Allwright had pulled the jack on his private phone.

They studied the telex tape.

The police in Trinidad-Tobago reported that Bertil Mård had been arrested on February 6, 1965, for beating to death an oiler of Brazilian nationality. He was brought before a police court that same day and found guilty of disturbing the peace and of what the report called "justifiable homicide," which was not a punishable offense in Trinidad-Tobago. For disturbing the peace, however, he was fined four pounds. The oiler had made advances to a woman in Mård's company and was thus considered to have caused the incident himself. Mård had left the country the following day.

"Fifty crowns," Kollberg said. "That's pretty cheap for killing a man."

" 'Justifiable homicide,' " Allwright said. "How do you say that in Swedish? Of course, we have the right of self-defense. That's the same thing in principle. But it's not a translation."

"It's untranslatable," said Martin Beck.

"There is no such concept," Kollberg said.

"You're wrong about that," Allwright said, and laughed. "They've got it in the States, believe you me. Just let a policeman shoot somebody, and it's always 'justifiable homicide.' Legitimate murder, or whatever we'd call it in Swedish. It happens every day."

There was a dead silence in the room.

Kollberg pushed away the plate with his half-eaten sandwich in distaste.

His eyes were vacant, and he sank down on his chair with his forearms resting on his thighs and his hands hanging between his knees.

"What happened?" Allwright said.

"You laughed in the wrong place," said Martin Beck.

Allwright didn't understand what he had done wrong, but he did realize that he shouldn't say anything more. Not right away, in any case.

Martin Beck kept a close and anxious eye on his old friend, but he too was silent.

Allwright finished his cigarette. He lit another one and smoked it too. Then he did nothing at all for a while.

Martin Beck continued to look at Kollberg.

At long last, Kollberg shrugged his fleshy shoulders and straightened up.

"Sorry, Herrgott," he said. "I get like that sometimes. It's a little bit like epilepsy. I just can't help it."

He took a big drink from his glass of beer and wiped away the foam with the back of his hand.

"Now where were we?" he said. "Mård's got a rotten alibi, or, rather, no alibi at all. And he has a history of violence. But does he have a motive?"

"Jealousy," said Martin Beck.

"Of whom?"

"Bertil Mård could be jealous of the cat," Allwright said, and laughed experimentally. "And so, sure enough, they didn't have a cat."

"Not much to go on," Kollberg said.

"Whoops," said Allwright, as Timmy took the ham sandwich out of his hand and gulped it down.

Martin Beck burst out laughing.

"Down, Timmy!" Allwright said. "What a police dog! It's a world's record. Did you see that? He just walked up and swiped my sandwich. Are you a soccer fan, Lennart?"

"No," said Kollberg, laughing so hard his stomach was bouncing up and down.

"Well, then I'll skip that story," Allwright said. "And so that brings us to Folke."

"Folke Bengtsson has no alibi at all and has a history of violence. But does he have a motive?"

"The motive would be that he's not all there," Allwright said.

"In the case of the murder of Roseanna McGraw, the motive was very deep-rooted and complex," said Martin Beck.

"Nonsense, Martin," Kollberg said. "There's something you and I have never discussed, but I've thought about a lot. You're convinced that Folke Bengtsson was guilty. I'm convinced of it too. But what sort of proof did we have? He confessed to you, of course, after I'd broken his arm, and after we'd enticed him like mad and trapped him. In the courtroom, he denied it. The only thing we could really prove was that he tried to rape, or possibly—but remember, *possibly*—strangle an undercover policewoman we had instructed to entice and seduce him, and who was practically naked when he entered her apartment. I've always thought that in a society of laws, Folke Bengtsson would never have been convicted of the Roseanna murder. The evidence just wasn't good enough. Moreover, he was a mental case, but they didn't send him to a hospital, they put him in prison."

"What are you getting at?"

"Don't you see? You and I and several other people, the judge who convicted him for one, were convinced that he was a murderer, but we didn't have any real proof. There's one hell of a difference."

"He had her sunglasses, among other things."

"A good defense lawyer would have made hash out of our evidence. And a real court would have dismissed the case. In a society of laws . . ."

Kollberg stopped.

"Maybe Trinidad-Tobago is a society of laws," Allwright said.

"No doubt," Kollberg said.

"In any event, tomorrow we have to talk to Folke Bengtsson," said Martin Beck, as if to change the subject to something more pleasant.

"Yes," Allwright said. "I guess it's about time."

"I think we'll have to hold some kind of press conference too," Kollberg said. "However dreadful that may sound."

Martin Beck nodded gloomily.

"Press conference," Allwright said. "I've never held one of those before. And how are we going to handle Folke? Shall I ask him to come in here?"

"I'd rather talk to him in his own home
Beck.

"And drive out there with a trail of re us?" Kollberg said.

"Yes, well, I guess it can't be avoided," said Martin Beck.

"Do we hold the press conference before or after?"

"After, I'd say."

"And how do we know when Bengtsson will decide to be at home?" Kollberg said.

"I can tell you that," said Allwright. "He leaves home at six in the morning and comes back at one in the afternoon. Then he goes out in the evening again and sets out his nets. He sticks to a schedule."

"Okay, then we'll drive out there at one-fifteen," Kollberg said. "And we'll talk to the papers at three o'clock."

Allwright appeared to be looking forward to an interesting and downright exciting day.

Martin Beck and Kollberg thought they knew better.

"You think we dare sneak over and go to bed?" said Kollberg, yawning.

"The restaurant's been closed for hours," said Martin Beck optimistically. "The ones who are still awake are probably having a card game somewhere."

10.

It turned out to be a very elegant procession. They filed out of the Anderslöv police station at precisely 1 p.m. on November 6, 1973. A uniformed police

...nt led the way. Kollberg felt like Abbott and Cos-
...o rolled into one as he marched along behind Martin
Beck and with Timmy sniffing at his heels. Allwright
brought up the rear in his usual green rubber boots, the
safari hat on the back of his head, and the dog straining
at its leash. It occurred to him that they ought to be
carrying little flags, since it was 341 years to the day
since Gustav II Adolf fell at the battle of Lützen.

"We'd better drive slowly, so we don't lose anyone,"
said Allwright with a grin.

Kollberg and Martin Beck took their seats in the patrol car, while Allwright wedged the dog into his
tomato-red Ascona and climbed behind the wheel to
lead the expedition.

But if Lennart Kollberg felt ridiculous, it was nothing
to what certain other people had good cause to feel.

No one had given it a thought in advance, but the
hour they had chosen for their departure fell in the
midst of what was, for most of the reporters, an almost
ritual event.

Lunch.

Nevertheless, someone had obviously been standing
watch, for the news spread like wildfire.

Men and women came tumbling out of the inn dining
room with their mouths full of herring salad or pork
knuckles and mashed turnips. One of them had his
camera in one hand and was still holding a long-
stemmed glass of aquavit in the other. They were followed by confused waitresses wondering what this mass
evasion of the check might mean, and by other guests,
who probably thought the building was on fire. The
confusion was compounded by the fact that some of
them had their cars parked in the square and others in
the long parking lot behind the inn garden.

But Allwright took it exceedingly slow and easy, as

promised, and when Kollberg looked around just as they passed the church, he saw no fewer than ten cars in line behind the patrol car. And he suspected all of them of containing members of what used to be called the Third Estate.

There was only one vehicle that was conspicuous by its absence, and that was Åke Boman's green Singer. The explanation was simple. In keeping with his promise of the day before, Kollberg had called Trelleborg and given him the schedule.

Halfway to Domme, Allwright slowed down, drove off onto the shoulder, and stopped. He climbed out, jumped the ditch, and disappeared behind a little shed. He appeared again about a minute later, calmly closing his fly in full view of everyone in the line of cars, some of whom were obviously in a quandary as to whether or not they might be expected to follow suit.

Without a trace of expression on his face, Allwright walked over to the patrol car and leaned down so he could talk through the window.

"Merely a diversionary maneuver," he said. "To be sure no one breaks ranks."

He studied the people in the following cars solemnly. Then he went back to his own car and drove on. Both Kollberg and Martin Beck could see his shoulders quivering. He was clearly up there having a good laugh all by himself.

"Christ, how I envy Herrgott!" Kollberg said. "Talk about a sense of humor!"

"Yes," said the sergeant suddenly. "He's an uncommonly funny man. It's a real joy to work for him, although, for that matter, you never have the feeling of being a subordinate. I'm four salary grades below him, but nobody gives it a thought. No, he's really all right— no pun intended."

Martin Beck knew the driver's name—Evert Johansson—but that was all.

"How long have you been a policeman?" he said.

"Six years. It was the only job I could get. Maybe I shouldn't say so, but I used to be on the force in Malmö and I thought it was sheer hell. People looked at me like I wasn't human, and I noticed myself that I was starting to get funny. I was at a demonstration there in 1969, and we were beating people with our billy clubs. I hit a girl myself. She couldn't have been more than seventeen, and what's more, she had a little kid with her."

Martin Beck looked at Evert Johansson. A young man with a bright, open face.

Kollberg sighed but said nothing.

"I even saw myself on TV afterward. It was enough to make you want to go hang yourself. And I decided to quit that same evening, but . . ."

"But what?"

"Well, I happen to have an uncommonly good wife. She came up with the idea that I ought to apply for a transfer out in the country somewhere. And I was lucky. I got this job. Otherwise I'd never have been a policeman today."

Allwright turned off to the right, and they were there.

The house was small and old, but looked well cared for. Åke Boman's sportscar was parked near the gate. He himself was sitting behind the wheel reading a book.

Folke Bengtsson was standing out by the hen house with a spade in his hand. He was wearing overalls and leather boots and had a checkered cap on his head.

Allwright walked around to the trunk of his car and took out a white plastic Co-op shopping bag.

Martin Beck wondered what he had inside.

"You watch the dog, Evert," Allwright said. "I know

it's a hell of an assignment, but ours isn't going to be much fun either. And try to keep all those people off his land."

Then he opened the gate, and Martin Beck and Kollberg followed him through. Kollberg was very careful to close it behind him.

Folke Bengtsson put down his spade and came over to meet them.

"Hi, Folke," Allwright said.

"Hi," said Folke Bengtsson.

"Shall we go inside and talk?"

"Talk?"

"Yes," Allwright said. "We've got all the papers and so forth. But you know me. I wouldn't come if it weren't necessary."

"Yes, well then, please come in."

"Thank you," said Martin Beck.

Kollberg was silent.

As soon as they were inside, Allwright took a pair of shoes out of the plastic bag and left his boots by the door.

Martin Beck felt chagrined.

God, how little he knew about manners and customs in the country! Besides which, it didn't say much for his powers of deduction. You go to visit someone wearing your boots. So, of course, you take along a pair of shoes.

Folke Bengtsson took off his boots too.

"We can sit in the living room," he said tonelessly.

Martin Beck glanced around at the room, which was spartan but neat. The only things that might be called luxuries were a large aquarium and a television set.

From outside came the sounds of cars being parked, and, right afterward, the low murmur of conversation.

Bengtsson had changed very little in nine years. In

any case, if prison life had marked him it was not apparent.

Martin Beck thought back to the summer of 1964.

Bengtsson had been thirty-eight years old at that time and had seemed healthy, calm, and strong. Blue eyes, with a little gray in his hair. A tall, well-built man, rather handsome, he had made a clean, neat, pleasant impression.

Now he was forty-seven and a little grayer.

Otherwise, the difference was nil.

Martin Beck ran his hand over his face. All at once it all came back to him. How terribly hard it had been to break through this man's facade, to get him to let down his guard, or make a slip of the tongue or an admission.

"Well now," Allwright said. "I'm not the one who's going to do the talking, but I suppose you know what this is all about."

Folke Bengtsson nodded. Possibly. In any case he made a slight movement with his head.

"I think you know these gentlemen," Allwright said.

"Yes," said Bengtsson. "I do indeed know Detective Chief Inspector Beck and Detective Kollberg. How are you?"

"They're superintendents now," Allwright said. "If that makes any difference."

"Well," said Kollberg, "technically, I'm just an acting superintendent. The correct title is actually Detective Inspector. But as Herrgott says, it really doesn't matter. Anyway, can't we use first names?"

"I'd be glad to," Bengtsson said. "For that matter, everyone around here is very informal. I've noticed, for example, that the children call the priest by his first name."

"Yes, that's right," Allwright said. "He comes steaming along in his vestments and everything, and the kids yell out, 'Hi, Karl.' And he knows all their names, so he always yells right back. 'Hi there, Jens,' for example."

"Things were very informal in prison, too," Bengtsson said.

"Don't you find it unpleasant to talk about that time?" said Martin Beck.

"Not at all. I enjoyed myself in prison. An orderly, regular existence. Better than home, much of the time. I've no complaints with the penal system. It was a good life. No complications, so to speak."

Kollberg sat down on one of the straight-backed chairs by the round dining table and covered his face with both hands.

The man is insane, he thought.

And:

Now this nightmare is going to begin again.

"Yes, well, let's sit down," Bengtsson said.

Martin Beck sat down, and so did Allwright.

None of them stopped to think that there were only three chairs.

"It's about Sigbrit Mård," said Martin Beck.

"I see."

"You know her, don't you Mr. . . . Folke?"

"Yes, of course. She lives only a few hundred yards from here, on the other side of the driveway."

"She's missing."

"So I've heard."

"No one has seen her since just after one o'clock on the seventeenth of last month. That was a Wednesday."

"Yes, that's just what I've been told."

"She had gone to the post office in Anderslöv. And then she was going to take the bus to the end of the driveway down here."

"Yes, I've heard that too."

"There are witnesses who say the two of you spoke to each other at the post office."

"Yes, that's true."

"What did you talk about?"

"She wanted to buy some eggs on Friday, if I had any."

"And?"

"I said I was fairly certain she could have a dozen."

"Yes?"

"That was what she wanted. A dozen."

"And what did she say then?"

" 'Thank you very much.' Or something to that effect. I don't remember exactly what she said, as a matter of fact."

"Sigbrit Mård didn't have her car that day."

"No, so I've heard."

"Now tell me . . . Folke, did you know she didn't have her car? When you ran into her at the post office?"

Folke Bengtsson said nothing for a very long time.

"Yes," he said finally.

"How did you happen to know that?"

"When you live like this, you notice things about your neighbors, whether you want to or not."

"But you had your station wagon with you in Anderslöv?"

"Yes, it was parked right out in front of the post office."

"You know, Folke, that's actually a no-parking zone," said Allwright with a mischievous look.

"I really didn't know that."

"There's a sign," Allwright said.

"I never noticed it, really."

Allwright took out an old silver pocket watch and snapped open the case.

"Sigbrit Mård would have been standing at the bus stop right about now," he said. "Unless, of course, someone gave her a lift."

Folke Bengtsson looked at his wristwatch.

"Yes," he said. "That sounds right. And it agrees with what I've been told."

"And with what was in the papers," said Martin Beck. "Right?"

"I never read periodicals," said Folke Bengtsson.

"Not even magazines? Men's magazines, or the sports papers?"

"Men's magazines have changed. I find them very tasteless these days. And the sports papers no longer exist. Anyway, magazines are so expensive."

"Well, now . . . Folke, since you happened to run into each other at the post office, and since she didn't have a car, wouldn't it be only natural for you to give her a ride? You were going the same way."

With rising irritation, Martin Beck noticed that he was having a hard time calling Bengtsson by his first name.

Once again there was a long pause.

"Yes," said Bengtsson finally. "I suppose that would seem natural, but that isn't what happened."

"Did she ask for a ride?"

This time Bengtsson paused so long before answering that Martin Beck finally felt he had to repeat the question.

"Did Sigbrit Mård say anything to you about getting a ride home in your car?"

"I don't recall anything of that kind."

"Is it possible that she did?"

"I don't know. That's all I can tell you."

Martin Beck looked at Allwright, who raised his eyebrows and shrugged his shoulders.

"Maybe it was the other way around, and you offered her a ride?"

"Absolutely not," said Bengtsson immediately.

Here, clearly, he was an firmer ground.

"So there's no doubt at all on that point?"

"No," said Folke Bengtsson. "I never pick up hitch-hikers. Every time I have ever given anyone a ride, it was always someone directly connected with my work. And that has only happened a few times."

"Is that true?"

"Yes, really."

Martin Beck again looked at Allwright, who made another face. His stock of facial expressions was clearly inexhaustible. The Anderslöv Chief of Police would undoubtedly have made a good mime.

"So we can rule out that possibility."

"Completely," Bengtsson said. "It's utterly unthinkable."

"Why should it be so utterly unthinkable?"

"Because of my disposition, I suppose."

Martin Beck thought about Folke Bengtsson's disposition for a moment. It was a subject that would bear some thought.

But this was not the time for brooding.

"How so?" said Martin Beck.

"I'm the kind of person for whom a regular routine is almost a necessity. For example, my customers can tell you that I am very particular about punctuality. If something holds me up, I try to hurry so as to get back on schedule."

Martin Beck looked at Allwright, who made a face that might almost have been worthy of Harpo Marx. Bengtsson's punctuality was clearly not in doubt.

"It irritates me when something disturbs the rhythm of my life. I must say, for example, that this conversation upsets me greatly. Nothing personal, of course, but a whole list of small tasks will suffer."

"I understand."

"So, as I said, I never pick up hitchhikers. Especially not women."

Kollberg took his hands away from his face.

"Why?" he said.

"I don't understand what you mean."

"Why do you say 'especially not women'?"

Bengtsson's expression changed and grew more serious. He no longer looked indifferent. But what was it in his eyes? Hate? Aversion? Desire? Severity?

Madness perhaps.

"Answer me, Folke," Kollberg said.

"Women have caused me a great deal of unpleasantness."

"We know. But that doesn't mean you can ignore the fact that more than half of all the people in the world are women."

"There are different kinds of women," Bengtsson said. "Almost all the ones I've met have been bad."

"Bad?"

"Exactly. Simply bad human beings. Unworthy of their sex."

Kollberg looked out the window in resignation. The man was insane. But what did that prove? For that matter, could the newspaper photographer who was hanging like a spider monkey from a pear tree fifty feet from the house be considered entirely sane? Presumably.

Kollberg sighed deeply and collapsed like a punctured weather balloon.

Martin Beck resumed his famous systematic questioning.

"Let's leave that subject for the moment."

"Yes, thank you," said Folke Bengtsson.

"Instead of speculation, we'll stick to facts. The two of you left the post office only a few minutes apart, is that right?"

"Yes."

"What happened then?"

"I got my car and drove home."

"Directly?"

"Yes."

"All right . . . Mr. Bengtsson, now we come to the next question."

"Yes?"

Martin Beck was disgusted with himself. Why couldn't he make himself say "Folke"? Kollberg had said it, and for Allwright it was apparently the easiest thing in the world.

"You must have passed Sigbrit Mård in your car, either at the bus stop or very close to it."

There was no reply, and Martin Beck heard himself say:

"Answer me, Mr. Bengtsson. Was Mrs. Mård visible at that time?"

Terrific. The best answer, of course, would be "No, she was invisible."

But Folke Bengtsson didn't seem to be aware of Inspector Beck's embarrassment. He said nothing at all, just stared vacantly at his big, sunburned hands.

Martin Beck was at a loss. The way he had asked it, the question was too idiotic to be repeated.

Finally Allwright came to his rescue.

"That's a pretty damn simple question, Folke. Did you see Sigbrit or didn't you?"

At long last Bengtsson said, "I saw her."

"A little louder, please," said Martin Beck.

"I saw her."

"Where, exactly?"

"At the bus stop. Maybe a few feet away."

"There is a witness who maintains that your car slowed down at that point. Maybe even stopped."

Seconds went by. Time passed. They all grew one minute older. Finally Bengtsson answered, softly.

"I saw her, and it's possible that I slowed down. She was walking along the right side of the road. I'm a very careful driver, and I usually slow down when I pass pedestrians. Maybe I was meeting another car. I don't remember."

"Were you driving so slowly that you actually stopped?"

"No, I didn't stop."

"Might it have looked as if you stopped?"

"I don't know. I really don't. All I know is that I didn't stop."

Martin Beck turned to Allwright.

"Didn't he say a moment ago that he tried to drive faster when he was late?"

"Yes," Allwright said. "That's right."

Martin Beck turned back to the murderer. Damn. He actually thought that word. Murderer.

"Wouldn't your visit to the post office have made you late?" he said. "So that you'd be hurrying afterward?"

"I always go to the post office on Wednesdays," said Folke Bengtsson calmly. "I always send a letter to my mother in Södertälje, for one thing, and there are usually other matters to attend to."

"Sigbrit Mård did not get into the car?"

"No. She did not."

It had been a leading question, but not quite in the right direction.

"Did Sigbrit Mård get into your car?"

"No. Absolutely not. I didn't stop."

"Another thing. Did Sigbrit Mård wave or signal to you in any other way?"

And then there was another of those painful, incomprehensible pauses.

Bengtsson didn't answer. He looked Martin Beck in the eye but said nothing.

"Did Sigbrit Mård make any sort of signal when she saw your car?"

Another few moments of their lives elapsed in silence. Martin Beck thought about women, and how those few moments might have been spent.

Once again, Allwright broke the silence. He laughed.

"Why the heck don't you answer him, Folke?" he said. "Did Sigbrit wave to you or didn't she?"

"I don't know," Bengtsson said.

So softly it was almost inaudible.

"You don't know?" said Martin Beck.

"No, I don't know."

Kollberg gave Martin Beck a resigned look.

He didn't have to say it.

Give up, Martin.

But there were more questions.

Hard questions.

"I remember when we were sitting at Kristineberg nine years ago," said Martin Beck.

"So do I."

"We talked a lot about women. Certain viewpoints were aired. Some of them were rather peculiar."

"I didn't think so."

"They seemed peculiar to me. Do you still have the same ideas about women, Mr. Bengtsson?"

A long silence.

"I try not to think about them."

Them.

"You know Sigbrit Mård, don't you, Mr. Bengtsson?"

"She's one of my steady customers. She's my closest neighbor. But I try not to think of her as a woman."

"Try? What do you mean by 'try,' Mr. Bengtsson?"

Allwright shook himself. He looked more distressed and unhappy than ever before in their six-day acquaintance. Which was not to say that he looked distressed or unhappy. Just a little less cheerful.

"Why don't you call him Folke? It sounds so damned formal."

"I can't," said Martin Beck.

It was true. He couldn't. At the same time, he was glad he could be honest about it.

"I see," said Allwright. "Well then, there's nothing to discuss. Truth can be blamed, but it can't be shamed."

Kollberg looked a bit startled.

"Local saying," Allwright said, and laughed.

Folke Bengtsson didn't laugh.

"In any case, you know Sigbrit Mård. And sometimes you must think of her as a woman. I want to ask you a question, Mr. Bengtsson, and I want an honest answer. What do you think of her? As a woman?"

Silence.

"Answer him," Allwright said. "Folke, you have to answer him. Be honest."

"Sometimes I see her as a woman. But not often."

"And?" said Martin Beck.

"I think she's . . ."

"She's what?"

Folke Bengtsson and Martin Beck looked into each other's eyes. Bengtsson's were blue. Martin Beck's were grayish blue. He remembered that from before.

"Disgusting," said Folke Bengtsson. "Indecent. Like an animal. She smells. But I see her often, and I've only thought that two or three times."

Insane, Kollberg thought.

"Lay off, Martin."

"That's what you wanted me to say," said Folke Bengtsson. "Isn't it?"

"Did you deliver the eggs?" said Martin Beck.

"No. I knew she was gone."

Gone.

They sat in silence for a while.

"You're tormenting me," said Folke Bengtsson. "But I don't dislike you. It's just your job. My job is selling fish and eggs."

"Yes," said Kollberg gloomily. "We've tormented you before, and now we're doing it again. I broke your shoulder once. Unnecessarily."

"Oh, it mended quite fast. I'm completely recovered, really. Are you going to take me with you now?"

Martin Beck had one last idea.

"Have you ever seen Sigbrit Mård's ex-husband?"

"Yes. Twice. He drove up in a beige Volvo."

Allwright made a mysterious face but said nothing.

"Shall we call it a day?" Kollberg said.

Martin Beck stood up.

Allwright took off his shoes and put them back in the plastic bag. And put on his boots.

He was the only one of them with the sense to say, "So long, Folke. Sorry."

"Goodbye," Kollberg said.

Martin Beck said nothing.

"You'll be back, I suppose," said Folke Bengtsson.

"Depends," said Allwright.

Outside the gate, the Nikon cameras started clicking like a hailstorm.

There was a voice coming from a car with a short-wave radio antenna.

"The chief of the National Homicide Squad and his right-hand man are just leaving the house of the Rose-anna murderer. Local police and dog-handlers are guarding the building. It doesn't look as if the Rose-anna murderer has been arrested yet."

Boman walked over to Kollberg.

"Well?" he said.

Kollberg shook his head.

"Gunnarsson," came a sudden, harsh voice. "If you brown-nose the cops we'll spread your ass all over the front pages. And then you can call yourself Boman till you're blue in the face. Just wanted you to know."

"You'll do it anyway, I imagine," Boman said.

Martin Beck threw a glance at the reporter who had spoken. A heavy-bellied man with a bushy gray beard and a patronizing manner. His name was Molin, and, of course, he worked for one of the evening tabloids. He seemed to have aged fifteen years since Martin Beck last saw him in 1966. Too much beer, probably.

"He was a buddy of Alf's," said Boman impassively.

Allwright cleared his throat.

"The press conference will be postponed for half an hour. We'll have it in the village hall. I think the library is our best bet."

11.

They had half an hour before the press conference was supposed to begin and they used the time to try and analyze what Folke Bengtsson had actually said. And not said.

"He's behaving exactly the way he did before," said Martin Beck. "Gives clear, unambiguous answers to questions he knows we can check."

"He's nuts," said Kollberg dejectedly. "It's as simple as that."

"And then sometimes he doesn't answer at all," Allwright said. "Is that what you mean?"

"Yes, by and large. He turns funny and evasive whenever you get to a really key question."

"As an amateur in this area . . ."

Allwright began, and then burst out laughing.

"What are you howling at?" said Kollberg, slightly irritated.

"Well, I don't mean that I love murder and that sort of thing," Allwright said. "And your true amateur, after all, is a person who loves something, right? From the Latin *amator* . . ."

"If we could skip the philology," said Kollberg, "it might be worthwhile to compare our impressions."

"Yes," said Martin Beck. "I think you're right. What do you think yourself?"

"Well, if we disregard Bengtsson's attitude toward women, which as far as I'm concerned shows that he's demented . . ."

"Sexually abnormal," Allwright said.

"Exactly. But if we disregard that . . ."

"Which can't be disregarded," Martin Beck interrupted.

"No. In any case, there were two questions where he really hesitated. First, what was actually said at the post office? And second, did Sigbrit Mård try to thumb a ride with him as he drove past the bus stop?"

"And both of those questions involve the same thing," said Martin Beck. "Did he give her a ride or didn't he? If she spoke to him in the post office about anything more than eggs, the obvious thing would have been for her to ask him for a ride home. Or does that sound farfetched?"

"Not at all," Allwright said. "They are next-door neighbors, after all."

"But would she really do that?" said Martin Beck. "Sigbrit Mård knew as well as most other people in the village that Bengtsson had been in prison and what it was they convicted him of, namely a sex murder."

"Well, yes," Kollberg said. "That's true enough. But in a way it's a logical somersault. After all, she was one of his so-called steady customers. Now that must mean that Bengtsson came over to her house every week to deliver whatever it was he delivered."

"Fish, mostly," Allwright said. "The prices are low, and the quality's high. That egg business is mostly just a sideline. He doesn't have all that many chickens."

"If she'd really been afraid of him, she never would have had him come to the house like that," Kollberg said.

"No," said Allwright. "I don't think Sigbrit's afraid of Folke. I've never noticed that anyone was afraid of him. On the other hand, everyone does know he's a little odd and prefers to be left alone."

"From my experience of Bengtsson, the way he's acting now is typical," said Martin Beck. "He's very wary about the conversation in the post office and what happened at the bus stop. He knows there are people who may have overheard what they were talking about and he also knows there may be witnesses who saw her try to hitch a ride."

"But he has no reason to lie if she didn't ask him for a ride," Allwright said. "And especially not if he didn't stop at the bus stop."

"You've got to remember that his experience of the police and the courts is pretty damn negative," Kollberg said.

Martin Beck rubbed the bridge of his nose with the thumb and index finger of his right hand.

"Let's try to imagine the situation," he said. "They just happen to find themselves at the post office at the same time. And it just happens that Sigbrit Mård doesn't have her car. And so she asks him for a ride home, and he says no and makes some kind of excuse. He's got something else to do, for example. She winds up her business and walks to the bus stop. When she sees Bengtsson coming along in his car, she waves at him to get a ride. He slows down but he doesn't stop."

"Or else he does stop and he picks her up," said Kollberg sadly.

"Right."

"But as long as we don't have a body, we don't have a murder, much less anything to accuse Bengtsson of."

"But you can't escape the fact that he's behaving oddly," said Martin Beck. "A third thing that struck me was that he didn't go over there with that dozen eggs. It was only two days later, and since Sigbrit Mård had such irregular working hours, it wouldn't be so terribly strange for him to assume she was home on Friday even if he didn't see her on Thursday."

"The story that she was missing spread awfully fast," Allwright said. "When she didn't go to work on Thursday and didn't answer the phone, there were quite a few people who started wondering where she might be. I heard on Thursday that she was gone, but of course

I figured what the hell, a person's got the right to disappear for a day or two. But still, they wondered at the garage why she didn't come pick up her car Thursday morning like she'd said. And that was a good question."

He took out his pocket watch and snapped it open.

"Is it time?" Kollberg asked.

"Pretty close," Allwright said. "There's just one little detail I'd like to point out—something you could hardly have noticed."

"What would that be?" said Kollberg, hanging his head dejectedly.

"Well," said Allwright, "Folke said that he knew Bertil Mård by sight and that he'd seen him there twice, in a beige Volvo. That doesn't jibe with what I know. Mård hasn't been around for a long time. He stopped coming out to see Sigbrit before Folke ever moved into that old house."

"Yes," said Martin Beck. "I did notice that. Because Mård told me that he used to come out here to lay her every now and then, but he said it was at least a year and a half since the last time he was here."

"Which might mean that your ship's captain is lying," Kollberg said.

"There were a lot of things in that conversation I didn't know whether or not to believe."

"We have to go downstairs now," Allwright said. "Shall we say anything about Mård?"

"Let's not," said Martin Beck.

The press conference was very impromptu and for Martin Beck and Kollberg it was very unpleasant, because they had so little to say.

But it was a necessity. It represented their only chance of being left alone to do their work in peace and quiet.

Allwright was more phlegmatic and good-natured about it all. He still looked almost as if he thought it was fun.

The very first question, with its simple brutality, set the tone.

"Do you think Sigbrit Mård has been murdered?"

Martin Beck felt obliged to answer, "We don't know."

"Isn't your very presence here—you and your colleague—sufficient indication of the fact that you suspect Sigbrit Mård has been murdered?"

"Yes. That's correct. That suspicion cannot be ruled out."

"Would it be accurate to say that you have a suspect but no body?"

"I wouldn't want to put it that way."

"How would the police like to put it?"

"We don't know where Mrs. Mård is, and we don't know what can have happened to her."

"One person has already been questioned. Is that correct?"

"We have spoken to a number of people in an attempt to determine Mrs. Mård's whereabouts."

Martin Beck detested press conferences. The questions were often infuriating and inconsiderate. They were hard to answer, and almost everything was open to misinterpretation.

"Is an arrest imminent?"

"No."

"But an arrest has been contemplated, is that right?"

"I wouldn't say that. We don't even know if any crime has been committed."

"Then how do you explain the fact that personnel from the National Homicide Squad are here at all?"

"A woman has disappeared. We are trying to find out what's become of her."

"I have the impression the police are beating about the proverbial bush."

"In that case, the press certainly is not," said Kollberg, to ease the atmosphere a little.

"Our duty as journalists is to supply the public with facts. If the police won't provide us with information, then we have to get it for ourselves. Why not put your cards on the table?"

"There aren't any cards to put," Kollberg said. "We're looking for Sigbrit Mård. If you want to help us find her, why, be my guest."

"Isn't it reasonable to suppose that she's fallen victim to a sex crime?"

"No," said Kollberg. "It isn't reasonable to suppose anything as long as we don't know where she is."

"I would like to know how the police sum up the situation. Would you mind?"

Kollberg didn't answer. He looked at the woman who had asked the question, a fair-haired girl of about twenty-five.

"Well?"

Neither Kollberg nor Martin Beck said anything.

Allwright threw them a look and then broke the silence.

"What we know is very simple," he said. "Mrs. Mård left the post office in Anderslöv around noon on Wednesday, October seventeenth. Since then no one has seen her. There is one witness who believes she saw her at, or on her way to, the bus stop. Period. That's all we know."

The reporter who had threatened Boman out at Domme cleared his throat.

"Beck?" he said.

"Yes, Mr. Molin."

"We've had about enough of this little farce."

"What farce?"

"This press conference is a travesty. You're the chief of National Homicide, but instead of giving us proper answers to our questions, you keep hiding behind your staff and the local police. Now are you planning to arrest Folke Bengtsson or aren't you?"

"We've talked to him. That's all."

"And what came out of that conversation? You were in there shooting the breeze for almost two hours."

"For the time being, we have no suspects."

Martin Beck was lying, and he didn't like it. But what was he supposed to say?

He liked the next question even less.

"How does it feel to be a policeman in a society where you have to arrest the same man twice in less than ten years for the same kind of heinous crime?"

Yes, how did it feel? Martin Beck had enough trouble analyzing his relationship to society without the newspapers asking him about it.

His only answer was to shake his head.

Kollberg fielded the rest of the questions, which were uninteresting and farfetched and to which he gave uninteresting and farfetched answers.

The wind was going out of the press conference. Everyone could see that, with the possible exception of Herrgott Allwright.

"Now that you're all here," he said suddenly, "from all the major newspapers and the radio and so forth, why don't you take the opportunity to write a little something about Anderslöv?"

"Is that supposed to be some sort of joke?"

"Not at all. Everyone's always talking about the miserable conditions in this country, and in the big cities—if you can believe the mass media—a person hardly dares stick his nose outdoors for fear of getting it cut off. But around here everything is calm and peaceful. We don't even have any unemployment or any junkies. It's pleasant. The people are mostly nice, and on top of that, it's pretty. Drive around and have a look at the churches in this district, for example."

"Just a minute," Molin said. "We've got feature writers to go look at churches. But I did like that question someone asked a little while ago. How does it feel to have to hunt down the same murderer for two sex murders within ten years? What's your answer to that?"

"No comment," said Martin Beck.

And that ended the press conference in the Anderslöv village hall.

Bertil Mård's name had never been mentioned.

The only person who hadn't said a word was Åke Boman.

12.

If the newspaper stories on Monday and Tuesday caused a certain amount of consternation, they were like a sea breeze compared with the cyclone that broke over the village on Wednesday.

The telephone rang continuously, upstairs at Herrgott Allwright's as well as down in the office, not to mention what it was like at the police station in Trelleborg.

Sigbrit Mård had been seen in Abisko and Skanör, on Mallorca, Rhodes, and the Canary Islands, and one voice even assured them that she had done a strip tease the previous evening at a sex club in, of all places, Oslo.

She was reported to have taken the automobile ferry from Ystad to Poland and the train ferry from Trelleborg to Sassnitz. She had also been observed in several different places in Malmö, Stockholm, Gothenburg, and Copenhagen. Especially persistent rumors placed her in the waiting hall at Kastrup and at Sturup Airports.

It was only in Anderslöv that no one had seen her.

Seven callers had seen her with Folke Bengtsson, in the most unlikely places, but not one of them could describe what she had been wearing. In other words, the police had not released this information, and every newspaper that had its own reporters on the case published completely misleading and mutually contradictory details of her attire, which ranged from red slacks and a white parka to a black dress, black stockings, and black shoes. And indeed this latter paper referred to her as "the woman in black."

But everyone agreed on the description of Folke Bengtsson. Actually, only the more unrestrained newspapers named him by name and proffered newly taken photographs. For the others, he was "the man in the cap" or "the sex murderer turned herring monger."

At three o'clock in the afternoon, Martin Beck was sitting in Allwright's apartment with a headache. He had just stirred up a great commotion by going to the pharmacy for aspirin, and he could already see tomorrow's headlines in his mind's eye. HEADACHE IN ANDERSLÖV, for example. He had also been on the verge of going to the liquor store for a pint of whisky, but had refrained because of the comments such an act would undoubtedly call forth.

HANGOVER IN ANDERSLÖV?

And now the telephone rang.

The infernal telephone.

With which he couldn't seem to manage to reach Rhea, not this morning and not the night before either.

"Allwright? . . . What? . . . No, I haven't seen him all afternoon."

The police inspector in Anderslöv was not unfamiliar with the administration of an occasional white lie.

But this time it didn't work.

"Excuse me? . . . Who? . . . Yes, just a moment, I'll see if I can find him."

Allwright covered the receiver with his hand.

"It's Superintendent Malm from the National Police Administration. Do you want to talk to him?"

Lord Jesus, thought Martin Beck, although he was not a religious man.

Malm was to him what the red flag is said to be to the bull.

"Okay," he said. "I'll take it."

What else was a poor civil servant to do?

"Yes, Beck here."

"Hi, Martin. How's it going?"

How's it going?

"For the time being, very badly."

Malm instantly changed his tone.

"I'll tell you something, Martin. This is turning into an outright scandal. I was just talking to the Commissioner."

They were probably sitting in the same room. The National Police Commissioner was known for not liking to talk to people who were capable of asking questions or talking back.

He especially disliked talking to Martin Beck, who had acquired a little too much prestige over the years.

In addition, the Commissioner suffered from acute paranoia. For a long time now, he had been convinced that the increasing unpopularity of the police force and its continuing stagnation were a result of the fact that "certain elements" did not like the National Police Commissioner personally. He now had the idea that such elements existed even within the police force itself.

"Have you arrested the murderer?"

"No."

"But the whole force is becoming a laughingstock."

How true.

"Our ablest detectives are in charge of the case. And nothing happens. The murderer strolls around giving interviews, while the police fawn all over him. The papers even have pictures of the place where the body is buried."

What Malm knew about the case was what he had read in the tabloids, just as surely as what he knew about practical police work was what he had seen in the movies.

He heard someone whispering in the background.

"What?" said Malm. "Oh yes. I can tell you that no effort has been spared from our side. We consider you to be our ablest homicide detective since Herbert Söderström."

"Herbert Söderström?"

"Yes, or whatever his name was."

Malm was presumably referring to Harry Söderman, a famous Swedish criminologist who ended his days as the Chief of Police in Tangier and who once offered to shoot Hitler in an attempt to put a stop to World War II.

There was more whispering in the background, and

Malm mumbled something with his mouth turned away from the receiver. And then he was back, as shrill as ever.

"The police look ridiculous. The murderer is telling his life story in the newspapers. The next thing we know he'll be writing a book about how he tricked the Homicide Squad. We've got enough troubles as it is."

At least the last part was true. The police did have troubles.

By and large, the difficulties began in 1965, when the police force was nationalized. Since then, it had begun to develop into a state within the state, and to become less and less popular with private citizens. During these eight years of national administration, the resources of the police force had increased several times over, which meant that the police had more power than ever before in Sweden's history. It also meant that Sweden maintained the most expensive constabulary in the world. On a per capita basis, the Swedish police force cost the taxpayers $65 per person per year. The corresponding figure in the United States was $25. Compared with the other Scandinavian countries, the disparity was grotesque. In Norway and Denmark, what's more, the police were comparatively popular.

Nevertheless, the crime rate continued to climb, and voilence steadily increased. There seemed to be no one within the police administration capable of grasping the simple truth that violence breeds violence and that, in fact, it was the police who had struck the first blow.

To this extent, then, Malm was right. People were beginning to get fed up. They had a hard time understanding why a Swedish policeman should cost the individual taxpayer more than three times as much as a policeman in neighboring Finland.

"Are you there?" Malm said.

"Yes, I'm here."

"You've got to arrest this man Bengtsson and get him under lock and key."

"There's no evidence against him."

"We'll attend to that detail later."

"I'm not so sure," said Martin Beck.

"Come now. If we forget that unfortunate business on Bergsgatan a year ago, why, your record of successful investigations is remarkable. Besides, it looks like an open-and-shut case."

Martin Beck smiled to himself. He had solved the murder on Bergsgatan, but an otherwise unsatisfactory investigation had led to the criminal's being convicted of another murder instead, a murder which he had not, in fact, committed. For Martin Beck's part, the whole affair had meant that he was excused from applying for a Division Commander's post that he had not wanted in the least. Stig Malm now had that post instead.

"Is he laughing?"

The voice was clearly audible. The potentate behind Malm's back was apparently losing his temper—not a rare event.

"Are you laughing?" Malm asked.

"Not at all," said Martin Beck innocently. "There's a funny noise on the line. You don't suppose your phone's being tapped?"

Another touchy subject that was better left alone.

And sure enough, Malm was annoyed.

"This is no time for jokes," he said. "This is a time for action. Immediate action."

Martin Beck didn't answer, and Malm grew more conciliatory.

"If you need reinforcements, Martin, you know we can help you at a moment's notice. Our new concentration strategy means . . ."

Martin Beck knew what the new concentration strategy meant. It meant that thirty busloads of policemen could be crowded into the village in less than an hour. It also meant automatic weapons, sharpshooters, tear gas bombs, helicopters, armored shields, and bulletproof vests.

"No," he said. "Reinforcements are the last thing I need."

"You'll be arresting this man today, I suppose?"

"No, I hadn't thought I would."

There was a muffled conference on the other end of the line.

"You're aware of the fact," said Malm finally, "that pressure can be brought to bear in other ways."

Martin Beck didn't answer.

"If you choose to be awkward."

He was all too well aware of what could be done. The Commissioner had only to call the State Prosecutor. He might not even have to make the call himself. Malm could probably do it.

"I don't think arresting Bengtsson is warranted at the moment," said Martin Beck.

"We have to put a stop to these newspaper stories."

"Our evidence is too feeble."

"Evidence!" said Malm contemptuously. "This isn't a Sherlock Holmes movie."

It could well be that Malm had seen an occasional Sherlock Holmes movie on television. On the other hand, there was no reason to suppose he knew anything of the literary background.

"Well?" Malm said. "Are you going to arrest the murderer or not?"

"I thought I'd try to find out what's happened to this woman instead. If there is a murderer, I hope we'll be able to link him to the crime."

"It looks like we're going to have to help you get started."

"I'd rather you didn't, thanks."

A door slammed in the room up in Stockholm. Martin Beck heard it clearly.

"I'm not the one who makes the decisions," said Malm apologetically. "And it really would look better for you if you'd get Bengtsson into custody."

"I'm not planning on it."

"Right away, at once," Malm said. "Before . . ."

"And definitely not right away."

"Well, in that case you've only yourself to blame," said Malm evenly. "And as for evidence, I'm sure you'll find what you need. Good luck."

"The same to you," said Martin Beck.

With that the conversation came to a close.

The process of going through channels in the so-called judicial system was usually tedious and troublesome and involved all sorts of paperwork and bureaucratic red tape.

But sometimes none of that seemed to exist. Someone picked up a telephone and said, This is the way it's going to be. And that was that.

The message came less than half an hour after Martin Beck's conversation with Malm.

Folke Bengtsson was to be taken into custody immediately.

Kollberg, who for some time had been trying to solve a chess problem in the Sunday paper, threw down his ballpoint pen.

"I'm not coming," he said.

"You're excused," said Martin Beck.

He and Allwright drove out to Folke Bengtsson's house in the patrol car. Several reporters followed them, and still more were already in position at Bengts-

128

son's place. In addition, a number of complete out-siders had taken the trouble to drive out for a look.

There wasn't much to see.

Dusk and a small cottage with a wooden hen house and a corrugated iron garage. And a man calmly shoveling beet greens onto his compost heap.

Folke Bengtsson was wearing exactly the same clothes he had on when they were there before.

He didn't seem surprised to see them, nor frightened, nor upset, nor angry.

He seemed the same as always.

It was an almost ridiculous repetition. Allwright rummaged around in the back seat and pulled out the Co-op bag with his shoes.

Martin Beck noticed that there was something else in the bag. But what?

He thought about it hard for a few seconds.

"Herrgott?" he said.

"Yes?"

"Have you got a flashlight in that plastic bag?"

"Sure do," said Allwright. "You need one living in the country. When there's no moon, you can't see your hand in front of your face."

Bengtsson put down his spade and walked over to meet them.

"Hi, Folke," Allwright said.

"Hi," said Folke Bengtsson.

"You're going to have to come along with us now. It's time."

"I see."

But he wasn't completely impassive, for he looked around in the failing light and said, "Awful lot of people here."

"Yes, it's bad," Allwright said. "Shall we go inside?"

"Yes, sure."

"There's no rush. You can change your clothes and get a few things together. Whatever you need. I can lend you a plastic bag if you need one."

"Thanks, but I've got a briefcase."

Allwright changed into his shoes.

"Take your time," he said. "Martin and I can sit here and have a little game of scissors-paper-stone."

Martin Beck was not familiar with this noble game, which requires no equipment but the human hand.

It took him thirty seconds to learn it.

Two fingers is a scissors. An open palm is paper. A fist is stone. Scissors cuts paper. Paper covers stone. Stone breaks scissors.

"Eleven to three, my favor," said Allwright a little while later. "You're too quick with your hands. That's why you're losing. You have to do it at exactly the same time I do."

And you think too fast, thought Martin Beck.

But, for that matter, he always lost. At all games from chess to Old Maid.

Another few minutes and Folke Bengtsson was ready to go.

For the first time, he looked a little uneasy.

"What's the trouble, Folke?" Allwright said.

"Someone has to feed the fish. And take care of the chickens. The aquarium has to be cleaned out now and then."

"I'll take care of it," Allwright said. "Word of honor."

He smiled uncomfortably.

"There's another thing, Folke, that you're probably not going to like. Some people are going to come out here tomorrow and dig up your garden."

"Why?"

"Well, I guess they'll be looking for the body."

"It's a shame about the asters," said Folke Bengtsson laconically.

"We'll try to be careful. Don't worry about it too much."

"I suppose you'll be the one to question me, Superintendent?"

"Yes," said Martin Beck. "But not today. Probably not tomorrow either. Unless Trelleborg wants to get started right away. But I don't think they will."

"Okey-dokey," Allwright said. "We'll drive in to my place in Anderslöv for starters. We can have a sandwich and a cup of tea. Unless you'd rather have coffee."

"Yes, I would, thank you."

"We can get some at the cafeteria. They've got hot cinnamon rolls there too. Are you ready?"

"Yes."

Folke Bengtsson seemed to hesitate.

"What'll we do about the eggs," he said.

"I'll take care of it," Allwright said.

"Word of honor again," he said with a laugh.

"Good," Bengtsson said. "You're a good person, Herrgott."

Allwright looked happily surprised.

"We do our best," he said.

"Am I under arrest now?" Bengtsson said.

"Not quite. We'll drive in to my place and shoot the shit for a while. They'll be up from Trelleborg in about a half an hour to pick you up and take you down there. Technically, we might say you're in custody, but it's not that formal. We'll go with you to Trelleborg. They'll book you down there. And then nothing will happen for a while."

Folke Bengtsson seemed a little apathetic as they left his house.

He locked the door and gave the key to Allwright.

"Will you keep this for me? In case I'm gone for a while? You'll need it anyway, to take care of the fish."

Allwright put the key in his pocket.

It was dark by now, and they climbed into the patrol car in a veritable crossfire of flashbulbs.

They were all three silent as they drove into town.

Allwright picked up some coffee and hot Danish pastry from the cafeteria next to the Co-op. He himself drank tea as usual.

Kollberg had gone back to his chess problem. He didn't even so much as glance at Folke Bengtsson when they came into the room.

Nor did Martin Beck say anything. They had been placed in a situation none of them wanted, and their freedom of choice in dealing with the case had been radically limited.

Allwright, however, had little bent for silence and somber meditation. He pushed a plastic mug of coffee over to their prisoner.

"Help yourself, Folke. Up here you can still consider yourself a free man."

He laughed.

"More or less. If you try to escape, I guess we'd have to stop you."

Kollberg grunted. He had a very clear memory of an occasion when Folke Bengtsson had tried to escape.

And it had been Lennart Kollberg, former paratrooper and hand-to-hand combat specialist, who had had to stop him.

"I wish I were home," he said suddenly.

He said it spontaneously, without really knowing what he meant.

It was true that he missed his wife and children, as it was also true that Folke Bengtsson and this whole case were things he wanted nothing to do with. But on a deeper level, his dissatisfaction was with life in general.

His house in Stockholm, a stone's throw from the subway, was not much to miss. And he certainly didn't miss his daily confrontations with policemen and people in revolt against the law. Sometimes it seemed to him that the only normal thing in his life was his wife and the children. Otherwise, the world seemed filled with policemen and criminals. And at this point in his life, his feelings toward the one category were as negative as toward the other.

It's not right, he thought. Life cannot be like a gangster film, with only two kinds of people.

The telephone rang. Allwright answered it.

"No, no one had confessed anything . . . Yes, we have taken a man into custody. That's all I can tell you."

He hung up and checked the time on his big silver watch.

"We don't have much time now, Folke," he said. "If you know anything about Sigbrit Mård, why don't you tell us now? It would make everything a hell of a lot simpler."

"I really don't know anything," said Folke Bengtsson.

Martin Beck looked at him. I don't know anything. Bengtsson hadn't changed. They would have to question him hour after hour, day after day, and he would admit nothing except when they had absolute proof. Maybe not even then.

"Except that I don't like her. No, I don't."

"That answer is not going to make your defense attorney especially happy," Allwright said.

He patted the dog lying at his feet.

"I'm damned if I'd want to defend you, Folke," he said.

The telephone managed to ring one more time before the detectives from Trelleborg arrived to make the formal arrest.

"It's your friend in Stockholm," said Allwright with his hand over the mouthpiece.

Martin Beck took the receiver.

"Everything's going nicely, I understand," Malm said.

"You think so?"

"Don't be misanthropic. You've really grown odd since you missed your promotion."

How stupid can you be? thought Martin Beck.

"But that isn't why I called," said Malm acidly. "There's another thing that seems peculiar. We've had some comments on it from higher up."

"What's that?"

"The papers report that you're showing favoritism for a man who is actually a murderer and who's now working as a reporter. A character named Gunnarsson."

"His name is Boman," said Martin Beck. "And I just happen to know him from years ago."

" 'Convicted of strangling a man, recently released, and now some sort of auxiliary to the National Homicide Squad,' is what it says here. I have the story in front of me. I don't suppose I have to tell you how bloody bad we think that looks."

Everything about Malm was ridiculous, even his expletives.

"And I don't suppose I have to tell you that I don't care what you think," said Martin Beck.

"No matter what I say, you take it badly," said Malm plaintively.

"Goodbye."

They spent the rest of the evening in Trelleborg, which was pretty much a waste of time.

Martin Beck said he would question the suspect later.

Folke Bengtsson was officially booked.

The next morning, the police began digging up his garden.

13.

There were no watchful reporters on hand when Martin Beck and Kollberg stepped out onto the steps of the inn early Thursday morning. It was only a little after eight o'clock, and the sun had barely had time to drag itself over the horizon. The air was cold and raw, and the cobblestones on the square still glittered with hoarfrost.

They climbed into Kollberg's car and drove down the road toward Domme. Kollberg drove carefully, with an occasional glance into the rear-view mirror. They were alone on the highway.

Allwright had given them a key to Sigbrit Mård's house. He himself had had a locksmith let him in, but once inside he confiscated an extra key that was hanging on a nail in the kitchen.

They drove in silence. Neither one of them was especially talkative in the mornings, and on top of that, Kollberg was unhappy at having missed his breakfast.

When they turned off and drove past Folke Bengtsson's house, there was already a Trelleborg police van parked in his yard. It had apparently just arrived. The rear doors were open, and two men in rubber boots and blue-gray overalls were unloading picks and shovels.

A third was standing in the middle of the yard scratching the back of his head as he surveyed the situation.

After another couple of hundred yards, Kollberg stopped the car, and Martin Beck got out and opened the gate to Sigbrit Mård's land. Kollberg parked in front of the door to the garage, which was built against the side wall of the house.

Before going in, they looked around outside. The yard in front was all gravel, with the exception of a circle of grass and rose bushes directly in line with the door, and a strip of topsoil about three feet wide that ran along the front wall of the house. It was stripped and bare; presumably flowers would be planted there for the spring.

Her piece of land was not especially large. Behind the house it consisted primarily of a large lawn with a couple of apple trees, some berry bushes, and, in one corner, a little kitchen garden inside a hedge. On the gravel walk between the kitchen steps and the cellar hatchway stood a lightweight metal rack for drying clothes.

Several pink clothespins were hanging from the lines.

Martin Beck and Kollberg walked back around to the front. It was not a very pretty house—yellow brick on a concrete foundation, with a red tile roof and green trim. Like a box, without embellishment or unnecessary decoration.

Three concrete steps and a green metal railing led up to the front door. Martin Beck opened it with the key Allwright had given him.

They came into a hall with a stone floor. There was a little bureau with curved, gilded legs and a slab of white marble against one wall, and above it hung a mirror in a gold frame, flanked by two crystal sconces. On either side of the bureau there were stools with embroidered cushions.

The living room had two windows facing the road and one on the side wall above the roof of the garage.

Martin Beck looked around the room and realized what Bertil Mård had meant when he said his wife was some kind of snob.

The room was not furnished for comfort; it was furnished to make an elegant impression.

The floor was covered with oriental rugs that might have been genuine, a crystal chandelier hung from the ceiling, the sofa and chairs were upholstered with wine-red plush, and the low oval coffee table was made of polished hardwood.

The walls were decorated sparingly. A few small, dark oil paintings, a couple of hand-painted china plates, and a large mirror in a broad, carved frame.

There was a mahogany cabinet with glass doors containing a collection of knickknacks and souvenirs that Bertil Mård had presumably brought back from his travels.

Kollberg went out to the kitchen and banged around slamming drawers and cupboards for a while before rejoining Martin Beck, who stood in front of the mahogany cabinet studying the objects inside.

"She keeps a damn tidy house," Kollberg said. "Almost meticulous. Clean and neat and everything in its place."

Martin Beck didn't answer. He was lost in admiration for the lines of a full-rigged ship cleaving the waves of a blue plaster of Paris sea in a large-bellied, small-mouthed quart bottle. Behind it was a tray made of the luminescent blue and green wings of butterflies.

As a boy, he had owned a butterfly tray of that same kind, given him by some relative just back from a trip to South America.

To him it had represented adventure: foreign ports, primitive jungles and great rivers, mystical places beyond the seven seas, all the distant lands he would definitely explore just as soon as he grew up. For a brief moment, he remembered those dreams and expectations with a sudden clarity that made him feel almost like a traitor to the boy he had once been.

He shook himself and turned his back on the cabinet and his memories.

"A funny living room," Kollberg said.

"How so?"

"There isn't a single book, no radio, no record player, not even a TV."

"There was an antenna on the roof," said Martin Beck. "She must keep the set in some other room."

"Herrgott did say she usually works nights," Kollberg said. "But she must spend the evening at home once in a while. What do you suppose she does here all by herself?"

Martin Beck shrugged his shoulders.

"Come on, let's have a look at the rest of the house," he said.

There was a small dining room between the kitchen and the living room. It was conventionally furnished with a round, white lacquered table and four chairs, plus four more chairs against the wall. Two sideboards and a corner cupboard full of glass and porcelain. White lace curtains and potted plants on the windowsill.

They walked through the kitchen and back out into

the hall, opened a couple of doors, and glanced into a closet and a lavatory. Then they went into the bedroom.

Like the living room, it faced the front of the house, but it was smaller and had only one window.

Through this window they could see the gate they'd forgotten to close and a bit of the road leading off toward Folke Bengtsson's house.

Behind the bedroom there was a spacious bathroom, from which another door led to a room with a window that faced the garden at the rear of the house. It was here, clearly, that Sigbrit Mård spent her free evenings.

In one corner stood a television set and, in front of it, a comfortable easy chair and a little table with an ashtray, a couple of magazines, and a brass cigarette box. Against one wall was a bookcase containing a fairly unimpressive library.

About thirty paperbacks, a dozen hardbound book club volumes, a black school bible, a world atlas, and several cookbooks.

The remainder of the bookcase was occupied by several piles of magazines, a sewing basket, a transistor radio, some ceramic bowls, and a pair of pewter candlesticks.

The room also contained a secretary, an armchair, a couch with a lot of pillows, and a low table in front of the window.

Kollberg opened a drawer in the table. Inside were a couple of fashion magazines and some tissue paper pattern pieces. The other drawer contained stationery, envelopes, a couple of ballpoint pens, and a deck of cards.

Then he turned to the drawers and compartments in the secretary, which were filled with letters, receipts, and various other documents, all carefully sorted into folders with clearly printed labels.

Martin Beck went back to the bedroom. He stood for a long time staring out the window toward Folke Bengtsson's house, which was almost completely hidden by the trees. All he could see was a little bit of the roof and the chimney. Behind him, he heard Kollberg go out in the kitchen and, a moment later, clump heavily down the cellar stairs.

The bedroom was as neat as the rest of the house.

Besides the bed and the night table, there was a dresser, a dressing table, a low easy chair and hassock, a couple of straightbacked chairs, and a rustic chest.

On the floor beside the easy chair was a basket of varicolored balls of yarn and the beginnings of a piece of knitting.

Martin Beck turned away from the window and caught sight of himself in a mirror that covered the space between the bathroom door and the closet. He seldom looked at himself in the mirror, especially not full length, and he couldn't help noticing that he really looked pretty disheveled.

His Levi's were wrinkled, his shoes weren't shined, and his blue Dacron jacket was starting to look worn and faded.

He left the mirror and started searching the room systematically. He began with the dressing table.

It was extremely well stocked with bottles, jars, and tubes of various kinds. Sigbrit Mård obviously spent a lot of time on her looks, and her supply of cosmetic preparations was impressive. In addition, there was a red leather jewel box containing a great many bracelets, rings, brooches, earrings, and amulets. There were necklaces, pendants, and strings of beads hanging on a couple of wooden pegs beside the dressing table mirror.

Martin Beck was no expert on precious stones and metals, but he knew enough to know that this was hardly a valuable collection of jewels. Most of them were inexpensive trinkets.

He looked in the closet, which was packed full of dresses, blouses, skirts, and suits, some of them in plastic bags to protect them from dust.

There were neat rows of shoes on the floor. On the shelf was a black fur cap, a sun hat of cotton batik, and a shoe box.

Martin Beck lifted down the shoe box, which was tied with twine. He undid the knot and opened the box.

It was full of letters and picture postcards, and he had only to glance through them to see that they were all written in the same hand and that they all had foreign stamps.

He looked at the postmarks.

They were in obvious chronological order—at the bottom, a thick letter dated 1953, and on top, a postcard from South Yemen that had been mailed six years ago.

Bertil Mård's collected letters home over fourteen years of marriage and an equal number at sea.

Martin Beck didn't bother to read them. For that matter, the handwriting was virtually illegible. He tied the string around the box and put it back on its shelf.

He heard Kollberg on the cellar stairs. He came into the bedroom a few moments later.

"Mostly old trash down there. A few tools, an old bicycle, a wheelbarrow, stuff like that. Garden furniture. A laundry room and a fruit cellar. Did you find anything interesting?"

"There are letters from Bertil Mård in a shoe box in the closet. Otherwise, nothing."

He walked over to the dresser and opened the drawers. The top one was filled with underclothes, handkerchiefs, and nightgowns in neat piles. In the middle one were jumpers, cardigans, and pullovers, and the bottom drawer contained a couple of heavy sweaters, a little book with blue covers labeled *Poetry* in ornate gold letters, and a thick diary with a clasp and a little heart-shaped padlock.

There were also two photo albums lying under some folded silk scarves.

All these documents dated from Sigbrit Mård's adolescence.

The poetry album contained the usual verses written in by girlfriends twenty-five years before.

Martin Beck opened to the last page and read the verse he had expected to find.

Here I am at the very end, last in the book but a first-rate friend. Anne-Charlotte.

Kollberg picked the lock on the diary with a hairpin he found in a bowl on the dresser.

December 25, 1949. Dear diary, Last night you were given to me for Christmas, and from this day on I will confide all my innermost thoughts to you.

Kollberg read several pages.

A third of the book was filled with the same round, childish handwriting, but by March 13 that same year, Sigbrit Mård had apparently grown tired of confiding in her diary.

The photo albums contained amateur snapshots of classmates and teachers, parents, siblings, and boyfriends. Way at the back of one of the albums were some loose photographs of a more recent date. A wedding picture—a young bridegroom, his hair plastered down with water, and an even younger bride with clear eyes and apple cheeks.

"Bertil Mård," said Martin Beck.

"Hell of a big man even way back then," Kollberg said.

There were also a couple of passport photos of Bertil Mård and several snapshots of Sigbrit apparently taken on the trip to Sassnitz.

They put everything back in the drawer and closed it.

Kollberg went into the bathroom.

Martin Beck heard him open the cabinet over the sink.

"A hell of a lot of make-up and curlers and stuff," he said. "But no pills or medicine. Only aspirin and Alka-Seltzer. Funny. Most people have tranquilizers or sleeping pills these days."

Martin Beck walked over to the night table and pulled out the drawer.

There was no medicine there either, but there was, among other things, a pocket almanac.

Martin Beck picked it up and flipped through the pages.

It contained mostly memoranda of the *hairdresser, laundry, dentist* type. The last one was under October 16: *Car to garage.* Otherwise there was nothing but her menstruation days, marked with a little cross, and the letter C, which recurred at regular intervals.

Martin Beck went through the book page by page. In January and February, the C appeared regularly every Thursday. The same in March, except that the second week it appeared on Friday as well, and the last week in March on both Wednesday and Thursday. In April there was no C on Maundy Thursday, and in May there was none on Ascension Day, also a Thursday, but on the other hand it did appear on three consecutive Saturdays. In June and July there were no C's at all, but in August it showed up three and four times a week. In September and October, the monotony resumed, with a C every Thursday up to October 11.

Martin Beck heard Kollberg return to the secretary

in the back room. He put the almanac in his pocket, thoughtfully, and looked down into the drawer of the night table. There was a little pile of folded papers under a jar of cold cream.

He put the papers on the tabletop and unfolded them one by one. They were mostly receipts, plus a few unpaid bills, all of quite recent date.

At the bottom of the pile were two pieces of paper of an entirely different nature. A couple of short letters or messages, handwritten on thin, lined, light-blue paper.

The first one read as follows.

Dearest, don't wait for me. Sissy's brother is in town, and I can't possibly get away. Call you later this evening if I can. Love and kisses, Clark.

Martin Beck read the brief message twice. The handwriting slanted slightly forward, but was smooth and easy to read, almost like printing.

Dearest Sigge, Can you ever forgive me? I wasn't myself, and I didn't mean what I said. You must come on Thursday so I can make amends. I long for you, I love you, Clark.

He took the two sheets of paper and went in to Kollberg, who was standing by the secretary studying a couple of bank books.

"She didn't have much money in the bank," he said without turning around. "Made deposits and withdrawals one right after the other. Like when you're trying to save money but can't. Before the divorce, she was in much better shape, financially. What have you got there?"

Martin Beck put the two sheets of paper on the secretary in front of Kollberg.

"Love letters, I think."

Kollberg read them.

"It sure looks that way. Maybe she's run off with this fellow Clark."

Martin Beck brought out the pocket almanac and showed it to Kollberg, who whistled.

"A lover with regular habits. I wonder why Thursday especially."

"Maybe he's got a job where he can only get away on Thursdays," said Martin Beck.

"Drives a beer truck," Kollberg said. "He delivers beer to the pub every Thursday—something like that."

"Funny Herrgott didn't know about it."

Martin Beck took an empty envelope from the drawer in the sewing table, put the almanac and the two letters into it, and put the envelope in his back pocket.

"Are you finished here?" he said.

Kollberg looked around.

"Yes," he said. "There's nothing of much interest. Tax forms, birth certificate, some uninteresting letters, receipts, and so on."

He put everything back where it belonged.

"Shall we go?" he said.

As they drove down the road they saw a long line of cars parked outside Folke Bengtsson's place. It was 9:30, and apparently the reporters were up and about.

Kollberg stepped on the gas and drove quickly past the crowd of journalists and out onto the highway. They had time to notice that another couple of police cars were parked in the yard beside the house and that the yard had been roped off.

On the way into Anderslöv, they sat for a long time without saying anything.

Finally Martin Beck broke the silence.

"It said, 'You must come' in one of those letters," he

said. "That must mean they didn't meet at her place."

"We'll talk to Herrgott," said Kollberg confidently. "Maybe he'll know something."

Herrgott Allwright was very surprised at Martin Beck's discovery.

He knew of no one named Clark.

There was no one by that name in all of Anderslöv. Wait. There was one, but he was seven years old and had just started school.

And as far as he knew, Sigbrit worked at the pastry shop in Trelleborg on Thursday evenings.

She didn't usually get home before eleven o'clock or so when she worked evenings.

"He calls her Sigge," he said. "I've never heard anyone call her that. Sigge. It sounds silly. Anyway, it's a boy's name and doesn't fit a woman like Sigbrit at all."

He stared at the light-blue sheets of paper and scratched the back of his neck. Then he chuckled.

"What if she's run off with her lover?" he said. "In that case, they can dig to their hearts' content, and Folke can turn his garden into a potato patch."

14.

There was a gentle, southerly wind, and the little bay lay smooth and shiny in the shelter of the land, but farther out in the lake, quick breezes drew dark veins across the calm surface of the water. A raw chill rose from the marshy ground wherever the slanting rays of the afternoon sun did not reach, and a light mist hung over the reeds along the shore.

It was November 11, a Sunday, and the sky continued blue and cloudless. The time was 1:30. The sun would warm for another couple of hours before dusk and the chill of evening took over.

A group of people came walking along the path that followed the southwest shore of the lake. Six women, five men, and two boys about eight to ten years old. They were all wearing rubber boots with their pants tucked into the tops, and most of them were carrying knapsacks or shoulder bags. They walked quickly and in single file, for the path forced its way between tall clumps of yellow reeds and a thicket of alder and hazel, and there was no room to walk two abreast. They all kept their eyes on the ground, which was a churned up mess of slippery black mud.

When they had walked this way for some distance, the thicket came to an end, and the path continued on along a fence of rotting posts and rusty barbed wire. On the other side of the fence was a fallow field, and beyond the field was a dense spruce forest.

The man at the head of the line stopped and surveyed the landscape with a squint. He was slim and wiry and fairly short and looked more like a boy than a fifty-year-old man. His face was tanned, and his brown hair was ruffled.

It took a while for the others to gather around him.

A tall man with a salt-and-pepper beard brought up the rear with long, leisurely strides. He had his hands in the pockets of his windbreaker, and he looked at the smaller man with a calm, jocular gaze.

"What are you up to now? Is it time to change course?"

"I thought we might cut across the field to those woods over there," said the man who seemed to be leading the expedition.

"But that takes us away from the lake," said one of the women.

She had thrown herself down on a rock, crossed her legs, and lit a cigarette.

"I mean, the whole idea is to walk around the lake," she went on. "But you're always trying to head us off in the wrong direction. Anyway, I'm hungry. Aren't we going to eat pretty soon?"

The others agreed. They were all hungry and wanted to lighten the loads in their knapsacks.

"We'll rest when we get across the field," said their leader.

He picked up the smaller of the two boys and put him down again on the other side of the fence. Then he climbed over it himself and set off across the grassy clumps with long strides.

When they reached the spruce woods they found the trees so close together that not even the children could get through easily. There followed a period of discussion, but since they couldn't agree on which way to go, the leader took the children and two of the women and headed off to the right along the woods, while the others, with the tall man in the lead, set off to the left in the direction of the lake.

Fifteen minutes later, the two groups met on the other side of the woods and started looking around for a good place to stop and eat.

This time they were all in agreement. They relieved themselves of their knapsacks and shoulder bags in a sunny little glade between a windfall and a stack of beech logs, and when one of the men, who was considered to be an expert on campfires, had selected a likely spot for the purpose, everyone began gathering fuel.

There were plenty of dry twigs and branches in the

windfall, and before long they were making themselves comfortable around a lively, crackling blaze. The rest was well-earned, for they had been walking over rather difficult terrain for three hours, almost without a break.

Thermos bottles, packets of sandwiches, and small flasks appeared, and they didn't permit the food to silence them. The conversation glided from one subject to another, and the mood was cheerful and relaxed.

A man in a green jacket and a knit cap stood warming his feet at the fire.

"This lake is too big," he said. "Let's take a smaller one next Sunday. Where there aren't quite so many muddy fields."

He paused to empty a little silver cup of rowanberry aquavit. Then he looked at the sky.

"Lord knows if we'll make it around before it gets dark," he said.

The fire began to die down and they speared sausages on sharp sticks and grilled them over the coals.

The two boys chased each other around the woodpile.

The botanist in the group had wandered off toward the woods looking for mushrooms. He had already gathered several handfuls of *Marasmius scorodonius* in the pocket of his parka, and he had a plastic bag full of muskmadder which, when dry, would spread its pleasant odor through his house.

The spruce woods were thinner on this side, and he peered in among the tree trunks and over the needle-strewn ground with a practiced eye.

He was not really expecting to find anything. It was late in the season, and the fall, like the summer, had been dry and warm.

Several yards into the woods he caught sight of what appeared to be a large and beautiful specimen of a parasol mushroom. He put down his bag of musk-madder on a mossy stone at the edge of the woods and started to push his way through the trees. He bent the sprawling branches aside and tried to keep his eye on the place where the mushroom stood.

Suddenly he stepped on soft moss that gave way beneath his weight, and his right foot sank up to the bootleg in what felt like a quagmire.

That's odd, he thought.

There shouldn't be any quagmire here.

He moved his other foot to a broken spruce branch on what he thought was solid ground. But the branch broke, and his boot slid down into the mud, though it sank only a few inches before striking solid support.

He pulled his right foot out of the ooze, which sucked at his boot and almost pulled it off. Then keeping his weight on his left foot, he took a giant step up onto solid ground.

He had forgotten the mushroom, and he turned around to look at this curious, moss-covered mudhole.

He saw black mud bubbling up into the holes left by his feet.

And then he noticed something else, rising slowly out of the mire and moss and spruce twigs about a yard from the depression where his left boot had been.

He stood very still and wondered what it might be.

The object took shape before his eyes, and it took a fraction of a second for his brain to register the fact that what he saw was a human hand.

And then he screamed.

15.

By Monday, November 12, everything had changed.

Sigbrit Mård was no longer missing. She was a rather badly decomposed corpse in a mud puddle in the woods. Everyone knew where she was, and she had been found roughly where a lot of people had expected to find her. She was beyond all good and evil, and had been so for almost four weeks.

Folke Bengtsson was arraigned that morning. He had not confessed to anything, but his own attitude and the vague testimony of the witnesses carried a lot of weight, and when his lawyer objected to the arraignment it was more of a gesture than a serious protest.

Martin Beck and the lawyer had even met and exchanged a few remarks. It was not a very profound conversation, but the lawyer did make one comment with which Martin Beck could agree wholeheartedly.

"I don't understand him," he said.

Folke Bengtsson was certainly not easy to understand. Martin Beck had talked to him on Friday—three hours in the morning and the same after lunch. It had not been a fruitful exchange. Both parties sank back in their chairs for long periods and repeated phrases they had already used only minutes earlier.

On Saturday, it had been Kollberg's turn. He had set to work with even less enthusiasm than Martin Beck, with commensurate results.

That is, none at all.

Virtually the whole interrogation was hung up on the

same points. First and foremost, what had taken place in the post office.

"You did speak to each other in the post office, didn't you?"

"Yes, she accosted me."

"Accosted you?"

"She came over to me and asked me if I would have any eggs on Friday."

"Would you really call that 'accosting' someone?"

"What else would you call it?"

"Didn't she ask about anything else?"

"I don't remember."

"Didn't she want a ride home?"

"I don't remember."

And then, of course, there was the famous moment at the bus stop.

"Did Sigbrit Mård make any sort of sign? Did she wave or anything?"

"I don't remember."

"And she didn't get into your car?"

"No. She did not."

Personally, Martin Beck was inclined to think that Herrgott was right. She had probably asked him for a ride home, and he had been evasive. It also seemed likely that she actually had made some sort of hitch-hiking gesture as he drove by the bus stop a few minutes later.

The trouble was that the witnesses were so poor.

Allwright had now spoken to everyone who had been in the post office at the time in question. Four people could attest to the fact that Sigbrit Mård and Folke Bengtsson had spoken to one another, but no one had heard what they said.

But, of course, Folke Bengtsson couldn't know that. The situation was similar with regard to the infamous

Signe Persson and what she had seen or not seen at the bus stop.

Only one thing was absolutely certain. Sigbrit Mård was dead, and whoever killed her had done their very best to hide the body.

"She could have been here all winter without ever being found," Allwright said. "If it hadn't been for those oddballs who hike around lakes."

They were standing at the scene of the crime—if, in fact, it *was* the scene of the crime—watching some policemen who were trying to secure clues within the roped-off area.

Another certain fact was that Folke Bengtsson's yard had been dug up to no purpose, unless it might make his garden grow better next spring. They had also ripped up some floorboards in his house, and in the nearly deserted chicken coop.

And now they had seized his station wagon for a laboratory examination.

Martin Beck heaved a deep sigh, and Allwright looked at him with clever, questioning brown eyes.

It was Kollberg's turn to continue the one-sided dialogue with Folke Bengtsson, and Martin Beck had forgotten that he was in Trelleborg. When Martin Beck sighed, Kollberg generally knew what he meant. They had worked together for such a long time that they thought the same way. Usually. They communicated thoughts and conclusions without words. Of course, it didn't always work that way.

And it seemed very unlikely that Allwright would understand why Martin Beck had sighed.

"What's the sigh for?" Allwright said.

Martin Beck didn't answer.

"God-awful place for a murder, isn't it? Assuming this is where it happened. But it probably is."

"We'll know after the post-mortem, if not before," said Martin Beck.

The lake hikers who found the body had been nature lovers. They hadn't littered, or damaged the terrain as such, but, of course, it was inescapable that the ground near the spot where the body was found had been trampled by a lot of feet. Policemen moving over the area had not made things any better, and on top of that, the find was almost four weeks old. The weather had been changeable, with rain and storms and frost.

From the laboratory point of view, the scene of the crime did not inspire optimism. There was a sort of road that led to the spot, at least as far as the windfall, but heavy forestry machinery had moved over it recently. In addition, they had information indicating that its present terrible condition was due to the fact that the army had churned it up with cross-country vehicles only about a week earlier when the road was wet and muddy.

In its present state, the road was not passable for any ordinary passenger car. But it might very well have been so four weeks earlier.

As for the question of whether or not this spot had been selected by chance, the answer had to be no.

By and large, it was only the owner and the people who worked here occasionally who knew the area in detail. The nearest building was a summer cottage, where no one had been since the end of September.

It was an inaccessible and difficult piece of terrain. No one would go there by car without knowing in advance that the car could get out again.

On the other hand, it was reasonable to suppose that anyone living in the vicinity had a good chance of knowing the place.

Folke Bengtsson and Sigbrit Mård lived not far away, and if you assumed that Bengtsson was guilty, which many people did and which no one at the moment could refute, the location of the body was an additional point against him. If the road were in good condition, he could get here from Anderslöv in ten minutes. Furthermore, it lay in the same general direction he said he had taken. He would only have had to turn off a little sooner and then gradually wind his way up to this path through the woods.

Martin Beck leaned back against a pile of logs and looked across the windfall toward the spruce trees.

"What do you think, Herrgott? Do you think someone could have driven in here in an ordinary car on October seventeenth?"

Allwright scratched the back of his head, pushing his hat askew.

"Yes," he said. "I think so. Someone could probably have driven as far as this stack of beech. You couldn't drive through that windfall even in a tank. Not now, and not then either. Sit, Timmy! Down, for heaven's sake! Yes, that's right. Good dog."

The men examining the scene of the crime had a German shepherd with them, a trained police dog, and Timmy was much too interested in the doings of this animal to stay calmly on his leash.

"Let him go, why not," said Martin Beck with an involuntary yawn. "Maybe he'll find something."

"And maybe we'll have a dogfight," Allwright said. "We'll see."

Allwright released the dog, who immediately started nosing around on the ground.

"Well, look who's here to nip at our heels again," said Evert Johansson a few moments later.

He was one of the men working with the lab crew.

"Yes, take care of anything he finds," Allwright said.

A little while later, Johansson walked over to where they were standing. He was wearing overalls and high rubber boots and moved slowly through the windfall.

"She looks pretty awful," he said.

Martin Beck nodded. He had been through this far too many times to let it bother him. Sigbrit Mård's remains were not the most appetizing sight he had ever seen, nor were they anywhere near the most repulsive.

"You can move her as soon as the girl with the camera's done," said Martin Beck. "Then we'll have a look at what the dogs have found."

"Timmy's found something odd," said Evert Johansson, extending a plastic bag full of something indescribable.

"Yes, take along everything that doesn't seem to be part of the natural vegetation," said Martin Beck.

"And I've just found this old rag," said Allwright, pointing with the toe of his boot.

"Bring it along."

They had walked around the woodpile and were approaching the rope barrier, where a few tireless reporters were on guard.

"There's one thing I would like to point out," Allwright said. "And that is that I wouldn't want to try and drive out here in Folke's old station wagon. Not even if the weather was good and the ground was fairly dry."

"Well, what about in your own car, for example?"

"Yes, I probably could have made it. Before the army tore up the road."

"Have you considered the fact that Bertil Mård must be familiar with this area too?"

"Yes, it did occur to me," Allwright said.

They came to the cordon and climbed over the rope.

Another of Allwright's sergeants was keeping the reporters company on the other side.

It was a very peaceful scene.

"Haven't you been up to take a look?" said one of the reporters.

"Good Lord, no. Ugh," said the policeman.

Martin Beck smiled. It was a miserable and tragic situation, but there was something rural and idyllic about it nonetheless. As opposed to the usual grim atmosphere of heavy suspicion and threatening billy clubs.

"Is she naked?" said the reporter to Martin Beck.

"Not completely, as far as I could see."

"But she was murdered?"

"Yes, it looks that way."

He looked at the reporters, who were ill-equipped for the terrain and the weather.

"We can't tell you much of interest until there's been an autopsy," he said. "There's a dead human being over there. All the indications are that it's Sigbrit Mård and that someone tried to hide her body. My personal impression was that she didn't have much on and that she'd been violently attacked. If you stay here and freeze long enough, you'll see us come by with a stretcher covered with a tarpaulin. And that's pretty much the story."

"Thanks," said one of the reporters and actually turned and started off with a shiver toward the line of cars parked several hundred yards away.

And that *was* pretty much the story, even for Martin Beck.

The lab report came through, and the results of the autopsy.

Nothing much had been learned.

Timmy had made the most curious discovery—a

piece of smoked goose breast, which, however, could be traced to the lake hikers. The funniest part of that, it seemed to Martin Beck, was that the dog hadn't eaten it.

A cotton rag that couldn't be traced anywhere.

Sigbrit Mård herself, her clothes, and her pocketbook.

Her wristwatch had a window for the date and had stopped at sixteen minutes, twenty-three seconds after 4 a.m. on October 18—as a result of not being wound.

Sigbrit Mård had been strangled, and there were indications of violence directed at the lower abdomen. There was a contusion on the pelvis, as if from a very hard blow.

The condition of her clothing was rather interesting.

Her coat and blouse had been found in one piece beside the body. Her skirt and pants, on the other hand, were torn. Her sexual organs had been exposed and her brassiere partially removed.

Martin Beck stayed on in Anderslöv, although the questioning was taking place in Trelleborg.

He sat and studied the lab reports. They could be interpreted in various ways, of course. One thing seemed fairly obvious.

Her coat and blouse were undamaged because she had removed them herself. This, in turn, might indicate that she had accompanied her murderer voluntarily.

Exactly where she died could not be determined. Probably in the vicinity of the mudhole, but that would have to remain a guess.

The contents of her handbag were not unusual.

Most of the evidence indicated that shortly after leaving the post office, she accompanied someone to the isolated spot where she was later found and that she was killed somewhere in that immediate area.

None of this made the outlook any brighter for Folke Bengtsson.

Roseanna McGraw had died under very similar circumstances a little over nine years earlier.

And Bengtsson continued to deny everything, apathetically, and without the least show of cooperation.

The investigation was bogging down.

The evidence was shoddy, but Bengtsson had public opinion against him and would probably be convicted.

Martin Beck was not satisfied. There was something that didn't fit, but what?

Maybe something about Bertil Mård.

Martin Beck often thought about him and his notebook. It really was an exceptionally fine notebook. The best notebook Mård had been able to find in 108 countries. Had he really made a note of everything? Had he, for example, recorded the death of the Brazilian oiler in Trinidad-Tobago?

Martin Beck had a strong feeling that he would have to talk to Mård once more. At least.

He also thought about what Sigbrit Mård had had in her over-the-shoulder pocketbook. A singularly commonplace collection. Handkerchief, a tin box of aspirin, keys, some receipts, a comb, a ballpoint pen, a little bottle of saccharin tablets, a mirror, driver's license, a coin purse with seventy-two crowns, and a make-up case containing powder, lipstick, mascara, eye shadow, and foundation cream. Plus a card of birth-control pills, one for each day of the week. She had taken the ones for Monday, Tuesday, and Wednesday, but not for Thursday. On Thursday, of course, she was dead.

Did the pills necessarily mean anything? Of course not.

Sigbrit Mård had been thirty-eight years old and

divorced. It was entirely possible that she went on taking the pill even though she had, in effect, stopped sleeping with men.

But all the same . . .

He thought about the almanac and the letters he had found in her house.

And there was a key on her key ring that didn't fit any of the locks he knew of.

There were bound to be things Mård hadn't told him. Martin Beck decided to go into Malmö and try to have another talk with him sometime when he'd be sober.

Friday morning sounded like a good time. Early, before he'd had even his first drink of the day.

If Martin Beck disliked the Sigbrit Mård case and the way it was developing, there was at least one other person who felt the same way.

Kollberg.

Lennart Kollberg bore his share of the investigation as if it had been a cross and the road to trial a veritable journey to Golgotha.

The sessions with Folke Bengtsson were becoming more and more fruitless. They had a terribly hard time talking to each other. The words seemed to vanish in the air between them, as if they lacked the buoyancy to make it across the table.

Kollberg maintained that Bengtsson was psychologically somewhat odd, or, to put it more bluntly, stark raving mad, but he also found the threads linking Bengtsson to Sigbrit Mård more fragile and the whole situation more abstract than did Martin Beck. Kollberg had never been as deeply involved in the Roseanna case, nor had he ever attempted to force his way into Bengtsson's head. At that time he was never in charge of the principal interrogation.

And now he had the feeling more and more that he

was merely tormenting a man who might be innocent, and who didn't really understand what it was all about.

Or perhaps he was tormenting himself. He would say something, and before it reached the other man, the words would dissolve and disperse in the air.

Kollberg often had business at police headquarters in Trelleborg and as he came out of the building on Friday the sixteenth, he ran into someone he knew.

Åke Boman.

"Hi," Kollberg said.

"We probably shouldn't talk to each other," Boman said. "We might both lose our jobs."

"I don't give a damn," Kollberg said. "Do you know a good place to eat?"

"Jönsson's tavern, The Three Hearts. You can really stuff yourself."

"Then let me take you to lunch."

"Or the other way around."

"We'll take each other to lunch. Fine and dandy. I see the Christmas madness has already begun," said Kollberg with a glance around.

Jönsson's tavern was excellent. It was exactly suited to Kollberg's intentions, i.e., to really stuff himself.

"Can you get a lot of food here?"

"Yes, you can eat till you burst. And it's good."

"Fine."

They sat down, and Kollberg appraised the menu carefully before he ordered.

"Don't you want a drink?" Boman said.

Kollberg looked at him. As usual, Boman had ordered mineral water.

"Yes," he said after a moment's hesitation. "A big son of a bitch. Miss, bring me a double acquavit."

His relationship to Boman required at least a big meal, a drink, and a talk.

"I've often had the feeling we ought to have a little talk," Boman said. "Just a few words."

"The same thing's occurred to me," Kollberg said. "Now especially."

"You did save my life," Boman said. "The question is whether it was worth saving. I really did want to die that time. And many times since."

"I didn't have any choice," Kollberg said. "The way it happened, there was nothing else to be done. What were those pills you took?"

"Vesparax."

"Right. I read somewhere that now they sell them only in suppository form. Very clever. As if people couldn't kill themselves through the ass."

Boman smiled sadly.

"There's one question I want to ask you," Kollberg said.

"What's that?"

"You were damned close to getting away with it. You were just about to get married, to a fine woman. What were you going to do? Live with it? Forget?"

"No," said Boman. "When I killed Alf, I ruined my life. I could have escaped unpunished, but I never could have lived with it. I know that now."

"Boman," said Kollberg.

"Call me Gunnarsson. It doesn't matter any more."

"You're Åke Boman to me. I'll tell you something. I killed a man once too. Not many people know about it. If you want me to, I'll give you the details."

Åke Boman shook his head.

"Okay. No details. I'd rather not, anyway. You know yourself how it feels. You can't live with it. Everything seems changed. You never get over it. And I didn't even get a reprimand. The Commissioner compared me to Charles the Twelfth."

He laughed hollowly.

"The truth is I hate being a policeman. And I won't be for very much longer, I'm afraid. You can quote me. What saved me is a good wife and two fine kids."

"I've considered something along those lines," Boman said. "But I don't really dare."

The herring and potatoes arrived.

Kollberg dug into it.

Boman did not have the same size appetite, but he seemed to be inspired by his companion.

"Do you want my opinion?" Kollberg said.

"Yes and no."

"Well here it is, free of charge. I think Bengtsson's insane, but I think he's innocent. Write that if you want to. I'm almost convinced."

"Do you think we might be friends?" Boman said.

"We are already," Kollberg said.

He lifted his glass of aquavit.

"Skoal!"

Boman took a drink of his mineral water.

It was a long lunch. Kollberg had nothing more to drink, but they talked for a long time.

About all sorts of things.

They sat there across the table from one another. A killer and a policeman who had killed.

They understood each other.

Maybe they would be friends.

"You saved my life," Boman said.

"I guess I did. What was I supposed to do?"

"I don't know."

"If you want to, you can write every word I've said."

"You'll be in a mess if I do."

"I don't give a damn," Kollberg said. "Take my word for it."

He had a sudden feeling of freedom.

He ate an order of ice cream with chocolate sauce.

"I'm too damned fat," Kollberg said.

"I don't think so."

"You're too thin."

"Maybe. I feel pretty good sometimes, in spite of everything."

"In spite of everything," Kollberg said.

"I've got a little apartment nearby," Boman said. "Do you want to come up for a while? It's only five minutes from here."

"Okay," Kollberg said.

"We'll both be fired," Boman said.

"Who cares?" Kollberg said.

Boman's apartment was pleasant.

On the table next to the telephone was a framed photograph.

He recognized it immediately.

An outdoor shot. Her head was thrown back, and she was laughing at the photographer. The wind tore at her ruffled blond hair.

"Anne-Louise, right?"

"The best thing that ever happened to me. She's married now. Nice guy, I understand. Two kids. A boy and a girl.

"Shit," he said suddenly.

They talked for a couple of hours.

About all sorts of things.

Two men who had killed.

16.

Nothing much had changed at Bertil Mård's. There was the same stink of liquor and unwashed bedclothes. The same semidarkness in the shabby little house. Mård was even wearing the same clothes he had worn the last time—an undershirt and an old pair of ship's captain's pants.

The only innovation was an old kerosene stove that smoked and did nothing to improve the general atmosphere of squalor and decay.

But in any case, Mård was sober.

"Good morning, Captain Mård," said Martin Beck politely.

"Good morning," Mård said.

He peered at his visitor, and the whites of his eyes were covered with an unhealthy, yellow film. But his brown gaze was raw and murderous.

"What do you want?"

"I'd like to talk to you for a little while."

"I don't want to talk."

Mård kicked the smoking kerosene stove.

"Maybe you can fix this thing for me," he said. "It doesn't work right, and at night it gets colder than nigger hell in here. I never was any good with machinery."

Martin Beck inspected the heating device, which looked to be ancient. It was years since he had seen anything like it. In principle, it seemed to be constructed like a primus stove.

"I think you ought to get yourself something newer and better," he said.

"Maybe so," said Mård absently. "Well, what the hell do you want to talk about?"

Martin Beck didn't say anything right away. He sat down on one of the chairs and almost expected a protest, but Mård only sighed heavily and sat down himself.

"Do you want a drink?" he said.

Martin Beck shook his head. The liquor was the same merchandise as the time before. Illegal Russian vodka of devastating potency. But there was only one bottle on the table, and it had not even been opened.

"No, that's right," Mård said.

"Where do you get that stuff?" said Martin Beck with a glance at the bottle with its blue label.

"That's none of your business," Mård said.

"No, I guess it isn't."

"It's hard to live in a country where a fifth of whisky costs fifteen dollars," said Mård philosophically.

"I suppose you've heard that we found your ex-wife?"

"Yes," Mård said. "That information reached me."

He unscrewed the cap of the bottle with a practiced motion and threw it on the floor.

Poured up half a tumbler and stared at it for a long time, as if it had been a living being or a flame.

"The funny thing is, I don't want any either," he said.

He took a small swig.

"And it hurts like hell," he said. "Can't even fucking drink yourself to death but it has to hurt. I guess that's the drinker's curse."

166

"So you know about Sigbrit?"

"Yes. Not that anyone exactly bothered to inform me. But the women at the beer shop read the papers, thank God."

"Are you sorry?" asked Martin Beck.

"What?"

"Are you sorry? Are you in mourning?"

Mård shook his head slowly.

"No," he said finally. "You can't mourn something you haven't had for such a long time. But . . ."

"Yes?"

"But it does seem funny that she's not there any more. I never thought Sigbrit would kick off before I did. And I know someone else who didn't think so either."

"Who's that?"

"Sigbrit herself. She's been acting pretty much as if I were dead for a long time now."

Mård banged his meaty right hand on the table, but the gesture didn't seem to mean very much.

"When did that start?"

"The minute I stopped giving her money."

Martin Beck said nothing.

"But there's a lot of life in me yet," Mård said. "I think this is going to take several years."

He stared darkly at Martin Beck.

"Several years," he repeated. "God knows how many. In this hellhole."

He drank down his vodka in a sort of rage.

"The welfare state," he said. "I heard about it all over the world. And then when you see this shit country, you wonder how in hell they've managed to spread all those lies and propaganda."

He refilled his glass.

Martin Beck didn't know exactly what he ought to do. He wanted Mård reasonably sober, but he also wanted him in a fairly good mood.

"Don't drink so damn much," he said experimentally.

"What?"

Mård looked perplexed.

"What the fuck did you say? Here in my own house?"

"I said you shouldn't drink so damn much. It's a hell of a good piece of advice. Besides, I want to talk to you, and I want some sensible answers."

"Sensible answers? How's a person supposed to be sensible in the midst of all this shit? Anyway, do you think I'm the only one sitting around drinking himself to death in this wonderful welfare state?"

Martin Beck knew only too well that Mård was not alone in his dilemma. For a large part of the population, alcohol and narcotics seemed to be the only way out. This applied to the young as well as the old.

"You ought to see the old men at my so-called restaurant. The hell of it is, not one of them has any fun drinking. No, it's about as much fun as turning on the gas for a while, and then turning it off again when you're groggy enough. And then opening it up again when you start to come around."

Mård stared heavily at his dirty glass.

"I've had some damn good times drinking. In the old days. That's the difference. That was in the old days. We used to have a hell of a time. But not here. Other places."

"In Trinidad-Tobago for example?"

Mård seemed utterly unaffected.

"Well," he said. "So you managed to dig that up. Well done. I'll be damned. I didn't think you were up to it."

"Oh, we usually find out a lot of things," said Martin Beck. "Most things, as a matter of fact."

"Well you wouldn't fucking believe it to see the cops around town. I often wonder why you use human beings at all. Over at Tivoli in Copenhagen they've got a mechanical man who pulls a gun and fires when you put in a coin. They ought to be able to fix him up so he'd lift the other arm too and hit you with a billy club. And they could put in a tape recorder that says, 'All right, what's going on here?' "

Martin Beck laughed.

"It's an idea," he said.

What he was really laughing at was the thought of how the National Commissioner would react to Bertil Mård's proposed reorganization of the force.

But he kept that to himself.

"I was lucky," Bertil Mård said. "Kill some son of a bitch and get a four-pound fine. In a lot of places, I might have been hanged."

"Maybe."

"Not here, of course. But here, on the other hand, a flock of bandits can sit around and spoil life for everyone. They don't even get a four-pound fine. They get made provincial governors and get free air fare to their banks in Liechtenstein and Kuwait. Nothing wrong with Liechtenstein and Kuwait, mind you. Fine countries, both of them."

Suddenly Mård groaned and pressed his right hand to his midriff.

"Are you all right?" said Martin Beck.

"No, but it'll go away."

Mård picked up his glass and emptied half of it.

He was breathing heavily. Martin Beck waited. A few moments later, his expression eased.

"But you said you wanted to talk about Sigbrit," he said. "Okay, she was murdered by that sex maniac who lived next door, and you've caught him and put him in the psycho ward where he belongs. If you hadn't got him, I would have gone out there and killed him myself. You saved me the trouble. What else is there to talk about?"

"That trip to Copenhagen."

"But you've got your murderer, for Christ's sake."

"I'm not absolutely sure we do. You say you went to Copenhagen on October seventeenth."

"Yes."

"On the train ferry *Malmöhus?*"

"Yes. And the men on board saw me. The mess steward and the deck crew, both."

"But they're not absolutely certain of the day. That's the trouble."

"What the hell am I supposed to do about that?"

"Well, what did you do in Copenhagen?"

"Went to a lot of taverns and drank myself good stinking drunk. I don't even remember how I got back home."

"Now listen, Captain Mård. You told us you sat in the forward saloon—what used to be the first-class smoking room."

"Yes. At the table amidships. Right behind the ship's bell."

"I've sat at that table myself. There's a marvelous view."

"Yes, it's almost like standing on the bridge. I suppose that's why I like to sit there."

"You're an old seaman and a practiced observer. Did anything happen on that trip?"

"Things always happen at sea. But nothing that would mean anything to you."

"Don't be so sure."

Mård stuck his hand in his back pocket and pulled out the worn leather notebook.

"I was at sea, after all," he said. "Even if I did sit there like a piece of baggage. I've got a notation here. I put down everything of interest in the log. Unless I'm dead drunk, of course."

He thumbed through the book to a special section.

"Here we are," he said. "Train ferry *Malmöhus* from ferry slip Malmö eleven forty-five hours October seventeenth, nineteen hundred seventy-three. Sixteen knots, estimated. Bound Copenhagen. I made notes of the ships we met."

"Oh?"

"Well, of course, you log your meetings, that's obvious."

"Wait a minute," said Martin Beck.

He took out a paper and pen, things he seldom made use of in his fieldwork.

"Eleven fifty-five, *MS Öresound* on course for Malmö harbor."

"Yes, that boat runs every day."

"I suppose so. Regular traffic."

"Twelve thirty-seven, *MS Gripen*, same thing there. Small cargo ship in regular traffic. I wrote 'blue ribbon' after the name. Which doesn't mean the Atlantic Blue Riband exactly."

"What does it mean?"

"Well, it means she had a blue ribbon painted along her plating."

"What's so special about that?"

"The ribbon used to be green. The shipping company must have changed its colors. Twelve fifty-five was more interesting, a freighter called the *Runatkindar*. Faroese flag."

"Faroese?"

"Yes, you don't see it very often. Then we were passed by two hydrofoils, thirteen-o-five and thirteen-o-six, *Svalan* and *Queen of the Waves*. Then I put down that there was an Italian destroyer at Langelinie and two small German freighters in Frihavnen. And that's all."

"I'll take down those names," said Martin Beck. "Can I have a look?"

"No. But I'll spell them for you."

He spelled out the name of the ship that had flown the flag of the Faroe Islands.

Martin Beck would have Benny Skacke check it. But in his heart of hearts he already knew that Bertil Mård's alibi would hold.

Now there were a couple of other subjects he wanted to go into.

"Excuse me if I ask you some more questions," he said. "But how did you know that Folke Bengtsson lived next door to your ex-wife?"

"Because she told me so herself."

"You said you hadn't been out there for at least a year and a half. Bengtsson moved in only a year ago."

"Who the hell said I was out there when she told me? Sigbrit came in here to try and get some money out of me. And I gave her some; I still liked her. I gave her a little cock too. Right here on the floor. Squealed like a stuck pig when she came. That was when she told me about that sex maniac. And that was the last time I saw her, for that matter."

Mård fixed his strange gaze on the floor.

"Goddam son of a bitch," he said. "Strangled her, right? Where have you got him?"

"Let's not talk about that."

"What the fuck do we talk about then? Whores? You

were interested in whorehouses, weren't you? Do you want some addresses?"

"No thanks."

Bertil Mård groaned again and pressed his fist hard against his right side, below the ribs. He poured himself some more vodka and drank it down.

Martin Beck waited.

"Captain Mård," he said, when the pain seemed to have passed. "There is one point on which you are obviously lying."

"I'll be damned if I've told a lie all day. What day is it?"

"Friday, November sixteenth."

"I ought to write it up in the log. 'No lies today.' Of course, the day isn't over yet."

"You said yourself that Bengtsson didn't move to Domme until after you had definitely stopped going out there, and yet he's seen you out there twice."

"Now there's your fucking lie! I haven't set foot on the place."

Martin Beck thought. He massaged the edge of his scalp.

"Do you know if your ex-wife was seeing anyone named Clark?"

"Never heard of him. Besides, I wouldn't stand for Sigbrit seeing other men."

"You don't know anyone named Clark?"

"Not offhand. I suppose I must have met someone by that name sometime. But it didn't have anything to do with Sigbrit. It's a silly fucking name anyway."

"I don't see why Bengtsson would lie about it. He definitely says he saw you at the house two different times."

"Typical," Mård said. "He's fucking crazy. He strangles two women. And here you sit—some kind of super-

173

intendent of police—wondering why the hell he would tell a lie."

Mård spit on the floor.

"Christ, that mechanical man I told you about would really make a better cop."

Suddenly Martin Beck put two and two together.

Very much too late, it seemed to him.

"What kind of car do you drive, Captain Mård?"

"A Saab. An old green wreck. I've had it six years. It's parked out there someplace with one of those little tickets on the windshield that says to send in your thirty-five-crown bribe. I'm rarely sober enough to drive it."

Martin Beck stared at him for a long time.

Mård didn't say anything.

After about a minute, Martin Beck broke the silence himself.

"I'm going now," he said. "And in all probability, I'll never come back."

"That suits me fine."

"In some funny way I like you," said Martin Beck. "Thanks for being so patient."

"I don't give a shit if you like me or not."

"Would you let me give you a piece of honest advice?"

"I suppose I could use it."

"Sell the restaurant and whatever else you may own. Put it in cash and get away from here. Buy yourself a plane ticket to Panama or Honduras and ship out. Even if you have to sign on as mate."

Mård looked at him with his dark-brown eyes, which could change so quickly from madness to utter calm.

"It's an idea," he said.

Martin Beck closed the door behind him.

He was always thorough, so he would ask Benny Skacke to check out that story about the ships.

But it wasn't very important any more.

Folke Bengtsson had seen a man in a beige Volvo at the house in Domme—twice.

And that man had not been Bertil Mård.

17.

When Martin Beck got back to Anderslöv, he went to the police station to talk to Herrgott Allwright.

There was no one in the office except an old man in wooden shoes, who was standing by the counter twisting a worn astrakhan cap in his hands. The door to Allwright's office was ajar, and he pushed it open and looked in. Britta, the clerk, was standing at the desk shuffling through some papers.

"Herrgott's gone to Hönsinge to see about something," she said. "He said he'd be back in an hour."

Martin Beck stood in the doorway and thought. He wanted to talk to someone, but he didn't want to wait a whole hour for Allwright, and Kollberg wasn't available.

"Tell him I've gone down to Trelleborg," he said finally. "I'll be back this evening."

He closed the door and went out to the outer office to call a taxi. The man in the wooden shoes put his cap down on the counter.

"Excuse me," he said. "I wanted to get a driver's license."

Martin Beck shook his head.

"I can't help you."

"But it's only for a horse and wagon," the old man pleaded.

"You'll have to talk to the clerk," said Martin Beck, picking up the phone.

The old man looked so crestfallen and unhappy that Martin Beck felt sorry for him.

"She'll be right back," he said. "I'm sure she can fix you up."

Driver's license for a horse and wagon, he thought.

Was there such a thing?

The cab driver was unusual—one of the silent type.

He drove and Martin Beck thought. He tried to summarize what he knew about the man who had been Sigbrit Mård's lover.

His name was Clark.

He wrote short notes to her on paper that looked as if it had been ripped out of a notebook. How did she get his messages? Not in the mail, certainly.

He was probably married to someone named Sissy, who had a brother.

He met Sigbrit on Thursdays. Once in a while, they might meet on some other day of the week as well, but always on Thursdays. Except for holidays, and the months of June and July. Maybe he had his vacation then. They saw each other unusually often during the month of August. Perhaps he had been a grass widow, with Sissy in the country.

It was possible that he owned a beige Volvo.

He called her Sigge.

It wasn't much to go on.

Martin Beck thought about the key in Sigbrit Mård's purse, the one that fit no lock. Herrgott had established that she didn't have a key to where she worked. Was it the key to Clark's apartment, or did they have a love nest?

He had a lot of questions, most of them pure speculation, based on the two handwritten messages and the letter C in Sigbrit's almanac.

The letter might stand for something entirely different. Coffee house? Did she work special hours those days? Class? Maybe she was involved in some kind of adult education course. But there was nothing in her house to indicate it, and no one she knew had mentioned anything of that kind. He had the taxi let him out at the square, and he walked the short distance to the pastry shop and coffee house where Sigbrit Mård had worked.

It seemed to be a popular place. The bakery section was full of customers, and all the tables in the café were occupied.

Martin Beck watched for a while, trying to figure out which one of the women behind the counter was in charge. There were new customers arriving all the time, and the women were very busy. He finally took a number and waited his turn.

The owner was a woman in her fifties. She was plump and seemed cheerful and motherly, and Martin Beck imagined her constantly surrounded by the aroma of fresh bread, meringues, and vanilla cream.

She showed him into a little office behind the kitchen.

"I simply can't tell you how dreadful it is, all this about Sigbrit," she said. "I had my misgivings when she just suddenly disappeared like that, but that anything so terrible might have happened to her, it's simply inconceivable."

"What sort of woman was she?" Martin Beck asked.

"Sigbrit? A wonderful girl, clever and conscientious and awfully good-natured. Everyone liked her, the girls she worked with, and everyone. The customers too."

"How long had she worked here?"

"Oh, it's a long time now. She was one of my oldest girls. Let me see . . ."

She closed her eyes and thought.

"Twelve years," she said finally. "She started here in the fall of sixty-one."

"Then you knew her quite well, I suppose," said Martin Beck. "Did she ever talk about her private life, about her marriage, for example?"

"Oh, yes, but that was such a peculiar marriage. I thought she did the right thing when she divorced that fellow. He was never at home anyway."

"Do you know if she was involved with any other men?"

The woman threw up both of her chubby hands.

"Sigbrit wasn't that kind at all," she said. "She was faithful to her husband, I can tell you that, Superintendent. In spite of the fact that he was always away at sea, and even though he was a no-good. That's what he was, in my opinion."

"I meant later, after the divorce," said Martin Beck.

"Well, Sigbrit was still young and good-looking, so actually it was funny she didn't find another man. But she didn't, as far as I know."

"What did her job involve? Did she stand behind the counter or did she wait on tables?"

"Both. The girls take turns; it depends on how much there is to do. Sometimes there's more to do in the shop, and sometimes we have so many for coffee that at least two girls have to wait on tables."

"What hours did she work?"

"It varied. We don't close till ten o'clock, so the girls work shifts."

"Thursday evenings, for example. Did she work then?"

The woman shook her head and looked at Martin Beck in surprise.

"No," she said. "Thursday was always Sigbrit's evening off. She was free on other evenings too, of course, but Thursdays in particular she always wanted off."

"She asked for them herself?"

"Yes, that's right. But she was always happy to work Fridays and Saturdays when the other girls all wanted off."

Martin Beck sat silently for a moment. He looked at the telephone standing on the desk.

"Did she ever get private phone calls here at work?"

"No, never. I'd really rather that none of the girls got personal calls here, but, of course, it does happen now and then in family emergencies and so forth. But Sigbrit never had any calls here at work."

Suddenly she looked at Martin Beck and knit her brows.

"Why are you asking all these questions, Superintendent? You've arrested the man, after all, that maniac who killed her. What good are all these questions?"

"There are still a few points that haven't been cleared up," said Martin Beck. "We think there was a man in her life, and we'd like to find him."

The woman shook her head.

"I don't think so," she said. "Sigbrit was always talkative and open. I'm sure she would have mentioned it if she'd met someone new."

"So no one ever came here to see her? Or picked her up after work?"

She shook her head again.

"Think hard," said Martin Beck. "It might be important."

"No," she said. "Never."

"Have you ever heard her mention anyone named Clark?"

"No. Never."

"And you've never seen anyone meet her in a car."

More head-shaking.

"Do you have any objection to my talking to the women she worked with? I promise not to keep them long."

"Yes, that would be all right," she said. "You stay here, and I'll send them in. Do you want to talk to Mrs. Johansson in the kitchen too?"

"Yes," said Martin Beck. "If it's all right, I'd like to talk to all of them. How many employees do you have?"

"Five. Four girls—I've had to get a replacement for Sigbrit—and then a woman for the buffet, to make the coffee and sandwiches. And then I have the bakery, of course, but that's in a different building, two blocks from here."

She stood up. When she opened the door, the smell of coffee and freshly baked bread drifted in from the kitchen outside.

Martin Beck saw a thin woman with white hair and very red hands decorating a plate of sandwiches. He watched in wonder as she speared a section of mandarin orange, an olive, and a cocktail cherry on a toothpick and jabbed the whole collection into a thick slab of headcheese resting on a piece of lettuce.

The owner came back with a tray and put it down in front of Martin Beck.

Coffee and a large plate of Danish pastries and cookies.

"I hope you'll like them," she said. "Ulla will be right here."

Martin Beck realized he was hungry, and although as a rule he wasn't fond of cookies and heavy Danish pastry, he managed to clean the plate before Ulla came in.

He spoke to the four girls and finally to the imaginative Mrs. Johansson.

Their opinions of Sigbrit Mård varied. Mrs. Johansson and two of the girls did not appear to share their employer's enthusiasm. They seemed to think she put on airs and was conceited.

None of them thought she was having a love affair or had anything to do with men at all. They had never heard of any Clark, not seen a beige Volvo in connection with Sigbrit Mård.

Martin Beck left the pastry shop and walked down toward the harbor. The ferry slip was empty.

He strolled slowly along toward the police building. It was two o'clock in the afternoon, which meant that his chances of finding Kollberg with Folke Bengtsson were slim. Kollberg was not in the habit of skipping lunch.

He was not looking forward to the coming interview with Bengtsson with any great delight, but it was a necessity, and this time he had concrete questions to ask and might possibly find Bengtsson a little more cooperative.

He looked in at the Cosmopolite, a restaurant in the same block with the police building. Kollberg wasn't there, but he recognized a couple of detectives sitting at a corner table eating Baltic herring and mashed potatoes. They nodded to him, and he raised his hand in greeting before closing the door behind him.

Folke Bengtsson was in the jail.

Martin Beck managed to borrow a room with a view of the harbor, and while he waited for someone to fetch Bengtsson, he looked at the view.

A small German freighter lay at the quay. A woman came out on deck and emptied a bucket of scraps over the outside rail. A solitary gull, sailing lazily against the wind, dove immediately to the surface of the water, grabbed something long and limp in its bill, and lifted again in an easy circle. The woman stood by the rail with the bucket in her hands and watched the gulls. In less than a minute, a whole flock of them had gathered and were screaming and flapping their wings as they fought for the best pieces. The woman disappeared down the fo'c's'le hatch.

Folke Bengtsson was calm and unruffled and greeted Martin Beck politely before taking a seat in the visitor's armchair in front of the desk.

"Detective Inspector Kollberg was here and questioned me this morning," he said. "I don't know what I can tell you that I haven't told you already. I really did not kill her, that's all I can say."

"I came to ask you about something in particular," said Martin Beck. "Something you said when we talked at your house in Domme ten days ago."

Folke Bengtsson looked attentively and expectantly at Martin Beck. He sat with his back straight and his hands folded in his lap, and Martin Beck was reminded of an obedient schoolboy waiting for the teacher's question.

"You mentioned at that time that you had seen Mrs. Mård's ex-husband on a couple of occasions, is that right?"

"Yes, that's true. I saw him twice."

"Can you tell me a little more about it?" said Martin Beck. "Can you remember when this was?"

Folke Bengtsson sat and thought for a long time.

"The first time was last spring," he said finally. "The last Sunday in May. I remember because it was Mother's Day and I had been into town to call my mother in Södertälje. I always call her on Mother's Day and on her birthday."

He stopped talking, absorbed in his own thoughts. Martin Beck waited, but finally broke the silence himself.

"Yes?" he said. "And that's when you saw Mård? Can you tell me how it happened?"

"Well, I had driven up to the house and then walked back to close the gate. Just then a beige Volvo swung into the road, and since he was going pretty slow I stood there thinking maybe he was coming to my place. Not that I was expecting anyone—and it was a Sunday too—but sometimes people come and want to buy fish or eggs."

"Which direction did the car come from?"

"From up toward Malmö."

"Did you see the driver?"

"Yes, it was him, her husband."

Martin Beck stared at the man in front of him.

"What did he look like?" he said.

Folke Bengtsson sat in silence again, as if he hadn't heard the question.

"I had heard that he was supposed to be a ship's captain," he said at last. "But it didn't seem to me that he looked like a seaman. He was very tanned, of course, but he was thin and looked frail. Rather small. His hair was wavy and almost white, and he wore glasses."

"Did you see him that clearly? Even if he was driving slowly, you couldn't have had that much time to study him."

"No, perhaps I didn't look at him so closely then. But I saw him once more, later on."

"When was that?"

Folke Bengtsson looked out through the window.

"I don't remember exactly, but it wasn't so long ago. At the beginning of September, maybe."

"And how did that happen? Did he drive up in his car that time too?"

"No, but the car was standing in Sigbrit's yard. I'd been down in the pasture to see if any mushrooms had come up. None had. There are often a lot of champignons down there. I can pick several quarts, and a lot of customers are happy to buy mushrooms. Especially champignons."

"So you walked down the road past Sigbrit Mård's house?"

"Yes, that's right. And then he came out on the steps and then he got into his car. Maybe that was when it occurred to me that he looked sort of frail and puny to be a seaman."

He fell silent again.

"Seamen are usually strong," he said. "But then, of course, he'd been sick, or so I'd heard."

"Did you see Mrs. Mård as well on that occasion?"

"No, I didn't. I only saw Mr. Mård standing on the steps buttoning up his coat, and then he walked over and got in the car. He passed me just before I reached my place."

"In which direction?"

"I beg your pardon?"

"In which direction did he drive off? When he got down to the highway?"

"Toward Malmö. That's where he lives. Or so I've heard."

"What was he wearing?"

"All I remember is the coat. It was one of those brown sheepskin coats with the fur on the inside. It looked new and smart, but it must have been warm on a day like that. He had nothing on his head."

He raised his eyes and looked at Martin Beck.

"It was a warm day. I remember that."

"Do you remember anything else about him?"

Folke Bengtsson shook his head.

"No, that's all."

"Did you see the license number on the car?"

"No, I didn't. I didn't think of that."

"Did it have old plates so you could see what province it was from?"

The Swedish automobile registry was just in the process of changing its numbering system.

"No, I don't remember."

Folke Bengtsson went back to jail, and Martin Beck got a ride in a police car to Anderslöv.

Kollberg had not come back, but Allwright was sitting in his office at the police station. Martin Beck told him about his visit to Trelleborg.

"Well," said Allwright thoughtfully, "I guess it must be this fellow Clark who drives the beige Volvo. I'll ask around town if anyone else has seen him or the car. But I doubt it. If anyone had known about him, surely they would have mentioned it before. While Sigbrit was still missing."

They sat in silence for a few moments.

"Which means," said Allwright finally, "that Folke is the only one who knows this man exists."

18.

It was not a good car. Much too conspicuous for the purpose. A big, light-green Chevrolet with three sevens in the license number, a lot of chrome, and a lot of lights.

On top of which it had been seen, and some nosy neighbor had already called the police.

It was early in the morning and rather cold, although it was going to be a warm day for some. The damp rose up from the ground and mixed with the mist drifting lazily in from the sea. The early morning light was grayish-white, hazy, and confusing.

In the back seat of the green car lay a pair of rolled-up oriental rugs, a television receiver, a transistor radio, and five bottles of liquor. The trunk contained several paintings, a figurine of doubtful origin, a pedestal, and some other odds and ends.

In the front seat sat two thieves. They were young and nervous and making a lot of mistakes. They both knew they'd been seen. And their luck was bad. The whole thing had begun badly and was going to get worse.

There were no street lights on at this hour, but the soft glow from the sky reflected in the film of dew that covered the car. The engine hummed gently and, with its lights off, the green car glided along between the hedges surrounding the private gardens on either side of the street. At the end of the block, it slowed and stopped. Then it swung out onto the highway, as cautiously as a circus tiger entering the ring. There had been no rain for some time, but the pavement was streaked with moisture and might have looked to the uninitiated as if it had just been cleaned. The initiated knew, however, that the Department of Sanitation didn't operate this far from town.

A light-green American car with its headlights off. It slid through the mist like a phantom, almost soundless, its contours blurred.

The patrol car, on the other hand, was frighteningly matter-of-fact.

A black and white four-door Valiant with spotlights and two blue flashers on the roof. It was unmistakable. But just to be sure, the actual word POLICE was spelled out in highly visible letters on the doors, hood, and trunk.

Automobile density in Sweden was still high, and patrol car density abnormally so. It was more and more common for these vehicles to stop suddenly and spew out oddly clad men with weapons in their hands, and yet the human element in these occurrences was virtually nonexistent.

Squad cars poked about in unlikely places or stood poisoning the air with idling engines, while the average patrolman inside had a bad back and a steadily decreasing IQ, even as he grew more and more alienated from society in general.

A policeman on foot was something of a curiosity these days, and in any case it was a sight that boded unpleasantness.

The patrol in question consisted of three policemen—Elofsson, Borglund, and Hector.

Elofsson and Borglund were an old patrol car team, and they looked like any other middle-aged policemen. Hector was younger and more gung ho. They didn't really need him, to put it mildly. He was along for the fun of it, and for a little extra overtime. He was very proud of his well-tended sideburns, which seemed to have become standard equipment for younger policemen.

Borglund was lazy and pudgy, and at the moment he was asleep in the back seat with his mouth open. Elofsson was drinking coffee from a plaid thermos bottle and drowsily smoking a cigarette. Hector disliked tobacco and had pointedly rolled down the side window. He sat with his hands on the wheel and stared silently out through the windshield with a morose and bored expression. All three men were wearing gray-blue uniforms of the jumpsuit variety, with shoulder belts and pistols and night sticks in white leather holsters.

The car was standing by the side of the road with its parking lights on. The engine was indeed idling, and poisonous exhaust fumes laid their shroud of death and suffocation over the languishing vegetation along the edge of the ditch.

None of the policemen had spoken for quite some time.

Hector had turned up the radio a little while ago, but Elofsson had immediately turned it down again, by right of several years' seniority. Hector had sense enough not to make a fuss, and the voice on the radio was now a subdued babble of almost sprightly remarks delivered in a foolish tone of voice. Elofsson wasn't listening at all, Borglund was breathing stertorously in the back seat, and Hector had to strain to hear what was being said.

"Good morning, good morning, good morning, dear friends and colleagues out on the highways and byways. We have a few little tidbits for you. A domestic disturbance on Björkgatan in Sofielund. Complaints about the noise, probably a drunken party. Closest patrol please check it out. What? Yes, music and singing. Björkgatan twenty-three. Suspicious hot rod outside an empty villa in Ljunghusen. Two-tone blue Chrysler, an A plate with three sixes in the number. Closest patrol will investigate. The address is Östersjövägen thirty-six. May be connected with a suspected burglary. A young man and two girls seen in the car. Routine check."

"That's right nearby," Hector said.

"What?" said Elofsson.

Borglund's only reaction was a slightly indignant snore.

"You fellows in the area might have a care," said the voice. "Usual procedure. Take no chances. Check out the vehicle if it shows up. Direction of travel unknown. Try not to attract attention. Take it a little easy if you spot this item. Ordinary routine checkout. Nothing more at the moment. Good morning, all."

"That's right nearby," Hector repeated.

Elofsson slurped some coffee from the mug of his thermos but didn't say anything. Borglund turned in his sleep.

"Right in this neighborhood," Hector said.

"Don't bust a gut, boy," Elofsson said, rooting around in his cookie bag.

He sank his teeth into a cinnamon twirl.

"Right close by," Hector said. "Let's go."

"Easy, boy. It's probably nothing at all. And if it is something, we're not the only cops in the world."

Hector flushed.

"What do you mean?" he said. "I don't get it."

Elofsson went on chewing.

Borglund sighed deeply in his sleep and whimpered. Perhaps he was dreaming about the National Commissioner.

They were no more than sixty feet from the intersection when the light-green Chevy swung onto the road ahead of them.

"There's the little bastards now," Hector said.

"Maybe," Elofsson said.

The word was muffled by a mouthful of food.

"Let's take 'em," Hector said.

He put the car in gear and tramped on the gas.

The patrol car leaped forward.

"What?" said Borglund groggily.

"Burglars," Hector said.

"Maybe," Elofsson said.

"What?" said Borglund, still half asleep. "What's going on?"

The youths in the green car didn't discover the patrol car until it was already beside them, and then it was too late.

Hector accelerated, cut in front, and jammed on the brakes. The police car skidded on the damp pavement. The green car was forced to the right and came to a stop with its front wheel three inches from the edge of the ditch. The driver didn't have much choice.

Hector was the first one out on the road. He had already unbuttoned his holster and drawn his 7.65 mm Walther.

Elofsson got out on the other side.

Borglund was last, disoriented and breathing hard.

"What's going on here?" he said.

"No headlights," said Hector in a shrill voice. "That's a violation. Out of the car, you little sluts."

He had his pistol in his right hand.

"And when I say 'Now' I don't mean tomorrow, by God. Move!"

"Take it easy," Elofsson said.

"No tricks," Hector said.

The people in the green car climbed out on opposite sides. Their faces were white patches in the fog.

"Just a little routine chat," Elofsson said.

He was closer to them than the others but still hadn't touched his revolver.

"Just take it easy," he said.

Hector was standing behind him to one side, his revolver in his hand and his finger on the trigger.

"We haven't done anything."

The voice sounded young. It could have come from a girl or from a boy whose voice was breaking.

"That's what they all say," Hector said. "Unlawful lighting, for example. What about that? Have a look in their car, Emil."

From where he was standing, only a few yards away, Elofsson could see that the suspects were two young men. They were both wearing leather jackets, jeans, and tennis shoes, but the similarity ended there. One of them was big and dark, with a crew cut. The other was below normal height and had billowing, shoulder-length blond hair. Neither one of them looked to be more than twenty years old.

Elofsson walked toward the taller of the two youths, fingering his holster but not opening it. Instead, he moved his hand, took out his flashlight, and shone it into the back seat. Then he put it away again.

"Mmm," he said.

Then he turned abruptly to the tall youth, grabbed for his clothing, and got a grip on the lapels of his jacket.

"All right, you little bastards," said Hector from behind him.

"What's going on here?" Borglund said.

And that was apparently the remark that set things going.

Elofsson was following normal procedure. He had grabbed the boy's jacket with both hands. The next step was to pull the victim closer and drive his right knee into the man's groin. And that would take care of that. The same way he had done it so many times before. Without firearms.

But Emil Elofsson had kneed his last arrestee. The young man with the crew cut had other ideas. He had his right hand at his belt and his left hand in his pocket. There was a revolver stuck in the waistband of his jeans, and he obviously had no doubts about what it was for. He pulled it and started shooting.

The revolver was a weapon constructed for short range, a nickel-plated Colt Cobra 32 caliber with six shots in the chambered cylinder. The first two shots struck Elofsson in the diaphragm, and the third and fourth passed under his left arm. Both of these bullets hit Hector in the left hip and sent him reeling backwards across the highway where he fell on his back with his head resting on a low wire fence that ran along the edge of the road.

Shots numbers five and six rang out. They were presumably meant for Borglund, but he had a very human fear of guns and at the very first shot had thrown himself headlong into the ditch on the north side of the highway. The ditch was deep and damp, and his large body bounced heavily to the bottom. He wound up on his stomach in the mud, not daring to lift his face, and almost at once he felt a cruel, stinging pain on the right side of his neck.

Elofsson had already pushed off with his foot, and his knee was an inch or so in the air when the bullets struck his body. He clung tightly to the leather jacket and only let go when the man with the gun took several steps back and opened the cylinder to reload.

He fell forward and landed on his side, where he lay with one cheek against the pavement and his right arm trapped helplessly under his body, along with his pistol, still buttoned in its holster.

In spite of the uncertain light, he could see the young man distinctly as he stepped back and loaded new cartridges, which he apparently had loose in his jacket pocket.

Elofsson was in great pain, and the front of his uniform was already soaked and smeared with blood. He could neither talk nor move, only observe. And still he was more dumbfounded than afraid. How could this have happened? For twenty years he'd been driving around shouting and swearing, pushing, kicking, hitting people with his billy club, or slapping them with the flat side of his saber. He had always been the stronger, had always had the advantage of arms and might and justice against people who were weaponless and powerless and had no rights.

And now here he lay on the pavement.

The man with the revolver was twenty steps away. It had grown lighter, and Elofsson saw him turn his head and heard five words.

"Get in the car, Caspar!"

Then the man raised his left elbow, rested the barrel on the crook of his arm, and sighted carefully. At what?

The question was superfluous. A ricochet glanced off the pavement less than a foot from Elofsson's face. At the same time, he heard a shot behind him. Was the other bastard shooting at him too? Or was it Borglund? He dismissed that idea. If Borglund wasn't dead already, he was lying somewhere pretending to be.

The man with the revolver was standing still. Legs apart. Aiming.

Elofsson closed his eyes. He felt the blood pulsing out of his body. He didn't see his life pass before his eyes. He merely thought: Now I'm going to die.

Hector hadn't dropped his pistol when he fell. He was lying on his back with his head propped up on the fence, and he too could see the figure with the revolver and the short black hair, though less distinctly and from a greater distance. What's more, Elofsson lay right in his line of fire, but pressed so tightly to the road that there was a free range above him.

In contrast to his colleague, Hector was not especially surprised. He was young, and this was roughly what his fervid imagination had always expected of this job. His right arm was still functioning, but there was something wrong with the left, and he had a hard time getting his hand on the housing of his pistol to cock it. And that had to be done, for in accordance with police regulations, he actually did not have a cartridge in the chamber. (Elofsson and Borglund did have, on the other hand, for all the good it did them.) He didn't succeed until the other man had fired the first shot of his second series.

Hector was in agony. The pain in his left arm and his whole left side was excruciating, and his vision was blurred. He fired his first shot carelessly and mechanically, and it went high.

This was not the time for wild shots, he could see that. Hector was generally a decent marksman on the range, but at the moment it would take more than decent marksmanship to save his life. The figure standing in the mist eighty feet away had all the advantages, and his behavior indicated that he wasn't about to go home until every policeman in sight was guaranteed stone dead.

Hector took a deep breath. The pain was so great he

nearly lost consciousness. A bullet hit the fence, and the steel wires reverberated. The vibration passed on through the back of his head, and for one instant, his vision became amazingly clear and concentrated. He raised the pistol and forced himself to hold his arm straight and his hand still. The target was indistinct, but he could see it.

Hector squeezed off the shot. Then he lost consciousness, and the automatic fell from his hand.

Elofsson, however, was still conscious. Ten seconds earlier, he had opened his eyes again, and nothing had changed. The man with the revolver hadn't moved. Legs apart, the pistol barrel resting on his elbow, he was carefully and calmly taking aim.

He heard another shot from behind.

And, wonder of wonders, the man with the revolver gave a jerk and threw his arms up over his head. The weapon flew from his hand. And then, in a continuation of the same motion, he collapsed on the pavement and went utterly limp, as if there had been no skeleton in his body. He lay there in a heap. Not a sound crossed his lips.

It would be wrong to call it pure chance, for Hector had aimed carefully and done his very best. But it was an almost incredibly lucky shot. The bullet struck the man's shoulder and followed his collarbone directly to his spinal cord. The youth with the revolver died ininstantly, probably while he was still on his feet. He didn't even have a chance to lie down and draw his final breath.

Elofsson heard a car peel out and speed away.

And that was followed by total silence, abstract and unnatural.

After what seemed like a very long time, someone moved nearby.

After another long wait, though it could not have been more than minutes or even seconds, Borglund came crawling over on all fours. He was moaning and looking about aimlessly with his flashlight. He stuck his hand in under Elofsson, flinched, and pulled it back. And stared at the blood.

"Jesus Christ, Emil," he said.

And:

"For God's sake, what did you do?"

Elofsson felt all the strength leave his body, and he could not talk or move.

Borglund got to his feet with gasps and groans.

Elofsson heard him clump over to the patrol car and switch the radio to the emergency frequency.

"Emergency! Come in! Highway 100 at Östersjövägen in Ljunghusen. Two men shot. I'm hurt myself. Gunfire. Shooting. Help!"

From a great distance, Elofsson heard metallic voices responding over the radio. First the nearby districts.

"Trelleborg here. We're coming."

"Lund district. We're on our way."

Finally the despatcher in Malmö.

"Good morning. Help on its way. It'll take about fifteen minutes. Twenty at the most."

After a while, Borglund was back, fumbling with the first aid kit. He turned Elofsson over on his back, cut open his uniform, and started stuffing compresses in at random between his stomach and his blood-drenched underclothes. He kept up a steady, monotonous, thick-tongued babble.

"Jesus Christ, Emil. Jesus Christ."

Elofsson lay there in the damp. His blood mixed with the dew. He was cold. It hurt even more than it had. He was still dumbfounded.

A little later he heard other voices. The people in

the house behind the wire fence had woken up and ventured out.

A young woman knelt down beside Elofsson and took his hand.

"There, there," she said. "There, there. They'll be here soon."

He was more dumbfounded than ever. A person was holding his hand. A member of the general public. After a while she put his head on her lap, and put her hand on his forehead.

They were still in that position when the scream of many sirens began to reach them, first very soft but soon shrill and piercing.

Just then the sun broke through the mist and spread a shallow, pale-yellow light over the absurd scene.

All of this took place on the morning of November 18, 1973, in the farthest corner of the Malmö Police District. For that matter, in the farthest corner of Sweden. Several hundred yards away, long shiny waves surged in against a curving sand beach that seemed to be endless in the fog. The sea.

On the other side was the European continent.

19.

Monday, November 19.

Clear, cold, and windy.

The day was called Elizabeth in the Swedish almanac, and it was Kollberg's turn to talk to Folke Bengtsson.

But a great many things were different this Monday

morning. It was as if Anderslöv had suddenly vanished from the map. The mass media were interested in other things.

What was a strangled divorcee compared with two bullet-riddled cops? And a third one injured, no one knew exactly how or why. One criminal was dead, and another was on a wild flight from justice.

Martin Beck and Kollberg both knew that being a policeman wasn't especially dangerous, even if the higher echelons and a lot of individual policemen did like to overdramatize their profession.

Of course, policemen did get shot. In fact, it happened a lot more often than the so-called general public knew. Because the accident rate at police firing ranges was alarmingly high, even though such accidental shootings were always hushed up. The trouble was that many policemen were trigger-happy young men who lacked the experience and caution in the company of weapons which usually characterizes civilian marksmen. They were simply careless, with the result that they often shot themselves or one another, though seldom fatally.

But otherwise it was not a dangerous job, not physically. In fact, a man's greatest risk was of ruining his back with too much riding around in automobiles. A great many other professions had infinitely more casualties on the job.

And this was true not only in Sweden.

To take an obvious example: In Britain, 7,768 mine workers have been killed since 1947, while in that same period only a dozen policemen have lost their lives.

This was perhaps an extreme example, but Lennart Kollberg was in the habit of using it whenever he got into a discussion of whether or not policemen should be armed. In England, Scotland, and Wales, as everyone knows, policemen are not armed. And there must be

some explanation for the fact that policemen are injured so much more often in a little country like
Sweden.

Martin Beck had to take the first phone call of the
day, and it came from someone he would rather have
avoided.

Stig Malm.

As a matter of fact, there was probably only one person he had a greater aversion to talking to.

"Your case is all wrapped up," Malm said.

"Well . . ."

"Isn't it? As far as I can see, it's solved. You've got
the murderer under lock and key. And you had him
even before you found the body. Though that was
hardly your own doing."

Martin Beck thought about the excavations in Folke
Bengtsson's garden, but he restrained himself from saying anything. The subject was possibly a little delicate.

"Isn't that right?" Malm said.

"I wouldn't exactly say the case is closed," said Martin Beck.

"What do you mean by that?"

"There are other possibilities. Some details that still
haven't been cleared up."

"But you have arrested the murderer?"

"I'm not at all sure of that," said Martin Beck. "Although it is possible of course."

"Possible? Could it be any simpler?"

"Oh yes," said Martin Beck with conviction. "Much
simpler."

Kollberg looked at him inquisitively.

They were sitting in Allwright's office.

Allwright himself was out taking the dog for its morning walk.

Martin Beck shook his head.

"Well, that's not actually why I called," Malm said. "You're welcome to keep your little mystifications to yourself. We've got more important things to do."

"What things?"

"Do you have to ask? Three policemen mowed down by gangsters, and one of the desperadoes still at large."

"I'm not familiar with it."

"That seems very odd. Don't you read the papers?"

Martin Beck couldn't resist.

"Yes, I do, but I don't base my judgments as a policeman on them. And I don't necessarily believe all the nonsense I read."

Malm didn't react. Every time Martin Beck stopped to think that this man was actually his boss, he felt the same mixture of distaste and amazement.

"The whole matter is very distressing by its very nature," Malm said. "The Commissioner is terribly upset, of course. You know how strongly he feels when something happens to any of our men."

This time, apparently, the National Commissioner was not there in his office.

"I know," said Martin Beck.

And, of course, the whole business really was as awful as it was significant. It was just that Malm's way of talking about it made it look like one of the pseudo-events used so often in recent years to make propaganda for the force.

"We're anticipating a nationwide manhunt," Malm said. "So far, not even the car has been found."

"Does this really concern the National Homicide Squad?"

"That is something which time and the next act in this ghastly drama will reveal."

Said Malm, with the stilted solemnity that so often marked his conversation.

"What sort of shape are those men in?" Martin Beck asked.

"At least two of them are still in critical condition. The doctors say the third one has a good chance of making it, although he'll have to figure on a good long convalescence, of course."

"I see."

"We can't ignore the possibility that this manhunt will spread over the whole country," Malm said. "We've got to catch this desperado at any price, and we've got to catch him soon."

"As I said, I'm not familiar with what happened," said Martin Beck.

"You can learn. Quicker than you suppose," said Malm with a short, self-satisfied laugh. "That's why I'm calling."

"I see."

"It has been decided that I will direct the manhunt personally," Malm said. "I will take charge of the tactical command."

Martin Beck smiled. That was very good news for him—and for the man being hunted.

He was going to escape an assignment where the National Commissioner would be breathing down his neck. The criminal, in turn, could now reckon on an excellent chance of getting away.

Putting Martin Beck on some sort of manhunt staff with Malm as the so-called tactical commander would presumably be going too far. In that respect, Martin Beck was privileged.

And so he wondered what Malm really wanted. But he didn't have to wonder long. Malm cleared his throat and assumed his most portentous tone of voice.

"Of course, it goes without saying that you will complete the assignment you're already working on. But we're just in the process of setting up a task force in Malmö. The Chief down there knows all about it. And we've just had a meeting here early this morning."

Martin Beck looked at his watch.

It was not yet eight o'clock.

Apparently the high command had been up early.

"And?"

"We've decided to transfer Lennart Kollberg to the task force effective at once. He's an exceptionally good man, and there's no good reason why you should need him on a case that's practically complete."

"Wait a moment," said Martin Beck. "You can speak to him yourself."

"That's not necessary," said Malm evasively. "You can give him the message. He's to proceed immediately to Malmö. Coordinator for Task Force Malmö is Inspector Månsson."

"I'll tell him."

"Fine," Malm said. "By the way, congratulations."

"For what?"

"For the way you've virtually wrapped up this sex murder. As quickly as ever."

"I don't even know if it is a sex murder," said Martin Beck. "The results of the autopsy aren't clear on that point."

"Your record of cases solved is masterful," Malm said. "Except when they involve locked rooms."

He laughed good-naturedly at his own little joke.

Martin Beck found it unusually easy to control his laughter when he saw Kollberg's suspicious glance.

"And you'll give Kollberg his orders . . . I mean, the message."

"I'll speak to him."

"Fine. Bye."

"Goodbye," said Martin Beck.

He hung up.

"What does that ass want now?" Kollberg asked.

Martin Beck looked at him thoughtfully.

"Well, I'll give you the good news first," he said.

"What's that?"

"You won't have to deal with Folke Bengtsson any more."

Kollberg's gaze became even more suspicious.

"Oh," he said. "And what's the bad news?"

"Two policemen were shot down toward Falsterbo early yesterday morning. And a third was injured some other way."

"I know."

"You're to report to Malmö."

"How come?"

"They're setting up a task force there. Månsson's co-ordinating."

"Well, that's something."

"There's one little catch. You're not going to like it."

"The National Commissioner," said Kollberg, with something like horror written on his well-fed face.

"Not quite as bad as that."

"How bad?"

"Malm."

"Christ."

"He's in charge of the tactical command."

"The tactical command?"

"Yes, that's what he said."

"What the hell is a tactical command?"

"Sounds military. They're turning us into some sort of a militia."

Kollberg frowned.

"There was a time when I liked being a cop. But that's a hell of a long time ago. Was there anything else?"

"Not really. You're supposed to get over to Malmö on the double."

Kollberg shook his head.

"Malm," he said. "What an asshole. Policemen shot. And that clown heading something called the tactical command. Terrific. I guess there's nothing to do but pack up my things and get out of here."

"What do you think about Folke Bengtsson? Your personal opinion?"

"Frankly, I think he's innocent," Kollberg said. "He's not all there, but this time he didn't do it."

They said goodbye a few minutes later.

"Now don't get all depressed," said Martin Beck.

"I'll try," Kollberg said. "So long."

"So long."

Martin Beck sat by himself for a while and tried to collect his thoughts.

He trusted Kollberg's judgment as much as he did his own.

Kollberg didn't believe Folke Bengtsson had strangled Sigbrit Mård.

Martin Beck didn't think so either. But he wasn't sure. Bengtsson was so damned odd.

On the other hand, Martin Beck did know one thing. Bertil Mård was innocent. Benny Skacke had checked on those ships. No easy task, per se, but not impossible for an energetic policeman with ambition and a pleasant telephone voice.

Mård's log was accurate. That detail about the Faroese freighter could be called decisive.

Allwright walked into the room, threw his hat on the desk and himself in the desk chair.

Timmy rose up on his hind legs and started licking Martin Beck on the face.

Martin Beck shoved the dog aside.

"Herrgott," he said. "Are you absolutely sure you don't know anyone named Clark, with a wife they call Sissy? Who's small and frail but suntanned? Who has wavy white hair and glasses?"

"There's no such person in the Anderslöv district," Allwright said. "You think that's the man who did away with Sigbrit?"

"Yes," said Martin Beck. "As a matter of fact, I think it's starting to look that way."

"Lie down, Timmy!" Allwright said.

The dog actually lay down beside his chair.

He scratched it behind the ears.

"Well, it would be nice it it weren't Bengtsson. People seem to miss him and his smoked herring. Besides, I'd rather it were someone who didn't live in Anderslöv."

20.

He drove all day Sunday, and in the evening he came to a place called Malexander.

He had avoided the main highways. In principle, he was headed for Stockholm, and he followed the signs as well as he could. But his knowledge of geography was sketchy, and he had no map, so he often went wrong. Sometimes he had the feeling he had passed through an area twice, driving south on one road where he had just driven north on another.

What had happened seemed abstract and unreal. He tried to recall the whole chain of events, but all he could call to mind were individual moments, like pictures frozen in a film.

At first he had been terrified, but the fear had subsided, and he had driven away without thinking.

He drove through Malexander, turned off onto a small road leading down to a lake, and parked the car. Then he day down in the back seat and pulled his collar up over his ears, put his hands between his knees, and fell instantly asleep.

The mist rose from the lake and covered the car with a dull film of moisture.

He was awakened by the cold. He didn't know where he was at first, but then he remembered, and his fear came rushing back.

It was still dark. He crawled over into the front seat, turned on the headlights, and started the engine. Then he made one shivering circuit of the car to loosen up his stiff joints. He stopped in front of the radiator, looked at the license plates, and decided he'd better change them as soon as he got a chance.

Then he got back in the car and continued north.

The boy called Caspar was short and delicate, with slender limbs, and the light hair that fell in waves to his shoulders accentuated the soft, childish lines of his face. He was often asked for his driver's license when he drove a car. It was hard for anyone to believe that he was eighteen years old. It annoyed him just as much every time it happened, and he hoped that by sticking to back roads he would avoid running into a patrol car.

His driver's license was okay. It was in the back pocket of his jeans, made out to Ronnie Casparsson, born 9/16/54.

He wondered what had happened to his friend. When he saw him collapse on the highway he'd been certain he was dead, but now he wasn't so sure any more. He'd been standing there in the middle of the road and had called out, "Get in the car, Caspar," as he took aim at one of the policemen. Then suddenly he'd been shot himself. Maybe he'd managed to kill one or two of the cops first, Caspar didn't know. He'd been scared and had driven away. He hadn't even known the other boy was armed.

Maybe he wasn't dead. Maybe he was squealing to the cops right now. But what could he squeal? He didn't even know Caspar's right name. Just as Caspar knew nothing about him, except what he was called.

They had met Friday evening in Malmö.

Caspar had come from Copenhagen that morning. He had really meant to go straight back to Stockholm, but his money was gone, and he hadn't been able to hitch a ride. So he had drifted around Malmö all day trying to think of some way to get some cash. Malmö was a strange city to him. He didn't know anyone there, and he didn't know where to go.

Finally he came to a park and ran into some other boys, who offered him a beer. That was how he had met Christer.

The other boys had gone off somewhere, and Christer and Caspar had sat on the bench and shared a beer. Christer hadn't had any money either, but he did have a car. It was not clear that the car was his own, but at least he had the keys to it. He lived in Malmö, and he knew where there were summer houses that could be broken into.

They had spent Friday night and Saturday morning driving around in the car and had made an unsuccessful attempt to get into a villa just outside of town. In the end they had broken into a summer cottage that appeared to be closed up for the winter. They found some cans of food and ate some of it, and then they had slept for a couple of hours. There was nothing of value in the house, but they took a couple of pictures and a plaster of Paris figurine on a pedestal.

They had driven back to Malmö, and Christer had stolen some LP's from a music store. Christer, who knew the city, managed to sell the records right away, and they had bought beer and a bottle of wine with the money. They sat in the park and drove around in the car until it got dark.

"Tonight we'll drive down to a place where there's nothing but rich people," Christer had said.

The place was called Ljunghusen, and they had been able to see from the houses that it was a wealthy neighborhood. They broke into a couple of villas and took things that would be easy to sell. A TV set and a transistor radio and a couple of rugs that Christer had insisted were genuine orientals. In one of the houses they had broken open a bar and taken a few bottles of liquor. They had even found some cash—some thirty newly minted five-crown pieces in a piggy bank that they shattered.

It had been a successful night's work right up until the patrol car appeared out of nowhere.

Caspar went over the chain of events in his mind, as he had done he didn't know how many times before. First the young cop, who had suddenly been standing there with a gun in his hand, then the older one who had grabbed Christer, and then the shots, which Caspar had first thought were coming from the young policeman's gun. Then he had seen the one policeman fall, and, right afterward, the other, and he had realized it was Christer who was shooting.

After that, everything had happened very fast. Caspar had been scared and had driven away without finding out whether Christer was dead or only wounded.

He had driven back toward Malmö the way they had come, but when he came to the expressway he had taken a different road.

He had realized that the alarm must already have gone out and that police cars and ambulances would be on their way from the city.

And then suddenly he had run out of gas.

Christer and he had just been talking about finding a car to siphon some gas from when the patrol car appeared. And then when he sped away in panic he completely forgot that the tank was as good as empty.

He had rolled the car down a short hill and parked it behind some dilapidated sheds. He left the things they'd stolen in the car.

Then he had walked down the side of the road until he came to a small community. He had heard the police sirens wailing in the distance, and the sound had made him desperate with fear. He had tried several cars before he found one he could take. It had been standing outside a large house, parked in an open carport, and its doors had been unlocked.

Caspar had been aware of the risks. The car's owner might suddenly have come out of the house. But it was Sunday, and still early in the morning, and it had only taken him a couple of minutes to get the motor started.

Since then he had been driving north.

Home. Toward Stockholm.

Caspar had lived in Stockholm all of his nineteen years, although he had never actually lived in the city itself. He was born and raised in a suburb, where he had lived with his parents and where he had gone to school until three years ago. Since then he had been looking for a job, somewhat halfheartedly, he had to admit. His parents had moved away two years before. They had bought a house outside Södertälje, and when he didn't want to move with them he had begun living a somewhat hand-to-mouth existence in the capital.

Getting an apartment of his own had been out of the question. He lived on unemployment and welfare and stayed mostly with friends or temporary girlfriends, young divorced women with apartments and bed space.

He had gradually come to move in circles that lived by the rule that crime does pay, so long as you run a small-scale operation and are clever enough not to get caught. He had taken part in burglaries, committed petty larcenies on his own, dabbled in car theft, and dealt a little in stolen goods, and for a couple of months he had lived on the income of a girl who frequented Malmskillnadsgatan and brought home customers while he sat in her kitchen drinking vodka and Pommac. He had two principles in regard to criminal activity—never deal in drugs and never carry a weapon. His childish appearance had often come to his aid, and he had been caught and convicted only once.

He stopped for gas near Katrineholm. He paid with shiny five-crown pieces, and the man at the filling station looked at them before putting them away in a special compartment in the cash register.

"Don't you hate to spend those things?"

Caspar shrugged his shoulders and thought about giving some sort of explanation, but he let it go.

He suddenly realized how hungry he was and went into the cafeteria next door. He had the special of the day, some kind of ground meat with a pasty, tasteless sauce, a dab of lingonberry jam, and four over-boiled potatoes. The food was bad and not even warm, but he was too starved to care.

After driving on for a while, he stopped at a kiosk and bought a pack of cigarettes, some gum, and a newspaper. On the way back to the car he saw the headlines on the front page.

He put it down on the seat beside him and drove into a side road, where he stopped the car and opened the paper over the wheel.

Christer was dead, but the three policemen were still alive. He himself was being sought by the police in a manhunt that covered the country. The newspaper article called him a "gangster," a "desperado," and a "cop-killer." He re-read the beginning of the story, where it told about the condition of the policemen. A couple of them were apparently in critical condition, but as far as he could see, none of them was dead. So how could they put "cop-killer"? Besides, he hadn't even been armed.

He read through the story carefully. Neither he nor Christer was identified, and they had not found the car. For the time being, the police were still searching for the big green Chevy, but he hadn't been able to hide it very well, so they were sure to find it before very long.

When he had read the paper, he sat for a long time and tried to collect his thoughts. The fear that had started to go away took hold of him again. He tried to think clearly and calmly.

All he was guilty of was a couple of burglaries and a car theft. It wasn't he who had done the shooting. Even if they caught him, they would have to prove it, and the penalty for what he had done couldn't be so severe. But at the moment the odds were still on his side, and if he just stayed cool, he had a chance of getting away.

After a while he wadded up the paper, threw it in the ditch, and drove on. He had decided what he would do.

He stopped at a department store and bought the makings of two license plates of the old type. He drove out of town, and on a little road through the woods he put together two plates, and then unscrewed the ones that were on the car and buried them in the trees. He screwed on the false plates and drove on toward Södertälje.

He parked the car in the garage of his parents' house. With luck, he could leave it there for several days. His father was a traveling salesman and was often gone, with his car, for days at a time.

He was in luck. His mother was at home, but his father wouldn't be back until the end of the week. He told his mother he'd borrowed the car from a friend.

She was happy to see him and still happier when he said he thought he'd stay for a few days.

For dinner she fixed his favorite foods—steak with onions, fried potatoes, and apple cake with vanilla sauce.

He went to bed early in his father's bed and, as he fell asleep, felt relatively safe.

21.

On the morning of November 21, Gustav Borglund died in the isolation ward at Malmö General Hospital. He had arrived at the hospital too late, and the doctors had about as much chance as a snowball in hell.

But Emil Elofsson and David Hector survived, thanks in great part to surgical acumen. They were given prompt, first-class medical attention and were treated as privileged patients.

They were both in bad shape, of course, especially Elofsson, who had taken a bullet through the liver and another in the vicinity of his pancreas. Surgery had made great strides, however, since the days of the ill-fated James Garfield, and the doctors really knew their business, even if they were overworked and chronically exhausted.

Elofsson and Hector were in no condition to be questioned on Monday or Tuesday, and Borglund didn't know anything, not even that he was dying.

The tactical command had made exactly as much headway as might have been expected. The getaway car had not been found, and the person who had been shot to death had not been identified.

Borglund crowned his long career of relatively good-natured fiascoes with a last sigh at about four o'clock Wednesday morning. He had not been a bad man. Once he had even encouraged Elofsson to give a Yugoslavian child a cough drop, in spite of the complications it might have caused.

In the course of a few hours, the news of his death made its way to the National Police Administration, where it produced a major paroxysm and provoked an immediate series of telephone conversations from Stig Malm to the Chief of Police in Malmö. The potentate himself stood behind Malm's back as he talked, and it was a wonder the wires didn't disintegrate from the vibrations.

What the National Police Administration wanted to see was activity.

What the National Police Administration meant by "activity" was the movement of busloads of policemen wearing bulletproof vests and helmets with adjustable plexiglass facemasks.

What it also meant was sharpshooters and automatic weapons and tear gas bombs, all of which were now available on permanent loan from the military.

What Lennart Kollberg meant by "activity" was talking to people.

He had spent Monday and Tuesday in passive observation of a stream of youths arbitrarily arrested by enthusiastic policemen either on the grounds that they were foreigners or because they were suspiciously dressed.

Kollberg was old enough at this game to know that you couldn't label someone a presumptive murderer simply because he hadn't been to the barber in six months. Besides, so far as he knew, no one had been murdered.

But there was so much excitement after Borglund's passing that someone was obliged to do something constructive.

And so Kollberg collected his car from the garage at the Hotel Sankt Jörgen, which is where upper echelon police officers were usually quartered, and drove to Malmö General Hospital.

He thought he would talk to Elofsson and Hector. The doctors had said it was okay, that both of them were as lucid as could possibly be expected.

Kollberg was a hardened man, but that didn't keep him from being slightly shocked when he stepped into the ward. He looked at the slip of paper Per Månsson had given him. Yes, he was in the right room, and of course he already knew he was in Sweden.

The building dated from the nineteenth century, and the ward he was in held approximately thirty men.

Many of them were obviously in serious condition, for the ward echoed with groans and whimpering cries for help. The stench was unspeakable, and the whole scene was strongly reminiscent of a first-aid station in the Crimean War. There were not even any screens or dividers between the beds.

A woman with a white coat and an absent expression turned out to be the cleaning woman. When he asked for the doctor, she stared at him with dreamy, clear blue eyes.

"Oh, the doctor," she said. "He's not here yet."

There was no more information to be had from that source.

But there was, in fact, a doctor on duty—a swarthy man with his shirt unbuttoned down to his navel. He was sitting in the staff room drinking coffee. The only trouble with him was that he came from Afghanistan, had a name that was impossible to pronounce, and spoke an English that might possibly have done credit to a sheepherder in the People's Republic of Mongolia.

If there was a shortage of doctors—and no one could doubt that there was—then the lack of nurses was even more flagrant.

But he finally found her. Because of vacancies, she was looking after two whole wards and had been at work for fourteen hours at a stretch, though she didn't show it. She was a serene, blond woman of about thirty-five, slim and strong, with clear eyes and muscular calves.

Kollberg, who was a sensualist, thought she was cute as hell.

Had he been ten years younger, he would have found her terribly exciting. But it was only his wife who aroused him any more. She was a brunette, and he had chosen her with great care for her ability to satisfy him intellectually and—of no less importance—sexually. She was a fine woman and made him as happy as he was capable of being.

Gun was pretty. She reminded him a little of Tatyana Samoylova, who was his favorite movie actress. He seldom went to the movies, but he never missed one of her pictures.

And yet he thought Gun was prettier than Tatyana Samoylova, which was saying a great deal.

He loved her. She was his whole life. She and the children. Bodil was just six and would soon start school. Joakim was only three. Good kids.

Earlier this morning he had looked at himself in the hotel room mirror. Naked and full length.

If Gun was pretty, he himself was fat and flabby. He didn't like it.

He looked at the ward nurse. How could she seem so fresh and healthy? With two wards to supervise?

She seemed cheerful enough. Clearly she must like her job.

More than fifty patients, many of them very ill, some of them dying.

In a disgraceful hospital.

He showed her his identification.

"You're in the wrong place," she said. "They're not here in the ward, they're in one of the old private rooms. We've got four of them. Two people in each. The policemen are in Number Two."

"Thanks."

"That's where we put cases that are really serious."

"And really privileged?"

"Yes, you might say that."

He looked at her calves and knees. He couldn't help it. She was wearing a brassiere under her white coat.

"You can talk to them if you want to," she said. "But not for long. Elofsson's in worst shape, but I think Hector's going to be in bed for a longer time."

"I'll be brief."

"The chief surgeon performed the operations himself. Four in a row. I don't think they would have made it otherwise. At least not Elofsson."

The room was a demonstration of the fact that the police do not forget their wounded. There were masses of flowers, chocolates, fruit, a radio, and a color TV.

Of the two, Hector seemed the more alert, although he had his left arm and both legs in traction.

Elofsson was attached to four different intravenous drips at once—one with blood and three with liquids of various other colors. He was a big, ponderous man with heavy features and a dull expression that was probably due to his condition.

Kollberg introduced himself. He had the feeling he had met Elofsson somewhere. He had never seen Hector before, but his appearance was typical of today's younger policemen, if appearances can ever be called typical.

He felt he ought to express his condolences, even though everyone else already had, from the Chief of Police all the way down to every patrolman who happened to be in the neighborhood.

"It's a damned shame, lying here in the hospital like this," he said, prosaically.

"Our time hadn't come yet," Hector said.

Perhaps he was religious.

"This man who shot you—he's dead."

"Yes. Just think, I got him," Hector said. "I mean, I did have two bullets in me, and Officer Elofsson was lying right in my line of fire, and it was dark too."

"But we haven't caught the other one," Kollberg said. "Did you see what he looked like?"

"It wasn't light yet," Elofsson said. "Just like Officer Hector said."

"But you did see him?"

"I never really saw him clearly," Hector said. "Officer Elofsson here was in between us, and then too I was concentrating mostly on the other one. But I remember he had light hair."

"We didn't have much time to look around," Elofsson said. "But it was a kid, I mean, not more than twenty at the most. And he had long blond hair."

"Did he say anything?"

"I heard Officer Elofsson speak to them," Hector said. "But I didn't hear what they answered."

"Neither one of them talked much," Elofsson said. "It was only the tall one said anything. I don't think the other one said a word."

"The tall one said he hadn't done anything," Hector said. "I remember that now. I pointed out that they were driving with no lights, and then he said he hadn't done anything."

"That's right," Elofsson said. "Officer Hector here said their headlights were in violation, and then he said they hadn't done anything."

"Is that all that was said?"

"No," Elofsson said. "After they started shooting, the tall one said something else. 'Jump in the car,' or something like that, and a name."

"Do you remember the name?"

"Wait a minute. It was a weird name, sort of. Started with K, or C. Claus, maybe."

"That's not especially weird."

"No, it was weirder than that. I'll think of it in a minute."

218

"Take your time," Kollberg said. "It'll come to you."

"I didn't hear any name," Hector said.

"We haven't found the car either," Kollberg said.

"They gave us the wrong description over the radio," Hector said. "They said it was a Chrysler, but I'm sure it was an old Chevvy."

"How do you know?" Elofsson said.

"I'm good at cars," Hector said. "The radio said it was a blue Chrysler, but I'm absolutely sure it was a Chevy. And it was green. And they gave us the wrong number too."

"Yes, that's always the way," Elofsson said. "They tell us wrong. But I don't remember exactly what they did say on the radio."

"I remember," Hector said. "They said it was a hot rod with old plates. That part was true, but from there on everything was wrong."

"Typical," Elofsson said.

He was breathing rather heavily.

"Are you in pain?" said Kollberg sympathetically.

"Yes, sometimes it hurts like hell."

Kollberg turned to Hector.

"You say the description was all wrong," he said. "We've got the make and the color, so far. Was there anything else?"

"Yes. They said there were two girls and a guy in the car. And, in fact, there were two men and no girls."

"Now I remember," said Elofsson suddenly. "Caspar."

"Caspar."

"Right. The guy who shot me said, 'Get in the car, Caspar.' It was Caspar."

"Are you sure?"

"Yes, absolutely. I said it was a weird name. Caspar's weird. I don't know anybody named Caspar."

"Neither do I," Kollberg said.

"And then there were the plates," Hector said. "They said they were A plates. You know, a Stockholm car with old plates. And they said there were three sixes in the number. But that was wrong, because the car had B plates, and the number started with two sevens. Then there was some other number, and then maybe another seven."

"I don't know about all that stuff," Elofsson said.

"This is important," Kollberg said. "You say it was a green Chevrolet, registered in Stockholm County, with two or three sevens in the license number."

"Yes, you can count on it," Hector said. "I generally try to notice things and get them right."

"Yes, that's right," Elofsson said. "Officer Hector's always on the job."

"And what was this Caspar wearing?"

"Dark jacket and jeans," Hector said. "Windbreaker. A small kid with light hair. Long, like he says."

"They all dress like that," Elofsson said.

A student nurse came in with a lot of test tubes on a cart. She busied herself with Elofsson. Kollberg moved out of her way.

"Are you feeling up to a few more questions?"

"Sure," Hector said. "There's nothing wrong with me. What do you want to know?"

"I'm thinking mostly about what actually happened. Okay, you stopped this car and got out. You'd already made a mental note of the make of the car and the color and the license number."

"Right."

"What did the men in the car do?"

"They got out too. Emil—Officer Elofsson here—he shone his flashlight in the back seat. Then he grabbed

220

the one who was standing closest. And then he started shooting."

"Were you hit right away?"

"Just about. I think Officer Elofsson was hit first. But it all happened incredibly fast. I got hit right afterward."

"But you did have time to draw your revolver?"

"I already had."

"You mean you had your revolver in your hand when you walked up to the car?"

"Yes, I must have had a feeling."

"Do you think the men in the car could see that you had your revolver in your hand?"

"They must have. But I didn't have a cartridge in the chamber—I mean, that's against regulations and everything. So I had to cock it before I could shoot back."

Kollberg glanced at Elofsson, who was beginning to look more and more insensible. The technical investigation had shown that he and Borglund had had cartridges in the chambers of their pistols. But neither one of them had fired, and as far as Elofsson was concerned, they could say definitely that he had never even unbuttoned his holster.

"Listen," Hector said. "I heard a rumor around here that Gustav Borglund was killed. Is that true?"

"Yes," Kollberg said. "He died early this morning. Here in the hospital. But he was in another ward."

"That's awful," Hector said.

Kollberg nodded.

"Yes," he said. "It's not good."

"I never saw him while it was happening," Hector said. "He was behind me. He must have been the first one hit."

"I saw him," said Elofsson thickly. "He came crawling over after you'd shot that desperado. He was the one who called for help. And he gave me first aid. He was hurt, I could tell. Is Gustav dead?"

Kollberg could see that Elofsson was starting to fade, but there were still a couple of questions he wanted to ask.

"Do you know whether both these men shot at you?"

"I thought the second one did too," Elofsson said. "While it was happening, I was sure they were both shooting at us. Because someone was banging away behind me. But now I realize that must have been David here, Officer Hector."

Kollberg turned back to Hector.

"What do you think?"

"All I know for sure is that I saw the tall dark one shoot at me and Emil while we were lying there on the ground. And then I shot him. After that I don't remember anything. But Emil was still conscious."

"Yes," said Elofsson weakly. "I saw the one who shot me throw up his hands and sort of crumple. And then I heard the car backing up and then peeling out."

"So neither one of you had the impression that this blond kid was shooting at you, or even that he had a gun?"

"No," Hector said. "Not that I could see."

Elofsson didn't answer. He seemed to have fallen into a stupor.

Kollberg looked at Hector. He formulated a question in his mind but didn't ask it.

Do you often have feelings like that? That make you draw your gun first and ask questions later?

But he didn't say it out loud. It didn't seem to be the right moment.

"Well, so long, boys," he said. "Try and get well now."

On the way out he tried to find the resident.

"He's in surgery," the nurse said.

"And that Dr. Aklam . . ."

"Aztazkanzakersky," she said. "He's in surgery too. What do you want to know?"

"I thought Elofsson looked pretty bad."

"He's weak," she said. "But he's been taken off the critical list. They're both going to make it, although . . ."

"What?"

"Those are serious injuries," she said. "Maybe neither one of them will recover completely."

Kollberg shook himself.

"That's a shame," he said.

"We have to try and look on the bright side," she said.

"I suppose so," Kollberg said. "So long."

His visit had been profitable as well as thought-provoking.

At the police building in Malmö, Per Månsson bit off the toothpick he had been chewing and threw the pieces in the wastebasket.

"Terrific. That means we've had a nationwide dragnet out for the wrong car for three days. Wrong make, wrong color, wrong county letter, and wrong license number. What more could you ask?"

"What did Borglund die of?" Kollberg asked.

"He was killed in connection with the shooting," said Månsson solemnly. "That's what it's going to say in the papers."

He took a fresh toothpick out of his breast pocket and slowly pulled off the cellophane.

"I just wrote it down on a piece of paper so there won't be any misunderstandings."

He gave the paper to Kollberg.

Sergeant Gustav Borglund, thirty-seven, died this morning of injuries received in connection with an exchange of fire between policemen and two armed men in Ljunghusen. Two other policemen were seriously wounded in the same gun battle. But, under the circumstances, their condition is satisfactory.

Kollberg put the paper down on the table.

"What did he really die of?"

Månsson stared out the window with an inscrutable expression.

"He was stung by a wasp," he said.

22.

Månsson and Kollberg were having a rough time. Stig Malm was on them like a hawk all Wednesday afternoon. The only comfort was that the head of the tactical command remained in Stockholm and confined himself to pestering his staff by telephone.

How's it going?

Have you found the car?

Has the killer been identified?

Who's the other desperado?

And then, of course, the predominating question:

Why aren't you doing anything?

It was Månsson who got that one, but he didn't let it throw him.

"Oh, we're doing a great deal—now."

Kollberg watched him from across the desk and admired his composure. Månsson calmly went on chewing his toothpick while Malm jabbered into his ear.

"Now that we've finally got something to go on," Månsson said.

And after a while:

"No, I wouldn't do that. It's better to have some central coordinator—someone who can keep his finger on everything. Yes, we'll let you know."

Månsson hung up.

"He's threatening to come down," he said. "If the damned planes are flying, we could have him here in two hours."

"Oh, no," said Kollberg despondently. "Anything but that."

"I don't think he really meant it," Månsson said. "Anyway, something's bound to break soon. And anyway he doesn't like to fly. I discovered that years ago."

Månsson was right. Malm did not appear, and on Thursday morning they got their break.

Kollberg had slept badly after an almost inedible dinner at a restaurant someone had recommended as being inexpensive. When he woke up, he thought enviously of Martin Beck, who had probably dined royally at the inn in Anderslöv and was now sitting with Allwright considering the Sigbrit Mård case.

But he ate a double portion of ham and eggs at the hotel and was in a somewhat better humor when he threw open the big copper door of the police building and trudged up to the second floor to see Månsson and get the morning's news. He had seen the words POLICE-MAN DIES in the morning headlines.

"Morning," Månsson said. "I didn't want to bother you at breakfast, but we now know who it was that shot Hector and Elofsson."

"Who?"

"His name was Christer Paulson. Central finger-printing finally managed to find the right card. They blamed it on some problem with the computer, as usual."

A problem with the computer. Kollberg sighed. Ever since police centralization, his life had been filled with such calamities.

"And on top of that we found the car. It was parked behind some old outbuildings on a farm near Vellinge. The farmer said it's been there since last Sunday, but he thought it was an old wreck that someone had left there to get rid of. He'd seen the description in the papers, of course, but what the hell, it was the wrong color and the wrong number and the wrong make. Benny drove down to take care of it. It won't take long to tow it up here."

"Mmm," Kollberg said.

The whole country was littered with old cars that people just abandoned. It was by far the cheapest and simplest way of getting rid of a worn-out automobile.

"What do we know about this Christer Paulson?" he said.

"Quite a bit. He was recently released from a penal institution. Twenty-four years old and he already had a long record. He's from central Sweden originally, but apparently he's been living down here for quite some time."

"And now he's dead."

"Yes, well, Hector shot him. Self-defense is the term. For the time being, we don't know much more than that. There was a statement from a psychiatrist who said he was a neurotic type . . ."

Månsson looked at one of the papers in front of him.

"Yes," he said. "Antisocial. In revolt against society.

He lacked education and never held a job. But he's never been convicted of a violent crime, although he's apparently been armed on other occasions. Wanted to look tough, I suppose. He was also a narcotics addict."

Kollberg sighed. This very type of person had become so common in the so-called welfare state that it was now utterly impossible to keep track of the individual cases. And, what was worse, no one had any idea what to do with them.

The contribution of the police was usually limited to a night stick on the head and a little working over at the station house.

"I wonder if he would have fired if Hector hadn't been waving that pistol around," Kollberg said.

"What did you say?"

"Nothing. I was just thinking out loud."

"I heard what you said," said Månsson after a short silence. "I've wondered the same thing myself. But I've stopped worrying about it. The fact is, we'll never know."

"Have you ever shot anyone?"

Månsson examined the toothpick he had just chewed to bits and chuckled to himself.

"Yes," he said. "Once. A cow. It escaped from the slaughterhouse and wandered into town. That was back in the days of streetcars, and the poor thing attacked the old coal car on Kreuger & Toll Bridge. A regular bullfight."

"Mmm," said Kollberg again.

"But that was a long time ago," Månsson said. "And besides, it was sort of a special case. I've always been sorry I didn't have my saber with me. I could really have played matador."

"I've never shot a cow," Kollberg said.

"You haven't missed a thing," Månsson said. "She

just lay there bleeding in the middle of the street and stared at me. No, I never carry my revolver any more. I've got it here in the drawer, of course."

He kicked the desk.

"I don't much believe in shooting," he said. "And that's what you wanted me to say. Anyway, my eyesight isn't good enough."

Kollberg was silent.

"I saw an interesting case a few years ago," Månsson said. "That was back in the days when I still believed in my chances of making Detective Superintendent, so I went on this study trip to England. Not London, but this other place—Luton, it was called. The men I was working with had a real tough case one evening. There was this maniac who'd broken into the house where his ex-wife lived and he was threatening her and making a hell of a row. He had a gun in one hand and a samurai sword in the other."

"What happened?"

"Well, these two constables, regular bobbies, were going to go in and get him. But he was pretty wild, swinging the sword around, and one of the constables got cut on the hand. Then he fired several shots in the air. So anyway, guess what they did."

"What?"

"They sent for two more policemen, who came over from the station house with a big net. And they threw the net over this guy and caught him like he'd been some sort of performing bear. A net. How about that?"

"Not a bad idea," Kollberg said.

"I thought about writing it up for the *Swedish Police Journal*," Månsson said. "But I suppose the fellows up in Stockholm would have laughed their heads off. For that matter, they probably wouldn't have printed it."

"We still don't know anything about this fellow Caspar," Kollberg said.

"No. But we've got a couple good leads. First off, we can talk to this Christer Paulson's friends. If they'll talk to us. Some kids are so funny these days."

"Not if you talk to them yourself," Kollberg said.

"And second, we ought to find his prints in the car. Or maybe something else."

Månsson drummed his fingers on the desk.

"This Christer Paulson was from Stockholm," he said. "Typical. Things have got so bad up there not even the crooks have the guts to stay. They come and make trouble down here instead."

There was something in what Månsson said, but Kollberg made do with a shrug of the shoulders.

The telephone rang.

Månsson waved generously toward the phone.

"Be my guest," he said. "It's your turn."

Kollberg grimaced mournfully and picked up the receiver.

But it wasn't Malm this time. It was Benny Skacke.

"Hi," he said. "I'm still down here in Vellinge waiting for the tow truck. It looks like she's out of gas. But it's the right car, that seems definite. The stuff they stole is still inside."

"Well, don't poke around and leave a lot of unnecessary fingerprints," Kollberg said.

"No," Skacke said. "I won't. Don't worry about that. But there's another thing I thought maybe you'd want to know."

Benny Skacke was always a little unsure of himself whenever he spoke to Kollberg. They had certain experiences in common which Skacke would like to have seen forgotten.

229

"Come on, Benny," Kollberg said. "What is it?"

"Well, Vellinge is still sort of a little town, where most of the people know all about each other, even if it is in Malmö District."

"What have you found out?"

"There's a man here had his car stolen Sunday. Although he doesn't seem to have reported it until yesterday. For that matter, it was his wife who called it in."

"Good work, Benny," Kollberg said. "Give me the number and everything, so we can send out a description."

Kollberg noted down the details and then sent the information out on the telex.

"This all fits together nicely," Månsson said.

"Mmm," said Kollberg. "It's beginning to."

"Right," Månsson said. "Christer Paulson and this here Caspar do a job together. They're seen breaking into the house. The radio patrol with Elofsson, Borglund, and Hector happens to be right there in the neighborhood. They stop the car with the thieves in it. Christer Paulson shoots Hector and Elofsson, but Hector gets his revolver out . . ."

"*Has* his revolver out," Kollberg said.

"Okay, *has* it out. In any case, he kills Christer Paulson. Caspar's scared shitless and jumps in the car and drives off. He manages to get across the bridge at Höllviksnäs—that's the only tough spot. From there on, he can stick to back roads, which we can't block or even watch effectively."

Kollberg was no great expert on Skåne, but he did know that Ljunghusen was on a promontory cut off by the Falsterbo Canal and that there was only one bridge over the canal.

"Could he get out before the first squad car arrived?"

"Easy. It only took him a minute or two to get to the bridge. Ljunghusen is right next to the canal. But as you can imagine, things got a little confused that morning. We had a lot of people in the area, but most of them were hustling down the expressway from Malmö at a hundred and ten miles an hour. On top of everything else, two of our cars broke down. Anyway, our friend Caspar makes it to Vellinge. And runs out of gas. He drives off the road. And then he steals another car and drives away."

"Where to?"

"As far as he can get, probably. That kid isn't still in *this* neck of the woods. But now we've got some data on his new car, we're bound to track it down."

"Yes," Kollberg said.

He was thinking about something else.

"Unless the owner gave us the wrong license number, the wrong make, and the wrong color," Månsson said.

"I want you to answer me a question," Kollberg said. "Even if it goes against the grain. It's not that I want to be disloyal to the official version, but for my own sake I have to know exactly what happened."

"Don't worry about me," Månsson said.

"Exactly what happened to Borglund?"

"I think I know, but it's only a guess," Månsson said.

"What do you think?"

"I think Borglund was asleep in the back seat when they stopped the car with the suspects. By the time he got out, everything was happening very fast. Christer Paulson and possibly this kid Caspar started shooting, and then Hector returned their fire, with the result we know of. As soon as that first shot went off, Borglund took cover, which is to say, he threw himself in the ditch. Apparently he landed right on a wasps' nest and a wasp stung him on the carotid artery. He tried to go on duty on Sunday, but he was so sick he had to go home. And on Monday he went into the hospital. He'd lost consciousness by that time, and he never regained it."

"An accident," Kollberg muttered.

"Yes. But not unique. I'm pretty sure it's happened before."

"Did you talk to him before he went to the hospital?"

"Yes. He knew practically nothing. They'd stopped a car, he didn't know why, and then one of the suspects started shooting. So he took cover. He was just scared, I imagine."

"Except for Caspar," Kollberg said, "I've now heard what everyone involved has to say. And there's no one who claims that this kid Caspar shot anyone or employed any kind of violence at all. It strikes me as extremely hypocritical to maintain that Borglund was murdered."

"Actually, no one does. All we've said is that he died of the injuries he received in connection with an exchange of fire. And that's true, as a matter of fact. What are you getting at?"

Månsson gave Kollberg a worried look.

"I'm thinking of this boy we're hunting," Kollberg said. "At the moment, we don't know who he is, but we're sure to find out pretty soon. He's the object of a pretty wild manhunt that might make anyone lose his head. But it may very well be that the only thing he did was take part in the burglary of an empty summer villa. I don't like it."

"No," Månsson said. "But there's not much to like in this job."

And then the telephone rang.

232

Malm.

How's it going? What have you done?

Kollberg handed the receiver to Månsson.

"He's better informed," he lied.

Månsson reported the news one item at a time, as cool as ice.

"What did he say?" asked Kollberg when the conversation was over.

" 'Excellent,' " Månsson said. "That's what he said. Plus that we should clap on all sail."

Clap on all sail.

An hour later, Benny Skacke arrived with the infamous car.

When the fingerprint experts were finished, it was time for an inspection.

"What a heap," Månsson said. "And here's the loot —an old TV, some rugs, this funny statue or whatever it is. A few bottles of booze. Trash. Plus some five-crown pieces from a piggy bank."

"And two dead and two in the hospital, probably crippled for life."

"Yes, that's sure a lot of needless casualties," Månsson said.

"What we can try to do is to see that there aren't any more," Kollberg said.

They went over the old Chevy again, with even greater care. Both of them were trained for this kind of job, and Månsson could even claim to be an expert at discovering things that no one else could find.

And he was the one who found it.

A thin piece of paper, folded several times, which had slipped down behind the cushion of the seat beside the driver. The upholstery was torn, and the little sheet of paper had lodged inside the padding. Kollberg was almost certain that he never would have found it.

On the other hand, he did find two picture postcards in the glove compartment. Both of them were addressed to Christer Paulson, at an address on Stenbocksgatan in Malmö. Two different girls seemed to have written them. The messages were of no interest. As clues, per se, they would have been a good deal more interesting twenty-four hours earlier. Not even the address was news. The police had already managed to find it through the social welfare authorities.

They took what they'd found to Månsson's office.

Kollberg unfolded the little slip of paper, and Månsson took out his magnifying glass.

"What is it?" Kollberg said.

"A money exchange note from a Danish bank," Månsson said. "The blue copy, at least. It's just the sort of thing you either throw away or else fold up and stuff in your pocket. And then lose it when you pull out your handkerchief to blow your nose."

"And you sign it? With your name?"

"Sometimes," Månsson said. "Sometimes not. It depends on the rules of the bank. This one is signed."

"Jesus, what handwriting!" Kollberg said.

"A lot of kids write like that these days. But what does it say?"

" 'Ronnie,' I think."

"And then something that starts with C. And then a little 'a,' and then an angleworm."

"It could be Ronnie Casparsson," Månsson said. "Or something like that. But that's just a guess."

"It does say 'Ronnie' in any case."

"We'll have to check and see if there is anyone named Ronnie Casparsson," Månsson said.

Skacke came into the room and shifted his weight from one foot to the other for a while. Kollberg looked up at him.

"You can cut that out now, Benny. The past is buried and forgotten. If we're going to work together you can't go around acting like a five-year-old who's been into the cookie jar. What is it?"

"Well, I've got some kids out here who knew Christer Paulson. A girl and two boys. Social welfare helped us get them over here. We found several, but these were the only ones who seemed like they might talk to us. Maybe. Does one of you want to talk to them?"

"Yes," Kollberg said. "I'd be glad to."

The young people looked very ordinary. That is to say, they would not have looked ordinary seven or eight years earlier. They had on long, embroidered leather jackets. The boys were wearing Levi's, also covered with embroidery, and the girl had on a floor-length skirt that looked to be Indian or Moroccan or some such thing. They all had leather boots with high heels and hair that reached down to their shoulders.

They stared at Kollberg with a listless indifference that looked as if it might blossom into open hostility at any moment.

"Hi," said Kollberg. "Can we get you anything? Some coffee and Danish or something?"

The boys mumbled affirmatively without actually saying a word, but the girl pushed the hair out of her face and spoke up in a clear voice.

"It's very bad for you to stuff yourself with coffee and a lot of sweet white bread. If you want to stay healthy in this society, you have to stick to the few pure natural products that are available, and avoid meat and all prepared foods."

"Right," said Kollberg.

He turned to the rookie who was standing in the doorway with an odd look on his face, torn as he was between trying to act overbearing and superior toward the three young people and obliging and obsequious toward Kollberg.

"Go get three coffees and a whole lot of Danish pastry," Kollberg said. "And then go down to the macrobiotic shop on the corner and get a biodynamic carrot."

The rookie went. The boys giggled, while the girl sat straight and silent and serious.

The hopeful rookie was a little red in the face when he returned with the coffee hamper and the carrot.

Now all three of them giggled, and Kollberg almost felt like grinning a little himself. Unfortunately, it was all too easy not to.

"Well, it was nice of you to come down," Kollberg said. "I suppose you know what it's about."

"Christer," said one of the boys.

"Right."

"Christer wasn't basically a bad person," the girl said. "But he'd been destroyed by society, and he hated it. And now the cops have shot him."

"He shot a couple of them too," Kollberg put in.

"Yes," she said. "It really doesn't surprise me."

"How so?"

After a long pause, one of the boys answered.

"He was usually armed," he said. "A switchblade or a gun or something. Christer said you had to carry something these days. He was sort of desperate, or whatever you call it."

"It's my job to sit here and look into things like this," Kollberg said. "It's an unpleasant and very thankless task."

"And it's our very unpleasant and thankless task to take over this rotten society, which we didn't help to ruin," the girl said, "and somehow make it habitable again."

"Did Christer dislike policemen?" Kollberg said.

"We all hate cops," the girl said. "Why shouldn't we? The cops hate us."

"Yes, they sure do," said one of the boys. "There isn't any place they'll leave us alone, and there isn't anything they'll let us do. As soon as you sit down on a bench or on the grass, the cops are there giving you a bunch of shit. And if they get the chance, they work us over."

"Or make fun of us," the girl said, "which is almost worse."

"Did any of you meet this fellow that Christer had with him in Ljunghusen?"

"Yes. Caspar," said the boy who hadn't said anything. "I talked to him, just for a little while. Then the beer was all gone, so I left."

"How did he seem?"

"Nice guy, I thought. Peaceable, like the rest of us."

"You knew he was called Caspar?"

"Yes, but I think his real name was something else. I think he said something like Robin or Ronnie or something."

"What do you think? About what's happened?"

"It's just typical," said the first boy. "It's always the way. Everybody hates us, the cops most of all, and then when one of us gets desperate, finally, and puts up a fight, well, it turns out like this. I don't see why a lot more guys don't get guns and knives. Why should we be the only ones to take a beating?"

Kollberg thought for a moment.

"If you had the chance to do anything you wanted," he said, "what would you do?"

"I'd be an astronaut and get spaced right out of sight," said the first boy.

But the girl took the question seriously.

"I'd move out to a farm and live right and healthy and have lots of animals and children and see to it they didn't get poisoned but grew up to be real human beings."

"Can I grow a little hash in your garden?" said the second boy.

Nothing else of any interest was said, and pretty soon Kollberg went back to Månsson and Skacke.

They were making progress.

There was someone named Ronnie Casparsson.

Who had been in jail and whose fingerprints were all over the steering wheel and the dashboard.

On top of that, there was an alert gas station owner near Katrineholm who had filled the tank on the car that was stolen in Vellinge on Sunday. The man also remembered that the driver had long blond hair and that he had paid with five-crown coins. He was almost unnaturally observant. He even knew the license number. Kollberg asked him how that had happened.

"I write down all the license numbers. An old habit of mine. Will there be a reward?"

"Yes, I'll buy gas from you next time I come that way," Kollberg said. "But don't be surprised if I put on a false beard and fake license plates."

By Friday they knew pretty much everything there was to know about Ronnie Casparsson—where his parents lived, where he had last been seen, in which direction he had been driving (north), even his social security number.

All of this moved the investigation one hell of a long way from Malmö Police District.

The cop-killer manhunt would continue in other parts of the country.

"Task Force Malmö is dissolved," said Malm, militarily. "Report to me here in Stockholm at once."

"Kiss my ass," said Kollberg.

"What?"

"Oh, nothing."

As he packed his bag and went to fetch his car, he realized that he had had just about enough.

23.

On Wednesday evening, Ronnie Casparsson learned that one of the policemen involved in the dramatic shootout in Ljunghusen was dead.

That was the way the woman on the news put it. The dramatic shootout in Ljunghusen.

He was sitting on the sofa with his mother watching TV, and he heard them read off his description. The man, who is the object of a nationwide manhunt, is about twenty years of age, below average height, has long blond hair, and was last seen wearing jeans and a dark windbreaker.

He glanced sideways at his mother. She was busy with her knitting, wrinkling her brow and moving her lips. Counting stitches, probably.

The description was not especially detailed, nor especially accurate. He had just passed his nineteenth birthday, but he knew from experience that people often took him for sixteen or seventeen. He had been wearing a black leather jacket. Moreover, his mother had cut his hair the previous evening, under simulated protest.

The newscaster also said that he was presumed to be driving a light-green Chevrolet with three sevens in the license number.

Funny they hadn't found the car. He hadn't taken any special pains to hide it. They were sure to find it any moment now.

"I've got to leave tomorrow, Mama," he said.

She looked up from her knitting.

"But Ronnie, can't you stay till Papa comes home? He'll be so unhappy when he finds out you've come and gone, and he didn't get a chance to see you."

"I have to give the car back. The kid I borrowed it from needs it tomorrow. But I'll come again soon."

His mother sighed.

"Yes, yes, that's what you always say," she said resignedly. "And then we don't see you for a year."

The next morning, he drove into Stockholm.

He didn't know where he was headed, but if the police managed to find out who he was, he didn't want to sit at home with his mother and wait to be arrested. In Stockholm, it was easier to disappear.

He didn't have much money, only a couple of the five-crown pieces and two tens his mother had given him. Gas was no problem. He had cut a section off the garden hose in his parents' garage, and as soon as it got dark, he could get all the gasoline he needed. Of course, most cars had locks on their gas tanks these days, but as long as you weren't in a hurry, things usually went fine.

A place to live was more of a problem. He had a couple of friends with their own apartment, and he would drive over and ask them if he could crash with them for a couple of days, but most of the other people he knew were in the same fix he was in. No place to live.

It was still early when he got to Stockholm, and he drove around aimlessly in the center of town before it struck him that he'd better look up his friends while there was still some chance of catching them in bed.

They lived in Henriksdal. He drove carefully, anxious not to break any laws or draw attention to himself. The car ran well and was comfortable and pleasant to drive.

There was a strange name on the door to his friends' apartment. He rang the bell, and a woman in bathrobe and slippers answered the door. She said she'd moved in a few days ago and that she didn't know what had become of the previous tenants.

Caspar wasn't particularly surprised. He had been to some pretty wild parties there himself, and he knew they'd been threatened with eviction several times.

He drove back downtown. There wasn't much gas left in the tank, and he didn't want to waste the last of his money on gasoline, which he could get for nothing that night. But luck was with him, and he found a free parking space on Skeppsbron.

As he stood waiting for the "walk" light by the statue of Gustaf III, he turned and looked back at the car. It was last year's model and still fairly shiny and clean, without a dent or a scrape anywhere on it. It was a common make and looked sober and middle-class. It wasn't conspicuous in any way. With its new fake plates, to go on driving it would be no great risk.

He wandered around in the Old City and thought about what he would do.

He'd been away from Stockholm for two weeks. It felt like an eternity.

Fourteen days ago, he'd had a little money and so he'd gone to Copenhagen with a couple of other guys. Then, when the money ran out, he'd gone to Malmö, where he'd had the misfortune of running into Christer. Who was now dead. It was still hard for him to grasp what had happened. Sunday morning in Ljunghusen had somehow been ripped out of his life. It had nothing to do with him; it was more like something he'd seen in a movie or heard someone tell about than something he'd lived through himself.

He felt a strong need to talk to someone, to see his friends, to get back to his normal life, and convince himself that nothing had changed.

But everything had changed. Oh, he'd been on the lam before, but not like this.

This time it was really serious. He was the object of a nationwide manhunt—that's what they'd said on TV.

He couldn't go looking for his friends. They hung out in Humlegården and Kungsträdgården and Sergel Square, the first places the police would go to look for him.

He was hungry and went into a shop on Köpmangatan to buy some rolls. A girl in jeans and a leather coat was standing at the counter paying for a box of tea that she was holding under one arm. She had short blond hair, and when she turned around, Caspar could see she was older than he'd thought. Thirty, at least. She looked him right in the face with her searching blue eyes, and for an instant he thought she recognized him and fear tied a knot in his belly.

"Mr. Beck still isn't back?" asked the clerk behind the counter, and the woman with the inquisitive gaze finally looked away.

"No, but he ought to be back any day," she said.

Her voice was a little hoarse. She went to the door without looking at Caspar and stepped out into the street.

"Thank you, Mrs. Nielsen," the clerk called after her. "Come again."

Caspar bought his rolls, but it was sometime before the knot in his stomach loosened enough for him to eat them.

I'm starting to crack up, he thought. I've got to pull myself together.

He left the Old City and crossed Slussen toward Södermalm Square. There were two Finns standing outside the entrance to the subway. He knew them slightly and had talked to them several times, but as he approached the steps leading down to where they stood, he caught sight of two patrolmen walking down Peter Myndes Hill. He changed direction abruptly and walked on toward Götgatan.

He came to Medborgarplatsen and stopped to stare at the newsbills outside the newspaper kiosk next to Björn's Garden. POLICEMAN MURDERED, said one, and WOUNDED POLICEMAN DIES another, in fat black type. He read the smaller subheads. *Desperado Sought Nationwide* read one of them, while the other evening tabloid stated more laconically, *Murderer at Large.*

Caspar knew it was him they meant, but he still couldn't see how they could call him a "desperado" and a "murderer."

He had never even held a gun in his hand, and if he had he wouldn't have had the nerve to use it on another human being, even if he were desperate.

It hadn't occurred to him all day to buy the papers, and now that he saw the newsbills, he was afraid to read what they had to say.

He thought of the green car, full of stolen property and with his fingerprints on the steering wheel. And not only the steering wheel. Once they found the car they would have his fingerprints, and once they had them they would know who they were hunting.

He remembered that time a year and a half ago all too well—the only time he'd been caught—and he could still see the stamp pad and the card they'd pressed his fingers on. All ten, one after the other.

Caspar didn't buy a paper. He went on walking, up one street and down the next, without being conscious of where he was. He racked his brains trying to think of someplace to hide.

His parents' house was out of the question. The police would go there as soon as they found out who he was. And they probably knew that already.

He felt sorry for his mother, and he wished he could explain to her what had happened. That he hadn't shot anyone. If he could find a place to hide out, maybe he'd write her a letter.

It was dark by four o'clock, and he started feeling calmer. After all, he hadn't killed anyone. It was all a misunderstanding, and you can't be punished for something you haven't done. Or can you?

Caspar was cold. He was wearing a thin pullover under his leather jacket, and his worn, washed-out jeans didn't afford much warmth. And his feet, in tennis shoes, were even colder than his legs. He considered going back to the car. He could try to siphon a little gas and drive out into the country and sleep in the back seat. But he remembered how cold the night had been by Lake Sommen three days earlier, and anyway, it was still too early.

In addition to the rolls, he had bought two hot dogs and a pack of cigarettes, but he still had nineteen crowns.

He went into a pastry shop on Ringvägen that he'd never been in before. He ordered coffee and two cheese sandwiches and sat down at a table next to a radiator.

As he lifted the cup to take his first sip of coffee, he heard a voice behind him.

"Well, if it isn't Caspar! What made you go get scalped like that? I almost didn't recognize you."

He put down his cup and turned around, his face drawn with terror.

"Don't look so scared," said the girl. "It's only me. Maggie. You remember me, don't you?"

Of course he remembered her. Maggie had been his best friend's girl for several years, and he had met her the very first day he came to Stockholm, almost three years ago. She and his friend had broken up six months before, and his friend had gone to sea. Caspar hadn't seen Maggie since then.

But she was a terrific girl, and he liked her.

She moved over to his table, and they talked about old times for a while, and finally Caspar decided to tell her about his problem. He told her everything, exactly the way it had happened. Maggie had been reading the papers, and she realized right away what a fix he was in.

"Poor Caspar," she said when he was through. "What a rotten mess! I suppose I really ought to advise you to go to the cops and tell them the whole story, but I won't, because I don't trust those bastards."

She thought for a while, and Caspar sat silently and waited.

"You can stay at my place," she said, finally. "I've got an apartment out at Midsommarkransen. My boyfriend isn't going to like it, of course, but he's not on such good terms with the cops himself, so he ought to understand. And he's a nice guy—deep down."

Caspar's vocabulary wasn't really adequate to express his relief and gratitude. But he did his best.

"You're one hell of a terrific chick, Maggie. I always said so."

Maggie even paid his check and then walked down to Skeppsbron with him to get his car.

"You can't afford to get a ticket in your boots," she

said. "And I've got money for gas, so don't worry about that."

They drove out to Midsommarkransen with Maggie at the wheel, and Caspar sang at the top of his lungs the whole way there.

24.

Herrgott Allwright reached behind his right ear with a thumb and two fingers and pushed his hat down over his left eye. It made him look like Huckleberry Finn, albeit thirty-five years older.

"Today we'll go out and shoot ourselves a pheasant. And then eat it. I'm one hell of a good cook. That's one of the advantages of being a bachelor."

Martin Beck mumbled something.

He himself was one of the worst cooks in the world. Maybe that was the result of becoming a bachelor too late. But probably not. Whenever he tried to do any kind of housework, he always had a strong impression that all of his fingers were thumbs.

"And where are we going to shoot it? Do you own hunting land?"

"I've got friends," Allwright said. "We have what amounts to a standing invitation. You can borrow some boots from me. And a shotgun—I've got two."

Allwright grinned and shuffled some papers on his desk.

"Unless, of course, you think it would be more interesting to refresh your soul in an exchange of views with Folke," he added.

Martin Beck shook himself. His conversations with Folke Bengtsson had now reached a state of total stagnation. Somewhat like a chess game where each of the players has nothing but a king and a knight left on the board.

"I read an interesting thing in here," Allwright said, picking up a foreign police periodical. "In Dayton, Ohio, a city roughly the same size as Malmö, there have been one hundred and five murders so far this year, which, on a per capita basis, is ten times as many as in New York. Detroit's the only city with dependable statistics that's worse. Seventy-one of those murders were committed with firearms. That must be worse than Stockholm."

"Does it tell how many robberies and assaults they've had?"

"No, it doesn't. Now, to compare that with Trelleborg Police District, we've had one murder here. And that's an unusually high figure."

"One," said Martin Beck. "But it's enough to spoil my sleep. Last night I dreamed about Bengtsson again."

Allwright laughed.

"About Folke? I wouldn't say anything if you dreamed about Sigbrit."

Allwright was touching on a psychological phenomenon that affected Martin Beck and, no doubt, a lot of other policemen in similar positions. Generally speaking, he could go out and inspect a massacred or mutilated corpse without turning a hair. Even if he did feel a certain inner discomfort, he was capable of throwing it aside like an old coat as soon as he got home. On the other hand, he was tormented by situations where he suspected that something wasn't right—like this matter of Sigbrit Mård and Folke Bengtsson. A man who had been convicted in advance and who could not defend himself. It was somewhat like a lynching.

"There's another piece of news from the lab today," Allwright said. "That rag that I personally found near the body when we were examining the scene of the crime. To tell the truth, I had completely and utterly forgotten about it."

He laughed.

"What did they find?" said Martin Beck.

"They subjected it to a complete battery of tests," Allwright said. "Here's the report. It contained cotton fiber, gravel, dirt, clay, fat, oil, and nickel shavings. The gravel and dirt had exactly the same composition as the sample we took from the mudhole where we found Sigbrit. But the ground where I picked it up, on the other hand, was of a completely different type. So we can advance the theory that whoever murdered Sigbrit used it to dry off his boots. Assuming he was wearing boots, and he must have been."

"Nickel shavings?" said Martin Beck. "That's sort of special."

"Yes, I thought so. In any case, it is not the sort of evidence that links Folke to the crime."

But Folke Bengtsson is going to be convicted, thought Martin Beck. Unless . . .

"Enough of that. Come on, let's go hunting," Allwright said.

The hunt was a peculiar experience for Martin Beck, who, as a matter of fact, had never been hunting before. Wearing jeans, a duffle coat, a cap knitted by Evert Johansson's wife, and Allwright's extra boots, he stalked across the meadows alongside Allwright, who held Timmy straining at his leash. Martin Beck had the shotgun—Allwright's extra—crooked in his left elbow, which was the way he had seen real hunters do it, probably in the movies.

"You get the first shot," Allwright said. "You're the guest, after all. I'll take the second."

The meadow was soft and springy underfoot, and the grass was tall and frosty after a cold night. Stubborn flowers defied the hastily approaching winter, and in several places there were great clumps of bluish mushrooms.

"Blue legs," Allwright said. "Highly edible. We can pick some on the way back. Give dinner a little *je ne sais quoi*. Is that the right word?"

The caps of the mushrooms were frozen, completely or in part, but for being so late in the year, it was a magnificent day. Martin Beck walked along in silence. He had heard that hunters were supposed to be quiet. And he gave very little thought to strangled divorcees, paroled sex criminals, keys that fit no locks, and rags containing nickel shavings.

The air was clean and pure, and the sky was blue with occasional ragged clouds. A glorious day.

Then they flushed their first bird, from a point about twelve inches from his feet. Martin Beck was taken completely by surprise, jumped back, fired, and the bird flew away as if shot from a catapult.

"Jesus," Allwright said, and laughed. "I wouldn't want you on my skeet-shooting team. Damn nice of you not to shoot Timmy or me."

Martin Beck laughed too. He had warned him that his experience in these matters was, to put it mildly, limited.

The next pheasant flew up about forty minutes later,

and Allwright shot it with such perfect ease that it was almost like something he had done in passing.

On the way back, Martin Beck devoted himself to picking mushrooms.

"Yes, mushrooms are easier," Allwright said. "They stand still."

They walked on back to Allwright's tomato-colored car.

"Nickel shavings," said Martin Beck when they reached it. "Where could they have come from?"

"Some sort of specialized machine shop, I suppose. How do I know?"

"It might be important."

"Could be," Allwright said.

He seemed to be thinking only about dinner.

Which turned out to be singularly delicious. Martin Beck had a hard time remembering when he'd had a better meal.

Even though Rhea Nielsen was a good cook—and proved it eagerly and often.

Allwright proved to have all sorts of odd things in his freezer. Morels, for example, that he had picked himself, and a wonderfully tasty mixture of blueberries, blackberries, and wild raspberries. It made a splendid dessert, especially with whipped cream, which, as Allwright put it, was "untouched by anything but human hands."

They had just wiped their mouths when the telephone rang.

"Allwright? . . . Is that right? . . . Well, that was really well done. Tell me about it . . . How? In a letter? . . . I'll pass it on. We'll probably be down sometime in the morning . . . If you keep that up you might even get a transfer to Anderslöv . . . You don't? That's the silliest thing I ever heard of . . . Okay, so long."

He hung up the phone and peered at Martin Beck.

"Who was that?"

"One of the boys in Trelleborg. They've found the apartment that belongs to that key in Sigbrit's purse."

Martin Beck was astounded and didn't bother to hide it.

"How the hell did they manage that?" he said.

"There's a saying in these parts that goes, 'The dumbest farmer gets the biggest beets.' Now you might suppose that would apply to a case such as this. But you'd be wrong."

Allwright started clearing the table as he talked.

"The fact is that some of the boys in Trelleborg made up their minds that, by George, they'd find that door if it was in Trelleborg to be found. They made a lot of copies of the key and put in a lot of overtime, and of course when you get down to it, Trelleborg's not Stockholm or Dayton, Ohio, to take a couple of examples. It isn't a hell of a big city, and if you're just pertinacious enough, you generally get where you're going."

He paused and chuckled under his breath. Martin Beck had pulled himself together and was helping with the clearing and the dishes.

"And there's another thing that I'd say was an important factor. Some of the boys down there are good. The Chief has a chance to pick them by hand. He doesn't have to take just anyone, like in Stockholm or Malmö."

Since coming to Anderslöv, Martin Beck had been made unusually conscious of the fact that there really were quite a few good policemen among the innumerable mediocrities and the frighteningly large number of complete incompetents.

"So the boys thought they'd show the big guns from Stockholm—you mostly—that they can do the job even down here south of the highway. And they kept at it till they found the right door. This afternoon. If I know them, they would have stayed with it until they could swear that there was no such lock in Trelleborg."

"Did you get any details?"

"Sure. The address, for example. And some other things. They haven't touched anything, just looked. A little one-room apartment, not much furniture. Rented by Sigbrit under her maiden name, which happened to be Jönsson. The rent was paid in cash in a stamped envelope with a typewritten address on the first of every month for three and a half years. For that matter, it was paid for this month too, although Sigbrit was dead then and could hardly have paid it herself. So someone else must have taken care of it."

"Clark."

"Maybe."

"I feel pretty sure of it."

"There were always two words and a letter typed on the back of the envelope—*Rent S. Jönsson.*"

"We'll have to go down and have a look in the morning."

"With pleasure. They've sealed the door."

"Clark," said Martin Beck to himself. "Hardly Folke Bengtsson."

"Why not?"

"He's too tight," said Martin Beck.

"Well, the rent wasn't much. Seventy-five crowns. Always the exact amount in the envelope, according to the landlord."

Martin Beck shook his head.

"Not Bengtsson," he said. "Wrong man. It just doesn't fit in his behavior pattern."

"Well, Folke's a creature of habit," Allwright said.

"It doesn't fit in with his attitude toward women. His view of the so-called opposite sex is different."

"Opposite sex," Allwright said. "You can say that again. Did I tell you about my lady friend in Abbekås? The flesh-eating plant?"

Martin Beck nodded.

"Speaking of Clark, he's a very shadowy figure," Allwright said. "He doesn't live here in this district. I can say that with ninety-nine percent certainty. And I happen to know that the boys in Trelleborg have gone in hard for this Clark business, the description and everything. In their opinion, there's no such person in the entire Trelleborg Police District."

"Mmm," said Martin Beck.

"So the possibility remains that Folke made up the whole thing about this man and his car in order to distract attention from himself."

"That's possible," said Martin Beck.

But he didn't believe it.

They drove to Trelleborg the next day and studied the premises.

The apartment was in a rather small building behind an old apartment house that looked worn but not run-down. The building was on a side street that appeared to be very quiet.

Sigbrit Mård's secret retreat was one flight up, on the second floor, as they say in South Sweden.

Martin Beck let Allwright break the seal. He had the feeling Allwright thought it would be fun, somehow.

It wasn't much of an apartment.

It smelled musty and probably hadn't been aired out for over a month.

There was some mail lying on the floor in the hall under the mail slot—various kinds of ads and notices addressed to Occupant.

The name on the door consisted of detachable white plastic letters forming the pseudonym S. JÖNSSON.

There was a lavatory on the right side of the hall, with a shelf above the sink for toiletries. Two toothbrushes in the same glass, a package of tampons, lipstick, pancake make-up, nail file, eye shadow. There was a diaphragm in a round plastic box. Sigbrit Mård had apparently not been one to take chances.

There was also a bar of soap, a shaving brush, and a razor, which did not necessarily mean that the place had been used by a man. Sigbrit had shaved her armpits.

The single room contained two chairs and a table. There was an ordinary foam rubber mattress against one wall, dressed up with a colorful spread from some bargain basement.

On the mattress was a pillow with a sky-blue pillow case.

Beside the table stood an electric heater. It was unplugged, and probably had been for some time.

They opened the drawers in the table without touching the knobs. Empty, except for some blank sheets of paper and a pad of thin, blue, lined stationery.

Martin Beck thought he recognized the quality.

In the kitchen they found the following: a coffee pot, two cups, two glasses, a jar of Nescafé, an unopened bottle of white wine, a half empty bottle of good whisky (Chivas Regal), four cans of beer (Carlsberg), and a tankard of indeterminate origin.

There was an ashtray in the kitchen and one in the main room. Both were clean.

"Not much of a love nest," said Herrgott Allwright.

Martin Beck said nothing. Allwright knew a great deal about the most disparate things. The one subject about which he knew very little was love.

There were no lampshades, only naked bulbs. It was all very clean and neat. There were a broom, dustpan, and rag in a cubby in the kitchen.

Martin Beck crouched down and looked at the pillow. There were two kinds of hairs on it.

Long blond ones, and others that were much shorter and almost white.

He studied the mattress. There were stains that could undoubtedly be analyzed, and frizzy hairs.

"We're going to want a lab report on this place. And it had better be damn thorough."

Allwright nodded.

"This is the place all right," said Martin Beck. "That's for sure. My congratulations to the Trelleborg police."

He looked at Allwright.

"Have you got the stuff to put a new seal on the door?"

"Yes, indeed," said Allwright slowly.

They left.

A little while later they found the patrolman who had discovered the apartment. He was walking a beat on the main street. He had red hair and did not speak the local dialect.

"Well done," said Martin Beck.

"Thanks."

"Did you talk to the neighbors?"

"Yes, but they didn't know anything. Mostly older folks. They'd noticed that there were people there in the evenings sometimes, but they were mostly the kind who go to bed at seven o'clock. They'd never seen any men there, just a woman. The old lady who'd seen her suddenly decided it might have been one of the girls from the pastry shop, but that was only when I gave her a hint. On the other hand, several of them had seen a beige car parked on the street now and then. A Volvo, they thought."

Martin Beck nodded. The pieces of the puzzle were starting to fall into place.

"Good work," he said, with a feeling of repeating himself.

"Oh, it was my pleasure," the policeman said. "Too bad we couldn't get a lead on this fellow Clark."

"If he exists," said Allwright.

"He exists," said Martin Beck as they walked toward the police building. "Rest assured."

"If you say so."

It was a bitterly cold day, even though the sky was still clear. An East German ferry lay at the slip. It was called the *Rügen*.

Uncommonly ugly, thought Martin Beck.

Boats had been getting uglier and uglier for years.

Clark, he thought. Rags. Nickel shavings. Beige Volvo. And the impossible Folke Bengtsson.

His view of all these things was more optimistic now.

25.

Karl Kristiansson and Kenneth Kvastmo did not make a good team. Although they had manned the same patrol car for a year and a half, they had little to talk about and even less use for one another.

Kvastmo was from Värmland, a big haystack of a man, with a blond mane, the neck of a bull, and a forehead like a washboard above a broad, meaty nose. As a policeman, he was thorough and persistent, eager and aggressive. In short, a stickler for duty. Besides which, he was very curious.

Kristiansson had always been lazy, and the years had made him more and more so. He almost never thought about duty, but rather about the soccer pools and food and sometimes about the pain from an old gunshot wound. Another policeman had shot him in the knee a couple of years before, on April 3, 1971, to be exact. That had been the most calamitous day of his life, and there were many unfortunate ones to choose among. He had lost his best friend on that chilly Saturday and had been shot himself. To top it all off, he had had a minimal four right on his infallible soccer pool system.

In Kristiansson's opinion, Kvastmo was an incurable blockhead, who did nothing but whine and complain about everything and everyone, and who complicated the job by constantly taking action. For his own part, Kristiansson never took action any more without a direct order, or unless he was very strongly provoked. And as long as he stayed inside the patrol car and contented himself with staring out through the windshield with unseeing blue eyes, he was not easily accessible, not even for the most notorious provocateurs.

But Kvastmo did everything he could to make life difficult. He fought an unending battle with gangsters. In spite of the fact that the Swedish police had a system of automatic promotions such that accumulating merits paid no appreciable dividends, he was constantly on the lookout for activities that called for police intervention. And given the society he lived in, he seldom had to look far. His dream was to be transferred to the notorious Östermalm Precinct, where, for no good reason, the police always arrested five times as many people as in all of the other Stockholm precincts put together. The new law gave over-zealous policemen a great opportunity to harass people, particularly young people who were, say, sitting on park benches talking to each other because they had nowhere else to go. People of this type were automatically regarded as suspect and could be apprehended immediately. The police could hold them for six hours, work them over at the station house, and release them again, only to make another military-style raid and drag the same people back into the paddy wagon. This was a good way to run things, Kvastmo thought, but unfortunately he was stuck in a precinct where the officers were not quite so bloodthirsty.

During their many months in the patrol car, Kristiansson had learned at least two things. One bad thing: it was impossible to borrow so much as five crowns from Kvastmo. But also one good thing: Kvastmo was addicted to coffee, and when the man got too insufferable he could always suggest a coffee break.

The brown liquid had an amazingly positive effect. Kvastmo could sit quietly for at least half an hour, often longer, slurping and smacking his lips and stuffing himself with Danish pastry and almond cake.

But as soon as they were back in the car again, the good effects were all undone. He returned at once to his incessant pursuit of suspects and his nagging complaints about the society of thieves they lived in.

Kristiansson did not like coffee, but he knew it was the price he had to pay for a few moments of relaxation.

At the moment, they had just finished a lengthy coffee session and found themselves back in the squad car, a black and white Plymouth with a spotlight and flashers and a short-wave radio and every other technical refinement.

The patrol car, in turn, found itself on Essingeleden, an elevated superhighway that sliced across bays and islands into the center of Stockholm from the south.

Kristiansson was driving at his usual phlegmatic pace, and Kvastmo was repeating one of his standard lines.

"Why don't you answer me, Karl?"

"What?"

"I'm talking to you about important things, and you're not even listening."

"Sure I'm listening."

"Are you? The hell you are. You're thinking about something else."

"I am?"

"What are you thinking about?"

"Oh . . ."

"Broads, I'll bet."

"Well . . ."

What Kristiansson had actually been thinking about was oat flakes with strawberry jam and cold milk, but, in order to control his hunger, he had trammeled up the vision of an uncommonly disgusting corpse that, thanks to Kvastmo's zeal, they had succeeded in discovering the previous summer. But not wanting to reveal his innermost thoughts, he made up another answer. Which he found an immediate use for.

"Well, what were you thinking about? And why don't you answer me?"

"I was thinking about how Leeds has played twenty-eight league matches in a row without a loss, and how Millwall has already been beaten five times at home. It doesn't make sense."

"You idiot," said Kvastmo. "How can a full-grown policeman think about crap like that? Those teams aren't even Swedish."

Kristiansson took this very badly. He was from Skåne, and in southern Sweden the word "idiot" is very bad. It is very nearly the worst thing a person can be called.

Kvastmo had no feeling for this at all and continued heedlessly.

"What I'm trying to say is that we don't have enough legal protection, and the police officials are a bunch of namby-pambies. A lot of our fellow officers don't dress properly, and no one does anything about it. Do you remember that motorcycle patrolman last summer? The one who didn't even have his cap on? And had his jacket strapped on behind?"

"But it was ninety-five degrees."

"What difference does that make? A policeman is a policeman in any weather. I read in the paper that in New York the patrolmen often get stuck in the asphalt when there's a heat wave. They stay at their posts, by God, and they have to pry them loose when they're relieved. If they ever get relieved."

By "paper" Kvastmo meant their magazine, *Swedish Police*, which often reported curious facts to its readers.

Kristiansson didn't respond. He'd seen a lot of American riot police in training films and he was wondering what it would look like if several hundred men were stuck to the street when the order came to charge.

"Are you listening, Karl?"

He was also wondering what clothes had to do with legal protection.

"Why don't you answer me, Karl?"

"I'm thinking."

"What about?"

"Oh . . ."

"It's really a waste of time talking to you. The fight against crime needs every man every minute of every day, and you just sit there thinking about soccer and all you can say is 'Oh . . .' and 'Well . . . ,' and when something happens, the most you can say is 'Jesus.' Can't you get it through your head what a tough spot we policemen are in? The Minister of Justice is the biggest namby-pamby of them all. That's why we don't have any decent legal protection. We've hardly got any protection at all. Like this shit about not having a cartridge in the chamber. Now suppose you're suddenly face to face wtih some armed gangster, what are you going to do? You don't have any cartridge in the chamber."

"Yes, I do."

"Well, that's crazy," said Kvastmo indignantly. "That's against police regulations. Well, anyway, you're not *supposed* to have. So there you stand, helpless. Done for. And whose fault is that? Whose responsibility? The Minister of Justice, that's who. How are we supposed to clean things up if we're not even allowed to have a cartridge in the chamber?"

"I fired my pistol once," said Kristiansson suddenly. "In a bus."

"Did you hit anyone?"

"Well, there wasn't anyone there. But I hit the bus, of course."

"What happened?"

"There was hell to pay. That tall, ugly guy from Violence really chewed me out."

"There, you see? No support from above. So it's no wonder. Look at those three guys down in Skåne. Cut down. What do you suppose their wives and children think of the Minister of Justice? And they haven't even caught the killer yet. You know what? I think he's hiding out someplace here in town. Goddam, if we could collar him. I hate those bastards. I wouldn't hesitate a second if I got the drop on him."

"Oh . . ."

"What do you mean, 'Oh . . .'? Two of our fellow officers are in the hospital, right? And one of them is dead. That guy Borglund. Dead. Murdered."

"Well . . ."

"What the hell do you mean, 'Well . . .'?"

"I heard he got bitten by some poison animal, a frog or something."

"How can you believe anything as dumb as that? Didn't you hear that lecture about the perversive forces in society? No, I mean *sub*versive. Communists and that kind of vermin. They spread lies like that to damage and weaken the police force. So they can destroy the very foundations, the very basis, of society. But I didn't really think we had anyone on the force who would fall for it. Sometimes you scare me, Karl."

"I do?"

Kristiansson had started thinking about something else. He had a constructive plan. Several days earlier, he had seen a gigantic loaf of marzipan in the supermarket. It was probably meant to be used in a bakery. But the next time he picked up any money on the soccer pools, he was going to buy it and put it down in the front seat between them. Kvastmo was exceptionally fond of marzipan and wouldn't be able to resist it. But there were two things that worried him. First, how long would the marzipan last? It was enough to last Kristiansson a lifetime, but maybe Kvastmo would wolf it down in half an hour. The second was equally serious. What if Kvastmo was such a great talker that he could rattle on uninterruptedly through a mouthful of almond paste?

He suddenly glanced at Kvastmo and said, "What is it that goes oink-oink and never gets to the door?"

"A pig."

"Wrong. A cat with a speech impediment."

"You scare me, Karl," said Kvastmo, shaking his head. "Why doesn't it get to the door?"

"Oh . . ."

"There's a limit," Kvastmo said. "There's a limit to

262

what a simple, ordinary policeman should have to put up with. Norman Hansson, for example. He's the limit. Last week when you were out sick I had to go check out this domestic disturbance and arrest this jerk who started resisting violently when I collared him. So I worked him over a little with the old night stick on the way down the stairs and then out in the car, you know, just to calm him down. Next morning Norman Hansson calls me in and wants to know if I've mistreated this editor what's-his-name. Well, I tell him, I used my night stick to calm him down a little, but there was no question of brutality. And you know what Norman Hansson said?"

Kristiansson was wondering what the enormous loaf of marzipan might cost.

"Why don't you answer me, Karl?"

"What?"

"Do you know what Norman Hansson said?"

"No."

"Well, he shook his head and he said, 'There's got to be a stop to this, Kenneth. The next time someone complains I'm going to put you on report.' I mean, he's going to put me on report because some son of a bitch gets drunk and plays his hi-fi too loud."

"I thought you said it was a domestic disturbance."

"Well, a disturbance is a disturbance. The guy was sitting home alone getting drunk and playing records. But that's not my fault, is it? They can't blame me for that, can they? Can I help it if the guy's a pantywaist and Norman Hansson's a milksop?"

Kristiansson stared wearily at the highway as it seemed to wind up and disappear beneath the car. Norman Hansson was one of the precinct commanders. By and large, Kristiansson liked him.

"I expect unswerving loyalty from other policemen, no matter what," said Kvastmo firmly. "Well, look at that. Look! Did you see that, Karl?"

They were passed by a red Jaguar. It was undeniably traveling very fast.

"After him, Karl!"

Kristiansson heaved a sigh and floored the accelerator, while Kvastmo flicked on the siren and the flashing lights.

"That might be our cop-killer," Kvastmo said.

"In a red Jaguar?"

"Stolen, of course."

Kristiansson happened to know how hard it was to steal a Jaguar, unless the door was open and the key in the ignition. Along with his late buddy Kvant, he had once been close to capturing a famous car-thief who specialized in expensive English cars and who was known respectfully as The Jag. The conclusion of the adventure was that Kvant drove into a haystack while The Jag disappeared in the distance.

The police car bellowed through the night. The tail lights of the car in front came closer. All around them, but especially to the right, lay Stockholm with its hundreds of thousands of glittering lights reflecting in dark bays and inlets. Church spires stood silhouetted against a starry sky. The moon was out.

"Now we've got the son of a bitch," Kvastmo said. "I was just waiting for something like this to happen."

Kristiansson glanced at the speedometer. Eighty-five. He held his foot down and pulled up alongside the red Jaguar. Kvastmo already had the STOP paddle in one hand and his night stick in the other.

And then something odd happened.

The driver of the car they were pursuing looked over at Kristiansson, smiled, and raised his right hand as if he were greeting him or maybe thanking him for something. Then he accelerated and pulled away from them.

"Well, I'll be damned," Kvastmo said. "Did you see that?"

"Yes."

"But now I recognize him, at least. Got the description. I never forget a face, as you know. You know that, don't you?"

"Did you get the number, too?"

"Sure. You think I'm asleep over here? FZK 011, right?"

"I didn't notice. Shall we call it in?"

"No, by God, we'll handle this bird by ourselves. Just stick with him. Can you do it, Karl?"

"Well . . ."

His chances would have been minimal except that the red rocket turned off the expressway and headed in toward the center of town. This forced the driver to reduce his speed, and Kristiansson managed to keep him in sight.

The chase screamed on through deserted night-time streets. As far as Kristiansson could tell, their bandit was not even trying to get away, and the patrol car was only a couple of hundred yards behind when the red Jaguar screeched to a stop outside a building on Nybrogatan in Östermalm. The driver jumped out and hurried across the sidewalk without even locking his car.

Before he was shot, Kristiansson had served in Solna —and before that in Malmö—so he was no expert on the capital. Had he known Stockholm a little better, he might possibly have been surprised to see the villain disappear into the Betania Foundation Hospital.

In the event that Kvastmo recognized the building, it raised no doubts in his mind. Nothing a criminal did could ever surprise him. He was fond of pointing out that a person could expect just about anything in this society of gangsters.

"No more than what you might expect, the way things are today," he said. "Right, Karl? But now we've got him where we want him. Is he ever going to be surprised! We'd better both go in."

Kristiansson had pulled up right behind the red car. He studied it through the windshield and then looked doubtfully toward the door where the man had entered the building.

"Well . . ." he said.

Kvastmo said nothing for once. He threw open the door and heaved himself out of his seat. The expression on his face was one of grim determination.

"The number checks," said Kristiansson. "FZK 011. It's the same car all right."

"What did you expect?"

"Well . . ."

"Hurry up," said Kvastmo.

Kristiansson sighed and stepped out of the car, straightened his shoulder belt, and followed Kvastmo reluctantly across the sidewalk.

Kvastmo marched firmly through the entrance, up a flight of stairs, and through a half-open door.

They found themselves in what appeared to be a waiting room. Directly in front of them was a door with an opaque glass panel. Behind it, someone was talking in a hushed voice.

Kvastmo threw Kristiansson a conspiratorial look that was all one-sided, grabbed the handle of the door, threw it open, and strode in.

Kristiansson stayed behind on the threshold. The scene before him filled him with uncertainty. He saw two people—the man from the Jaguar, who was now wearing a green gown of some strange material, and a middle-aged woman. The woman was also dressed oddly. She looked like a nurse, or perhaps a nun. She was holding up a pair of plastic gloves which the man obviously intended to put on.

He also saw Kvastmo, who moved his right hand from his holster to his breast pocket and took out a notebook and pen.

"All right, what's going on here?" he bellowed.

The man threw a distracted and slightly astonished look at the two policemen. Then he pushed his hands into the transparent gloves.

"Thanks for the help," he said.

And then he turned his back on them and started to walk away.

Kvastmo turned red in the face.

"Don't get smart with us," he said loudly. "What's your name? And let's see your driver's license. We're just doing our job. My partner here can vouch for that, can't you Karl?"

"He's just doing his job," Kristiansson mumbled, shifting his weight from one foot to the other.

The man seemed to have lost interest in them altogether. The woman had just covered his face with a mask, and he was taking a step toward a large double door, when Kvastmo grabbed him by the arm.

"Now that's enough of this bullshit. Or maybe you'd just like to come with us?"

The man in green turned around, gave Kvastmo an uncomprehending look, and hit him.

It was a good blow, quick and hard. It caught him right on the chin, and Kvastmo dropped on his seat with a meaty thud. Pad and pen fell from his hand and his stare grew even more vacant, if that was possible.

Kristiansson didn't move a muscle.

"Jesus," he said.

267

The man and the woman left the room. The massive doors closed behind them. A key turned in a lock.

Kvastmo remained seated on the floor. He looked a lot like Harry Persson after the famous knock-down in the match with Johnny Widd.

"Jesus," Kristiansson repeated.

Kvastmo seemed to recover somewhat after a minute or so. But the recovery was uncertain and, in any case, hardly perceptible. He crawled around on all fours for a while and then got to his feet, heavy and unsteady.

"This is going to cost that son of a bitch," he said very groggily. "Assaulting an officer of the law."

He took hold of his chin and whimpered like a sick dog. It obviously hurt him to talk.

"Karl," he whispered, almost inaudibly. "I can't talk."

Too good to be true, thought Kristiansson.

And then he was seized by gloom.

Now there were bound to be complications again.

Why were there always so many difficulties? he wondered misanthropically. Even though he never did anything to cause them.

He put his arm around Kvastmo to hold him up.

"Come on, let's go," he mumbled.

"Yes," Kvastmo said. "We've got to write the report. He'll get thirty days for this. At least. No, ninety days and damages for pain and suffering."

He sounded as if he were trying to talk through a mouthful of almond paste.

26.

Gunvald Larsson was furious. He couldn't remember having been this angry for several years. He pounded his big hairy hand on the desk and demanded silence.

They had finally promoted him to Chief Inspector one year earlier. The automatic promotion program hadn't left them much chance—they either had to kick them upstairs or get rid of him.

But his new title hadn't changed him. It was only the years, forty-eight of them now, which were slowly leaving their mark. He had not grown any taller, but he now weighed a good 230 pounds, and the blond hair combed back across his head had begun to recede at the temples. He was stronger than ever, or at least he felt he was, and would make a formidable physical opponent.

Even as a verbal opponent, he was no picnic.

"Don't stand there mumbling, man," he said to Kvastmo. "Can't you talk?"

"Only with great difficulty," said Kenneth Kvastmo in a much clearer voice than he had just been using.

Gunvald Larsson turned to Kristiansson.

"It's funny how often we've found ourselves in this situation over the last ten years. Is that possibly a result of the fact that you are an even bigger blockhead than all the other idiots that infest the police force in this town?"

"I wouldn't know," said Kristiansson unhappily.

The two policemen were standing at attention by the door. For Kristiansson, this situation was by no means unique, but it was new to Kvastmo, and he seemed to be taking it more to heart.

"Would you be so kind as to tell me exactly what happened?" said Gunvald Larsson in a tone of voice that he himself would have characterized as gentle and understanding.

"Well . . ."

Said Kristiansson and looked appealingly at Kvastmo, who, however, remained silent for the time being.

"We were patrolling as usual on Essingeleden," said Kristiansson softly. "And then all of a sudden we were passed by this . . . gentleman, who came tearing along in a red Jaguar."

"At an excessive speed," said Kvastmo.

"What did you do then?"

"We caught up to him," Kristiansson said.

"And what was his response."

"He waved at me," said Kristiansson. "And then he pulled away from us."

His expression was so sheepish that Gunvald Larsson felt suddenly several years older and many pounds heavier. He sighed heavily.

"And so you gave chase?" he said.

"We thought he was the cop-killer," Kvastmo said.

"Did he have blond hair? Did he look to you like an unusually youthful nineteen-year-old?"

Kvastmo didn't answer.

"Now the fact is," said Gunvald Larsson, "that this man is fifty-seven years old and a professor of medicine. He was on his way to perform a very urgent and complicated Caesarian section of twins. Do you know what that is?"

Kristiansson nodded. He and his wife had had several children.

"He was still driving too fast," said Kvastmo stubbornly.

"Cretin," said Gunvald Larsson.

"That's insulting an officer of the law," said Kvastmo. Kristiansson frowned.

"Not when one of your superiors says it," he said.

"Moreover, this professor called the police ten minutes earlier and asked for an escort," Gunvald Larsson said. "And so he figured you were there to help him. What were you doing ten minutes earlier?"

"Taking a coffee break," said Kristiansson dismally. "We weren't in the car, so we couldn't hear the radio."

"I see," said Gunvald Larsson woefully. "And so then you chase him into the hospital and try to prevent him from entering the operating room. And what's more, you've got the gall to report him for assaulting an officer of the law. Personally, in that situation, I would probably have killed you."

"I didn't report anybody," Kristiansson mumbled.

"The National Commissioner himself said that . . ."

Began Kvastmo grandly, but was immediately interrupted by Gunvald Larsson.

"You leave him out of this, or I'll throw you bodily through that window," he bellowed.

"That's not a very loyal attitude," said Kvastmo.

Gunvald Larsson rose to his full and considerable height and extended his arm like Charles XII, although he was pointing at the door and not at Russia.

"Out!" he thundered. "And see to it you withdraw that report pretty damn quick."

An hour later he received a telephone call that made his clear blue eyes stiffen in anger.

"Malm here. The Chief tells me you haven't been showing proper loyalty to the patrol units. He doesn't like it. As long as you're under my command, you're going to have to control yourself. Because I have to suffer the consequences."

"What?" said Gunvald Larsson.

That was all he could get out.

"By the way, we've got that cop-killer surrounded out at Midsommarkransen," said Malm blithely. "Along with some gangster named Lindberg. You and Kollberg might drive on out, if you've got the time. We're going to move in any moment now. I'm personally in command, from down here at Södra police station."

Gunvald Larsson banged down the receiver and rushed into the office next door, where Kollberg and Einar Rönn were playing tic-tac-toe.

Rönn was another detective, notable for his red nose and his Lapland dialect. He had long experience in the Violence Division and had therefore been detailed to Malm's special command.

"Quick," said Gunvald Larsson. "The desperado himself just called and told me they've got Ronnie Casparsson and The Breadman surrounded out at Midsommarkransen."

"The desperado?" said Rönn.

"Yes, Malm, of course. Come on, let's get out there. We'll take my car."

"Poor kid," Kollberg said. "But I've got a score to settle with The Breadman."

Ronnie Casparsson stepped right into a trap when he went with Maggie to Midsommarkransen, but there was no way he could have known.

For Maggie's new boyfriend was Lindberg in person,

better known as The Breadman, and the apartment was under surveillance night and day.

Admittedly, this stakeout was being handled by a group of unusually listless and uninspired plainclothesmen, who, for fear of The Breadman's well-known impudence and audacity, stayed too far from the building and who, moreover, lacked the necessary experience.

But The Breadman sensed that they were there, and when he saw Ronnie Casparsson he shook his head.

"This is not a good spot for you, Caspar," he said.

But Ronnie Casparsson had nowhere else to go, and even if The Breadman was a crook, he was a good-tempered crook, which he immediately demonstrated.

"But stick around, Caspar. I've got a really terrific place to hide out if they try to take us here. Anyway, no one's going to recognize you with that haircut."

"You don't think they will?"

Ronnie Casparsson was discouraged and frightened, and his sense of alienation was now complete. He had only been disturbed before, according to the social welfare psychologist.

"Come on," said The Breadman. "Don't be downhearted. So you shot a cop. I shot an old woman, who popped up out of nowhere. It can happen to the best of us."

"The only thing is, I never shot anybody."

"That doesn't make any difference to them, so it's nothing to worry about. Anyway, like I said, no one's going to recognize you."

Lindberg himself had been sought by the police any number of times, and he didn't think it was at all unlikely that they were watching him now, but he accepted the situation with studied calm and an almost exaggerated sense of humor.

"They've already been here to search the place," he said. "Twice. So they probably won't be back for a while. The only trouble is that now Maggie has to support you too, and she's already got me to carry."

"Don't be silly," Maggie said. "You're getting unemployment and welfare—we'll make do. Of course, it's going to be mostly blood pudding and spaghetti and like that."

"As soon as it's safe for me to get out to the cabin in Södertörn, it's going to be *pâté* and champagne," The Breadman said. "You can count on that. And it won't be long now. And then, Caspar, my boy . . ."

He put his arm around Caspar and squeezed his shoulders to cheer him up. He was more than twenty years older, and it wasn't long before Caspar began to look up to him as a sort of father, or at least as an adult who understood. There had not been many such adults in Ronnie Casparsson's life. His parents were straight out of the Stone Age. The very most a person could do was feel sorry for them, sitting there in their splendid suburban house with their installment-plan car in their garage, bored to death, their eyes glued to their color TV. They never thought about anything but how they were going to make ends meet and how badly their son had turned out.

After all they'd done for him.

That was a constantly recurring theme.

Ronnie Casparsson had always had a hard time sitting still. It had never been easy for him to wait patiently for things to happen, and now, afterward, it seemed to him that it was exactly the passive atmosphere in his parents' home that had driven him away.

He saw himself in the mirror and realized that he looked like thousands of other young people.

274

Maggie and The Breadman were probably right. No one would recognize him.

And so on Friday he went out. Took the subway downtown and strolled around for a while in the usual places. Nevertheless, he avoided spots like Humlegården, where he knew the police made regular raids, mostly just for the fun of it. He wasn't about to give the cops a chance of getting him by accident, by coincience, simply because he happened to sit down on a park bench or talk to someone who was about to be arrested.

He left the house for a few hours on Saturday and Sunday too. He knew that all the papers had carried his picture and that the police had been to his parents' house and that they had raided a lot of clubs and apartments where he used to hang out. He also knew he was being pictured as some sort of public enemy number one. A cop-killer, pure and simple. A person who had to be put out of action by any and all means.

The Breadman was a somewhat calmer soul than Caspar, but he'd been forced to lie low for a long time now, and he too was beginning to long for some sort of activity.

As the three of them sat watching television Sunday night, The Breadman made Caspar an offer.

"If the cops track you down and try to take you," he said, "let's get out of here together. The two of us. I've got a good plan that I made for myself, but it'll be easier for two."

"The cabin in the woods, you mean?"

"Right."

Maggie said nothing. But she thought, Well, boys, they'll catch you pretty soon, and that's the end of the fun this time around.

On Monday, Caspar was finally identified.

275

The man who spotted him was an older Chief Inspector in plain clothes who had really come out only to see that the men on the stakeout weren't sloughing off completely.

The man's name was Fredrik Melander. He was an old, trusted confederate of Martin Beck's, but had been in the Robbery Division for several years. It was one of the dreariest jobs a man coud have on the Stockholm police. Theft, burglary, and robbery were being committed at a furious and steadily accelerating rate, and the police had not the slightest chance of keeping up, but Melander was a stoic man with no inclination to neurosis or depression. He also had the best memory on the force and was worth a great deal more than any computer.

He parked his car near the building at Midsommarkransen and immediately caught sight of Ronnie Casparsson, who was on his way home after a brisk, aimless afternoon walk. Melander followed him in and made certain that the boy entered the apartment where The Breadman and his girlfriend lived.

But it took him some time to find the policeman presently in charge of surveillance. This was an individual named Bo Zachrisson, notorious for his incompetence, and he found him asleep in his car two blocks away.

Zachrisson was just the type of man who would probably not have noticed either Caspar or The Breadman had they come parading out of the building at the head of a herd of elephants. To the best of Melander's knowledge, he had never done anything right. But his peculiar ability to misjudge every possible kind of situation had caused great difficulties from time to time.

Melander now found himself in a somewhat delicate predicament. His long experience and sound judgment told him there was only one sensible course to follow. That would be to take Zachrisson with him—preferably in handcuffs—and go up in the building and arrest Caspar and The Breadman before they had time to take any counter-measures. In order to do this, he would need a ballpoint pen and a pad of paper, utensils which he always carried with him.

On the other hand, Melander knew that strict orders had been issued regarding what was to be done if and when an individual policeman spotted Ronnie Casparsson. The matter was to be reported instantly to Division Commander Malm, who would then take over and effect an arrest.

And so Melander used the radio in Zachrisson's car to report what he had seen and let it go at that. Then he walked tranquilly back to his own car and drove home for a lunch of mutton stew.

And thus the apparatus was set in motion.

Malm's tactical command had planned carefully for just such an eventuality as this. The necessary force had been assessed at fifty men, half of whom would be equipped with helmets, face masks, automatic weapons, and bulletproof vests. They were to be transported in seven police vans and would have at their disposal two specially trained dogs, four tear gas experts, and a frogman, in the event the criminals attempted some counter-move. In addition, there was a helicopter ready for immediate takeoff. What its mission might be, Malm would not reveal. Perhaps it was his secret weapon.

Stig Malm had a weakness for helicopters, and now that the police had been equipped with no fewer than twelve of these machines, they were an unavoidable feature of any action organized by the upper echelons.

The tactical command also had four observation and surveillance specialists, who would be dispatched to the scene at once and hold the position until the main force could be brought into play.

Caspar and The Breadman were sitting in the kitchen eating cornflakes wth lingonberry jam and milk when Maggie came hurrying in.

"Something's happening," she said. "There are two trucks outside. I think it's the cops in disguise."

The Breadman walked quickly over to the window and looked out.

"Right," he said. "It's them all right."

One of the policemen was dressed up as a telephone repairman and was sitting behind the wheel of a bright yellow telephone van. The other was wearing a white coat and driving a worn-out ambulance. They both sat stock still at their posts.

"Let's get out of here," The Breadman said. "You'll cover for us, Maggie?"

She nodded, but at the same time she made an objection.

"Breadman, you really don't have to go," she said. "It's Caspar they're after, not you."

"Could be," The Breadman said. "But I'm starting to get sick of them running after me day in and day out. Come on, Caspar."

He hugged Maggie and gave her a kiss on the nose.

"Now don't take any chances," he said. "I don't want you getting hurt. Don't put up any resistance."

Aside from the bread knife, there was nothing in the apartment that even resembled a weapon.

The Breadman and Caspar went up to the attic, opened a trapdoor, climbed out onto the rear slope of the roof, and then crawled across to the next building. They moved across five buildings before descending through another trapdoor and leaving through a kitchen entrance. From there, they had to climb over a couple of fences before they finally reached the street where The Breadman had parked his getaway car.

It was an old black taxi with false license plates, and The Breadman even had the cap and jacket to a uniform so he could pass as a cabbie without attracting attention.

As they turned onto another street and headed south, they heard the wail of a great many sirens in the distance behind them.

The big police action went wrong right from the start.

The neighborhood wasn't cordoned off until fifteen minutes after Caspar and The Breadman had left that entire section of the city.

When Malm drove up in his command car, he managed to run over one of the special dogs.

The dog's hind legs appeared to be seriously injured, and it lay on the ground whimpering. Malm climbed out and began the day's operations by bending over and patting his wounded colleague on the head. He had probably seen some American police chief do something similar in the movies or on TV. It would doubtless be a popular gesture, and he looked around to see if any press photographers had reached the scene. But they had not, which was probably just as well, for an instant later the dog bit his hand. It couldn't seem to distinguish between criminals and Division Commanders from the National Police Administration.

"Good for you, Grim, by God," said his handler.

He was obviously very attached to the animal.

"Good dog," he added, for good measure.

Malm threw him an astonished glance and then wound a handkerchief around his bleeding right hand.

"Get me a dressing," he said to the men standing nearby. "And carry on with the operation as planned."

The plan was rather complex. First, policemen with

automatic weapons were to enter the building and try to evacuate people from the neighboring apartments down to the basement. Then sharpshooters were to break the windows to the apartment, whereupon tear gas bombs would be hurled in through the shattered glass.

If the criminals did not surrender instantly, the apartment would be stormed by five policemen in gas masks, supported by the two dogs and their handlers. Or, as now seemed to be the case, one dog and its handler. When all of this was completed, a policeman would give the all-clear sign from the window and Malm himself would enter the house along with a couple of higher police officials. Meanwhile, the helicopter people would keep watch over the entire block for the possibility of some attempt by the two criminals to leave the building.

The plan proceeded beautifully. Terrified neighbors were herded into the cellar, and the windows were shot to pieces. The only real error committed was that the tear gas personnel managed to lob only one of their grenades into the apartment, and that one turned out to be a dud.

Maggie was standing in the kitchen, washing dishes when the windows were shot to bits. At this point, she grew really frightened and decided to escape through the front door and try to give herself up.

Before she got that far, they stormed the apartment.

This was easily done, as it happened, because in her desire that nothing be damaged she had left the door unlocked.

Maggie was just on her way out to the hall when five heavily armed men and a dog burst in upon her.

The dog was obviously in a vile mood after the calamity that had befallen its associate.

It threw itself directly at the woman and knocked her to the floor on her back. Then it bit her on the left thigh, in the groin.

"By God, that dog sure knows where to bite a whore," said one of the policemen, laughing.

Since they could see right away that Caspar and The Breadman were gone, they let the dog bite her again in roughly the same spot.

"Well, at least we'll have some use for the ambulance," said the policeman with the sense of humor.

Gunvald Larsson and Kollberg arrived just as the operation was beginning and were thus too late to be of any help or hindrance.

And so they remained sitting in the car and observed what took place.

They saw the accident with the dog and Malm being wounded and eventually bandaged. And they watched as one of the ambulances was backed up to the building and Maggie was carried out.

Neither one of them said a word, but Kollberg shook his head sadly.

When everything seemed to be over, they climbed out of their car and walked over to Stig Malm.

"No one home, I see," said Gunvald Larsson.

"Only that girl."

"How was she hurt?" Kollberg asked.

Malm glanced down at his own bandaged hand.

"Apparently the dog bit her," he said.

Malm was an unusually well-dressed, vigorous man, even though he was approaching fifty. He had a ready, winning smile, and anyone who did not know he was a policeman—which, in fact, he was not—might easily have taken him for a film director or a successful businessman. He ran his good hand through his curly hair.

"Ronnie Casparsson and Lindberg," he said. "Now we've got two desperadoes to hunt. And both of them are apparently prepared to use a gun."

"Are you sure of that?" Kollberg said.

Malm ignored the question.

"I'll have to have more personnel next time," he said. "Twice as many men and quicker concentration. Otherwise, the plan worked beautifully. Just as I had imagined."

"Ha!" said Gunvald Larsson. "I've read through that damn plan. In my opinion, it borders on pure idiocy. Are you really so stupid you think an experienced man like The Breadman wouldn't recognize two policemen in disguise, lurking there in a telephone van and an old discarded ambulance?"

"I've never liked your choice of words," said Stig Malm resentfully.

"I can well imagine. Because I happen to say what I mean. Where the hell did you get this concentration idea? This isn't the Battle of Breitengfeld, you know. If you'd sent me and Lennart over here alone, we'd have Caspar and The Breadman now."

Malm sighed.

"I wonder what the Chief will say about all this," he said.

"You could always take that damn attack dog with you," said Gunvald Larsson. "If you don't dare face him by yourself. It might bite his balls off. That would be something."

"Larsson, you're vulgar," Malm said. "That's uncalled for."

"What is called for? Running over the specially trained livestock?"

"The concentration strategy is a good idea."

Malm ran his hand through his curly hair.

"Only numbers can annihilate," he said.

"Are you thinking of going to sea?"

"Hardly," Malm said. "I get so seasick."

"Do you know who coined that expression?"

"No."

"Nelson. The guy on the column in Trafalgar Square."

"He was right," Malm said. "And it's equally true on land."

"I doubt it. Anyway, he wasn't a policeman."

"We believe in it," Malm said.

"So it seems."

For a moment, Malm seemed almost human.

"I wonder what the Chief is going to think about all this," he said.

"He probably won't be too happy. Chew on the carpets a little."

"Don't say that," said Malm gloomily. "I'm the one he'll yell at."

"You'll get them next time."

"Maybe," said Malm pessimistically.

Kollberg hadn't said anything for a long time. He was lost in thought.

"What are you worrying about, Lennart?" Gunvald Larsson asked.

"About Caspar. Can't help it. He must feel like a hunted animal. He's bound to be scared. And he probably hasn't done anything especially criminal."

"We don't know that, do we?"

"It's what they call an intuition."

"Ugh," Malm said. "I've got to get over to headquarters. So long."

He climbed into the tactical command car and was driven away.

He made one more comment before he disappeared.

"Try to see to it that nothing gets out. Absolutely nothing must get out."

Kollberg shrugged his shoulders miserably.

"Being Division Commander probably isn't all that much fun when you get right down to it."

They stood in silence for a few moments.

"How are you feeling, Lennart?"

"Poorly. But I think I've discovered something. Maybe. Anyway, Christ! what a group we work with!"

"And Christ! what a rotten job!" said Gunvald Larson.

27.

On Tuesday morning, Lennart Kollberg got up early, put on his bathrobe, shaved, and went out to the kitchen and brewed himself a cup of coffee. For once, he was up before the children. There wasn't a sound to be heard from Bodil and Joakim's room. Gun was still sleeping too. He had kept her awake half the night, and it was only an hour since she'd fallen asleep.

When he had gone to bed the night before, following the abortive operation at Midsommarkransen, he had not been able to get to sleep. He had lain on his back with his hands clasped behind his head, stared up into the darkness, and thought. He could hear Gun's steady breathing beside him, and now and then a subway train would roar into the nearby station and then slowly roll away again. He had lain like this many times this past year, going over the same problem, but tonight he definitely felt he'd had enough.

At about three o'clock, he went out to the kitchen to get himself a beer and a sandwich, and pretty soon Gun came padding out to keep him company. Then they went back to bed, and he told her about his decision. It did not come as any great surprise to her. They had discussed it many times before, and Gun supported his plans wholeheartedly and energetically. He had been in a grim and restless mood ever since coming back from Skåne, and she had sensed that he was reaching a decision.

They talked for a couple of hours and then they made love, and after a while Gun fell asleep in his arms.

When Bodil and Joakim woke up, he made them breakfast, and when they had eaten, he sent them back to their room and urged them not to wake Gun. Not that they generally did what he told them—it was only Gun who could make them take notice—but he was hoping they would leave her in peace for at least a little while longer.

He got two sticky kisses and drove to work.

As he walked down the hall to his office, he passed the door to Martin Beck's empty room, and it occurred to him, as it had so many times before, that working with Martin was the only thing he would really miss.

He hung his jacket over the back of his chair, sat down, and pulled the typewriter over in front of him. He rolled in a sheet of paper and wrote:

> *Stockholm*
> *November 27, 1973*
> *To: National Police Administration*
> *Subject: Resignation*

285

He rested his chin in his hand and stared out the window. As always at this hour, the expressway was crowded with cars, three lanes of them rolling in toward the center of town. Kollberg gazed out at the apparently inexhaustible flow of shiny private automobiles. There probably wasn't another country in the world, he thought, where drivers were so particular about their vehicles as they were in Sweden. There was a constant washing and polishing, and a scratch in the paint or a dent in the coachwork was regarded as catastrophic and called for immediate repairs. The automobile was an important status symbol, and in order to keep up with the neighbors, a lot of people traded in their cars unnecessarily and more often then they could afford to.

He suddenly thought of something, ripped the paper out of the typewriter, and tore it into little pieces which he dropped in the wastebasket. He wriggled into his jacket and walked quickly out to the elevator. He pressed the button for the garage where he'd left his car—seven years old, battered, covered with *skånsk* mud—but he changed his mind and stopped the elevator at the street level.

Midsommarkransen wasn't far away. He could almost have watched yesterday's fiasco from his window.

It stood in the parking area behind the apartment house where Maggie lived. A beige Volvo, with a different license number from the one reported by Skacke and the gas station owner in Katrineholm. But they were the old plates that were easy to put together by hand, and Kollberg had no doubt it was the right car. He jotted down the number and walked back to Södra Police Station.

When he was seated at his desk again, he pushed aside the typewriter and pulled over the telephone.

The Department of Motor Vehicle Registration gave him a prompt reply. The number did not exist, and never had existed. The county letter was AB, which meant the City of Stockholm, but the number that followed was higher than the registry had ever reached. For that matter, the number never would exist, because all of the vehicles in Stockholm had already been assigned one of the new national license numbers.

"Thanks," said Kollberg.

He was a little surprised to be given such quick and definite confirmation of the fact that the Volvo had false plates. As a rule, he didn't have much faith in computers.

Spurred on by his success, he lifted the receiver again, dialed police headquarters in Malmö, and asked to speak to Benny Skacke.

"Inspector Skacke," said a self-assured voice.

The title was so new that he couldn't disguise his pride.

"Hi, Benny," Kollberg said. "I expect you're just sitting there twiddling your thumbs as usual, so I thought I'd give you an assignment."

"Well, as a matter of fact, I'm sitting here writing a report. But it can wait. What's it about?"

He was sounding a bit less cocky now.

"Can you get me the chassis and engine block numbers on that Volvo that was stolen in Vellinge? Quickly?"

"Sure. Right away. Hold on a second."

Kollberg waited. He could hear Skacke rummaging through his desk—drawers slamming, papers rustling, Skacke mumbling—and finally Skacke's voice back on the line.

"Here they are. Shall I read them to you?"

"Jesus Christ," Kollberg said. "Why do you think I asked?"

He noted down the numbers as Skacke gave them to him.

"Are you going to be there for another hour?" he said.

"Yes. I've got to finish this report. It'll probably take all morning. Why?"

"I'll call you back," Kollberg said. "There's a couple of other things I want to talk to you about, but I don't have time right now. So long."

Kollberg didn't hang up the phone, just broke the connection, waited for another dial tone and dialed another number.

Everyone seemed to be at their jobs and on their toes this morning. The head of the State Crime Lab answered on the first ring.

"Crime Lab. Hjelm."

"Kollberg. Hi."

"Hi. What do you want now?"

Hjelm's tone of voice was resigned. It implied that Kollberg did nothing but call him and disturb him and make his life miserable. As far as Kollberg could remember, he hadn't spoken to the man for weeks. But Oskar Hjelm was a misanthrope who felt he was taken for granted by the ungrateful detectives who overwhelmed him with impossible problems. He almost always managed to solve these problems, however, and he was esteemed for the clever professional he was—scrupulous, persistent, and ingenious. But not everyone knew enough to show their appreciation, or to take the time to listen to his unnecessarily involved and, for the layman, incomprehensible descriptions of the fine points of laboratory analysis and technical investigation.

Kollberg knew exactly how he ought to be handled—with gentle persuasion and flattery—but he lacked the patience for cajolery, and flattery wasn't in his line.

"Well, it's about a car," he said.

"I see," Hjelm sighed. "In what condition? Totaled? Incinerated? Submerged?"

"No, none of those. It's a perfectly ordinary car, parked at Midsommarkransen."

"And what do you want me to do with it?"

"It's a beige Volvo. I'll give you the address and the license number, plus the chasis and engine block numbers. Have you got a pen?"

"Yes, I have a pen," said Hjelm impatiently. "And I also have a piece of paper. Well?"

Kollberg gave him the information and waited for him to write it down before he went on.

"Could you send over one of your boys to see if those numbers check? On the chassis and the engine block? If they do, have him take it out to Solna. And if they don't, have him call me immediately."

Hjelm didn't answer right away. And when he did he was annoyed.

"Why don't you go over there yourself and have a look? Or send somebdy? This address you gave me is right across the street from you! If it isn't the right car, then one of my people will have come all the way in from Solna for nothing. We've got a full load of work out here . . ."

Kollberg interrupted his tirade.

"In the first place, I'm quite sure it is the right car, and in the second place, I have no one to send, and in the third place, the car is your department because it's going to have a complete lab examination."

He caught his breath and went on in a gentler tone of voice.

"Besides, you and your people know how to handle things like this. We'd only mess it up and leave fingerprints all over the place and destroy important evidence. We're all better off if you take charge of it right from the start. You people are experts."

He was sure he sounded false and insincere.

"Yes, well, then I guess I'd better send someone," Hjelm said. "What exactly is it you want us to find out? Any special tests you want performed?"

"Just move it out there and let it stand for the time being," Kollberg said. "Martin will call you later and tell you what he wants."

"Okay," Hjelm said. "I'll send a man over right away. Although I don't really have anyone I can do without. And Lord knows where we'll find a place to put it. We've got five cars out here now that we have to work on. And there's all sorts of trash piled up in the lab that we've got to analyze. Do you know what we got in yesterday, for example?"

"No," said Kollberg feebly.

"Two barrels of herring in brine. Someone had split the fish open and sewed them up again, and every little herring stomach contained a plastic bag of morphine. Do you know what a person smells like when he's been up to his elbows in herring brine all night?"

"No, but I can imagine," said Kollberg laughing. "What did you do with the fish? I can give you a terrific recipe for fried herring with onion sauce."

"Yes, very funny I'm sure," said Hjelm in an injured tone. "We manage to control our laughter in this job."

He hung up the phone in Kollberg's ear, but Kollberg was still chuckling as he put down the receiver.

The thought of fried herring made him hungry, in spite of the fact that he had just had breakfast.

He sat and drew curlicues on the pad in front of him while he thought about his next call. Then he picked up the phone again.

"Inspector Skacke."

"Hi, Benny, it's me again. Finish your report?"

"No, not quite. What was it you wanted to talk about?"

"That Volvo that Casparsson stole in Vellinge," Kollberg said. "Have you got the theft report handy?"

"I've got it right here in my drawer," Skacke said. "Wait a minute."

He didn't put the receiver down this time, and it took him only thirty seconds to find the form.

"Yes," he said. "Here it is."

"Good," Kollberg said. "What's the owner's name?"

It seemed like an eternity before Benny Skacke answered.

"Clark Evert Sundström."

That's the right answer, Kollberg thought.

He was not the least bit surprised, but felt the familiar thrill of satisfaction at having figured things out correctly. Plus, maybe, a quiver of something that was more deeply rooted in human nature—the hunting instinct, the smell of prey.

That is something of the red fox still within you—and something of the hare, he thought. Ekelöf. Later, when I've got the time, I'll try to remember the whole thing. It's a marvelous poem.

"Lennart?"

"Yes, I heard you. Clark Evert Sundström. But he wasn't the one who reported it missing, was he?"

"No, that was his wife. Her name is Cecilia Sundström."

"Weren't you out at their place in Vellinge?"

"Yes, they've got a house out there. The car was in the garage, which is open toward the front yard. And there aren't any doors, so Caspar could see it from the road."

"Did you meet both of the Sundströms when you were there?" Kollberg asked.

"Yes, but I mostly talked to her. He didn't say much."

"What did he look like?"

"In his fifties. Five feet seven, I'd guess. Thin—not wiry, but rather as if he'd been sick. Blond hair, starting to go gray. Or white, almost. He was wearing glasses with dark rims."

"What does he do?"

"Manufacturer."

"What kind of manufacturer?"

"I don't know," Skacke said. "That's what his wife listed as his occupation when she made the report."

"Did he give you any reason why he hadn't reported it earlier?"

"No, but his wife told me she wanted to go to the police on Monday morning, but that he'd said the car would turn up and they should wait and see."

"Can you remember anything else that was said? Did they talk to each other at all?"

"Well, it was mostly about the car. I asked them if they'd seen or heard anything that Sunday morning, but they hadn't. I really only talked to the wife. She let me in, and then we stood in the hall. He just came out for a minute and said all he knew was that the car was gone when he went outside sometime around noon."

Kollberg looked at the curlicues on his scratch pad. He had tried to draw some sort of a map of Skåne, with little dots for Vellinge, Anderslöv, Malmö, and Trelleborg.

"I got the impression he worked in Trelleborg," said Skacke uncertainly. "I think his wife said something about it."

Kollberg drew a line between Anderslöv and Trelleborg, and another from Trelleborg to Vellinge.

He made a triangle, with its apex at Trelleborg, and its long base the line from Vellinge to Anderslöv in the north.

"Good, Benny," Kollberg said. "Excellent."

"Have you found the car?" Skacke said. "I heard he got away. Caspar, I mean."

"Yes, he did," said Kollberg dryly. "And I think we've found the car. Have you spoken to Martin lately?"

"No," said Skacke. "It's been a while. But he's still in Anderslöv, isn't he?"

"Right," said Kollberg. "And as soon as I hang up, I want you to call Martin and tell him everything you've just told me. About this Clark Evert Sundström and what he looked like and all that. And then tell him he can call Hjelm at the Crime Lab and find out if he's got the car yet. Do it now, right away."

"Okay," Skacke said. "What's the story on this guy Sundström? Has he done something?"

"We'll see," Kollberg said. "You just talk to Martin. He'll make the decisions. Got it? And then finish your report. And if anything comes up, I'll be right here in my office. I've got a kind of report to write myself, as it happens. Say hello to Martin for me. So long."

"Goodbye."

Kollberg made no further calls. He pushed the phone to one side and put away the scratch pad with the inverted triangle and the wavy lines depicting Skåne.

Then he pulled over the typewriter, rolled in a piece of paper, and wrote:

28.

Lennart Kollberg typed slowly, with two fingers. He knew that this letter, which he had thought about for such a long time, had to be considered a formal document, but he didn't want to make it too long-winded. And as far as possible, he tried to keep the tone of it informal.

After long and careful consideration, I have decided to leave the police force. My reasons are of a personal nature, and yet I would like to try and explain them briefly. Right at the outset, I feel compelled to point out that my decision is in no way a political action, even though many people will see it in that light. To be sure, the police establishment has been increasingly politicized over the last few years, and the police force itself has been exploited for political purposes more and more often. I have observed these developments with considerable alarm, even though I, personally, have managed to avoid coming into contact with this aspect of police activity almost completely.

Nevertheless, during the twenty-seven years that I have served on the force, its activities, structure, and organization have altered in a manner that has convinced me that I am no longer suited to being a policeman—assuming that I ever was. Above all, I find that I cannot feel any sense of solidarity with the kind of organization the police department has become. Consequently, it seems to me that my own best interests and those of the department would be best served by my resignation.

The question of whether or not the individual policeman should be armed has long struck me as an especially important one. For many years, I have held to the opinion that, under normal circumstances, policemen should not be armed. This applies to uniformed patrolmen as well as to plainclothesmen.

The great increase in the number of violent crimes over the last decade is, in my opinion, largely due to the fact that policemen invariably carry firearms. It is a known fact, and can be demonstrated with statistics from many other countries, that the incidence of violent crime immediately increases when the police force sets, as it were, a bad example. The events of recent months make it seem more obvious than ever that we can expect our situation to deteriorate even further with regard to violence. This is especially true of Stockholm and other large cities.

The Police Academy devotes far too little time to providing instruction in psychology. As a result, policemen lack what is perhaps the most important prerequisite for success in their profession.

The fact that we nevertheless have so-called police psychologists, who are sent out in difficult situations to try and bring the criminal to reason, seems to me to be nothing but an admission of defeat. For psychology cannot be used to camouflage violence. To my way of thinking, this must be one of the simplest and most obvious tenets of the science of psychology.

I would like to emphasize in this connection that

for many years I myself have never carried a gun. This has often been a direct violation of orders, but I have never had the feeling that it hampered me in the execution of my duties. On the contrary, being forced to carry arms might have had a strong inhibiting effect, it could have caused accidents, and it could well have led to even poorer contact with persons outside the police force.

What I am trying to say, essentially, is that I cannot continue to be a policeman. It is possible that every society has the police force it deserves, but that is not a thesis I intend to try and develop, at least not here and now.

I find myself confronted with a *fait accompli*. When I joined the police department, I could not have imagined that this profession would undergo the transformation or take on the direction that it has.

After twenty-seven years of service, I find that I am so ashamed of my profession that my conscience will no longer permit me to practice it.

Kollberg rolled the paper up an inch or two and read what he had written. Once he had started, he had the feeling he could have gone on indefinitely.

But this would have to do.

He added two more lines:

I therefore request that this resignation be accepted effective immediately.

Sten Lennart Kollberg.

He folded the sheets of paper and stuffed them into an official plain brown envelope.

Wrote the address.

Threw the letter into his Out basket.

Then he stood up and looked around the room.

Closed the door behind him and went.
Home.

29.

The cabin in the Haninge Woods near Dalarö
was a good hideout. It was so isolated that no one was
likely to come upon it by accident, and it was outfitted
in a way that showed Lindberg The Breadman had no
illusions. There was food and drink, weapons and ammunition, fuel and clothing, cigarettes and piles of old
magazines—in short, everything that might be needed
for a lengthy period of seclusion. It might even be possible to withstand a not overly ambitious siege. Hope-
fully, of course, nothing of that kind would occur.

When the police stormed the apartment at Midsommarkransen, Caspar and The Breadman had escaped
almost too easily. This cabin, on the other hand, was
their very last resort.

If they were trapped out here, there were by and
large only two choices—to surrender or to fight.

The third possibility—another escape—was not even
worth considering. For it would be a solitary flight, on
foot, and straight out into the forest. The rapidly approaching winter made this prospect less than inviting,
especially since it would entail leaving a large stash of
valuable stolen goods behind.

The Breadman was no great luminary in the criminal
sky, and his plans were of the simplest possible nature.
He had buried valuables and money in and around the

cabin. Now he could hope only that the police manhunt would quieten down enough for the two of them to venture back into Stockholm. Once there, they could quickly convert their goods into cash, buy false papers, and flee the country.

Ronnie Casparsson had no plans at all. He knew only that the police were hunting him with every means at their disposal for a crime he had not actually committed. As long as he stuck with The Breadman, at least he wasn't alone. Besides, The Breadman took an optimistic and uncomplicated view of life. When he said their chances of getting away were good, he honestly meant it, and Caspar believed him. The reason Lindberg had not retired to the cabin earlier was simply that he didn't want to be alone.

Now there were two of them, which immediately made everything more cheerful.

For Caspar, there was really only one serious problem, namely, that The Breadman always got caught. But they both reasoned that sooner or later the wind had to change and that all they needed was a little luck. Over the past few years, quite a few habitual criminals had succeeded in getting out of the country after successful jobs and had managed to disappear somewhere in Western civilization with their money and their health intact.

The cabin had a number of advantages. It lay in the middle of a clearing with an uninterrupted view in all directions. There were only two outbuildings—an outdoor toilet and an old ramshackle barn where they had hidden The Breadman's car.

The cabin itself was in good condition. It was an ordinary Swedish crofter's cottage with three windows in front, one in the back, and one on either side. The lower floor consisted of one main room with a kitchen and a bedroom opening off of it. There was only one road to the cabin, and it led directly into the front yard and up toward the little porch in the middle of the house.

The very first day, The Breadman carefully inspected their weapons. They had two Army model submachine guns and three automatic pistols of varying make and caliber. They also had plenty of ammunition, including two whole boxes for the tommy guns.

"The way the police are these days," said The Breadman, "there's only one thing to do in the unlikely event they find us and surround us out here."

"What?"

"Shoot our way out, of course. If we hit a cop or two, it won't change our situation one little bit. It'll be hard for them to get us unless they set fire to the house. And if they try tear gas, I've got some gas masks over there in that trunk."

"I don't even know how one of these things works," said Caspar, picking up one of the submachine guns.

"It takes about ten minutes to learn," The Breadman said.

He was right. A quick ten-minute course was all he needed. They tested all their weapons the next morning with excellent results. The house was so isolated they didn't even have to worry about the noise.

"So now there's nothing to do but wait," The Breadman said. "If they come, we'll give them a warm welcome. But I don't think they will. Where shall we celebrate Christmas? On the Canary Islands or somewhere in Africa?"

Ronnie Casparsson had never thought as far ahead as Christmas, and didn't do so now. Christmas was still several weeks away. But he did think about what it would be like to shoot at someone. It was hard to imagine that it would be difficult or strange to put a couple of bullets into one of those bloodthirsty sons of bitches.

From what he'd seen of the police in raids and street fights, it was hard to think of them as humans or even as distinct individuals.

They listened to the radio constantly, but it didn't have much to tell them that was new. The hunt for the cop-killer continued with unabated energy. It was now known for certain that he was in Stockholm, and the tactical command considered an arrest imminent.

It was a completely unpredictable factor that did them in.

Maggie.

If Maggie hadn't been injured, she would have been no danger to them whatsoever, for she was a good, loyal friend, who knew how to keep her mouth shut.

But the fact was that she had been injured and was now at Söder Hospital.

The dog bites were not critical, but they did have a wicked look to them, as the doctors put it.

They operated, and following surgery she developed a high fever and became delirious.

Maggie talked a great deal in her delirium. She didn't know for sure where she was, but she did have the feeling she was talking to someone she knew, or at least to someone who was interested and attentive.

And true enough, at the head of her bed sat a person equipped with a tape recorder.

This person was Einar Rönn.

Rönn asked no questions. He merely listened and put Maggie's chatter on tape.

He realized immediately that he had been given some important information, but he didn't know exactly what he ought to do with it.

After thinking it over for a few minutes, he searched

out a telephone and called Gunvald Larsson in his office at police headquarters on Kungsholmsgatan.

"Yes, Larsson here. What do you want?"

He could tell right away that Gunvald Larsson was not alone. He sounded brusque and irritable.

"Well, this girl over here is delirious. She just told me where The Breadman and Caspar are holed up. In a cabin out toward Dalarö."

"Did you get any details?"

"Yes, a very precise description of how to get there. If you gave me a map I could probably point to the house."

Gunvald Larsson was silent for a long moment before he answered.

"This is a very complicated, technical decision," he said cryptically. "Are you armed?"

"No."

There was another pause.

"Don't we have to tell Malm?" Rönn said.

"Yes, you must definitely do that," said Gunvald Larsson. "Naturally."

And then he added, in a lower voice:

"But not until you see my car drive up outside the door. Do it then. Quick as hell."

"Okay," Rönn said.

He went down to the huge hospital lobby and took up his post by a coin telephone.

He did not have to wait more than ten minutes before he saw Gunvald Larsson drive up in front of the entrance. He immediately called Kungsholmsgatan again, and after a brief delay he got through to Malm. Rönn reported exactly what Maggie had said.

"Splendid," Malm said. "You may return to your post."

Rönn walked straight out to Gunvald Larsson, who reached over and opened the door for him.

"There's a map and a pistol in the glove compartment," he said.

Rönn hesitated for a moment and then stuck the pistol inside the waistband of his trousers. Then he studied the map.

"Yes," he said. "Here's the house."

Gunvald Larsson examined the network of roads and then threw a glance at his watch.

"We'll have about an hour's start," he said. "Then Malm will move in with his so-called main force. That staff of his has planned for this very situation, God help us. He'll have a hundred men, two helicopters, and ten dogs. Besides that, he's requisitioned twenty huge shields of armor plate. It's to be a massacre."

"Do you think those boys will put up a fight?"

"Pretty likely," Gunvald Larsson said. "Lindberg's got nothing to lose, and this manhunt has probably driven Casparsson half out of his mind."

"I suppose," said Rönn philosophically, fingering his pistol.

He was no lover of violence.

"For that matter, I don't really give a damn what happens to Lindberg," Gunvald Larsson said. "The man's a professional criminal, on top of which he just recently committed murder. It's the boy I'm thinking of. So far, he hasn't shot or injured anyone, but if Malm has his way you can be damned sure he'll either get himself killed or else kill a couple of cops. So we've got to get there first and act quickly."

Acting quickly was one of Gunvald Larsson's specialties.

They drove south, through Handen and the latest ghastly high-rise development, called Bandhagen.

Ten minutes later they reached the turnoff, and ten minutes after that they saw the house. Gunvald Larsson stopped the car in the middle of the road, about 150 feet from the cabin.

He studied the situation for a moment.

"This will be hard but okay," he said. "We'll get out here and walk toward the house, on the left side of the road. If there's any shooting, we'll take cover behind the shithouse over there. I'll move right on around and try to take them from behind. You stay under cover and fire slowly toward the roof or the eaves to the left of the porch."

"I'm such a miserable shot," Rönn mumbled.

"You must be able to hit the house, for Christ's sake."

"Yes. At least I hope so."

"And Einar . . ."

"Yes?"

"Don't take any chances. If something goes wrong, stay under cover and wait for the great invasion."

Inside the cabin, The Breadman and Caspar had heard the car even before they saw it. Now they stood looking out the window.

"Funny car," The Breadman said. "Never seen one like that before."

"Maybe they're just out for a drive and got lost," Caspar said.

"It's not impossible," said The Breadman dryly.

He picked up one of the submachine guns and gave the other one to Caspar.

Rönn and Gunvald Larsson got out of the car and started toward the house.

The Breadman checked them out with his binoculars.

"Cops," he sighed. "I recognize both of them. Violence Division in Stockholm. But this'll be an easy match."

He knocked out the middle pane of the window with his elbow, took aim, and started firing.

Rönn and Gunvald Larsson heard the glass breaking and knew what it meant. They reacted quickly, ran to one side, and dove down behind the outhouse.

The salvo would have missed in any case, since The Breadman was unused to the weapon at such a distance and held it too high. But he seemed pleased nevertheless.

"Now we've got them right where we want them," he said. "All you've got to do, Caspar, is cover the rear."

Gunvald Larsson didn't stay behind the outhouse for more than a few seconds. He crawled on under the cover of some low blackberry bushes.

Rönn was well protected behind the stone foundation of the privy. He stuck out his pistol and one eye and fired off two shots toward the roof. The answer came at once. A longer salvo this time, and more accurate. Cascades of gravel flew up into his face.

Rönn fired again. He probably didn't hit the house, but it didn't matter much.

Gunvald Larsson had reached the cabin. He crept swiftly along the back wall, twisted around the corner and stopped below the side window. He rose to his knees and drew his Smith & Wesson 38 Master, which he carried clipped to his belt. Then he raised himself a little farther, held his pistol ready, and peered in. An empty kitchen. Ten feet away, a door standing ajar. Presumably Caspar and The Breadman were in the room beyond.

Gunvald Larsson waited for Rönn to fire again. He waited thirty seconds and then he heard Rönn's pistol bang twice.

The answering salvo came immediately and ended with a metallic click indicating that the magazine was empty.

Gunvald Larsson planted his feet and threw himself in through the window with his arms in front of his face for protection.

He landed on the floor amidst a shower of glass and wood, rolled over once, came to his feet, kicked open the door, and rushed into the adjoining room.

Lindberg had taken one step back from the window and was bent slightly forward, changing magazines. Ronnie Casparsson was standing in the corner behind him with another submachine gun in his hands.

"Shoot for Christ's sake, Caspar," The Breadman yelled. "There's only two of them. Shoot him!"

"That's enough, Lindberg," Gunvald Larsson said.

He took one step forward, raised his left hand, and struck The Breadman a heavy blow across the collarbone right next to his throat.

Lindberg let go of his weapon and dropped like a sack.

Gunvald Larsson stared at Ronnie Casparsson, who let the submachine gun slip from his grasp and covered his face with both hands.

That's right, said Gunvald Larsson to himself. That's the way.

Then he opened the front door.

"You can come out now, Einar," he called.

Rönn came into the cabin.

"Better put handcuffs on that character," Gunvald Larsson said, pointing to The Breadman with his foot.

Then he looked at Ronnie Casparsson.

"You don't need handcuffs, do you?"

Ronnie Casparsson shook his head. He was still holding his face in his hands.

Fifteen minutes later, they had their prisoners in the back seat and had driven up in front of the cabin to turn around. Lindberg had recovered from the blow and even regained some of his good spirits.

Just then a man in a sweatsuit came running into the yard. He was holding a compass in one hand and stared stupidly from the car to the house and back to the car.

"Sweet Jesus," said The Breadman. "A cop dressed up for orienteering. But why has he got a compass and no map?"

He laughed loudly.

Gunvald Larsson rolled down the window.

"Hello there," he said.

The man in the sweatsuit came over to the car.

"Have you got your two-way radio on you?"

"Yes, sir."

"Then inform Malm that he can call off the maneuver. All we need is someone to drive up and go through the house."

The man fussed with the radio for a long time.

"You're to turn over your prisoners to Division Commander Malm at his command post," he said. "Two thousand meters east of the second 'e' in 'East Haninge.'"

"Well, then, that's what we'll do," said Gunvald Larsson and rolled up his window again.

Malm looked very pleased as he stood there surrounded by subordinates.

"Smartly done, Larsson," he said. "I must admit. And why isn't Casparsson in handcuffs?"

"He doesn't need them."

"Nonsense. Put them on."

"Don't have any," Gunvald Larsson said.

And he and Rönn drove away.

306

"I hope the boy gets a good lawyer," said Gunvald Larsson after a while.

Rönn didn't answer. He changed the subject.

"Gunvald," he said, "your jacket's torn. It's cut."

"Yes, what a pain in the ass," said Gunvald Larsson joylessly.

30.

As soon as Martin Beck got the phone call from Benny Skacke, the rest of it went quickly.

After a preliminary search of the biege Volvo at the Crime Lab in Solna, Hjelm could report that a white cotton rag had been found in the trunk. The laboratory analysis showed this to contain nickel shavings of the same type as those in the rag found at the scene of the crime.

That same afternoon, there was a search of Clark Sundström's factory, which made machine parts and precision tools. Nickel was an essential element in several of these products, and particles of that metal were found in abundance on the premises. Furthermore, a cardboard box filled with white cotton rags containing nickel shavings was found in a corner of the factory where Clark Sundström usually parked his car.

A comparative study of handwriting showed, as anticipated, that the two letters found in Sigbrit Mård's night table had been written in Sundström's hand.

In his desk, they found a packet of envelopes of the same type used to send in the rent for the one-room apartment. The typewriter used to type the words *Rent. S. Jönsson* stood on the shelf beside the desk.

The Helsingborg Crime Lab had made a minute examination of the apartment that had been used as a love nest, and among other things, they had secured fingerprints.

With that, the evidence could definitely be said to link Clark Evert Sundström to the murder of Sigbrit Mård.

The factory was located in Trelleborg, but Cecilia Sundström had inherited the firm, and it still bore her father's name, which might explain why the industrious Trelleborg detectives had not succeeded in finding Clark Sundström. Technically, he was employed by his wife as factory manager.

Sundström was not in his office during the search of the factory on Tuesday afternoon. He had not been feeling well after lunch and had taken a taxi home.

Martin Beck wondered if he really was sick or if he had had a premonition of what was about to happen. Before any news of the decision to search the factory could reach Clark Sundström, Månsson sent two of his men to Vellinge to keep a discreet eye on the house.

By the time all the samples had been taken, analyzed, and compared, and enough evidence had been assembled to issue an arrest warrant, it was evening.

Martin Beck and Benny Skacke took the new expressway and arrived in Vellinge just before eight. First they searched out the two plainclothesmen, who had parked their car on a side road where they had a good view of the Sundström house without calling attention to themselves.

"He's still in the house," said one of them when Martin Beck walked over to their car.

"His wife went out and did some shopping about

five," the other one said. "But no one's left the place since then. The girls came home an hour ago."

The Sundström couple had two daughters, twelve and fourteen years old.

"Good," said Martin Beck. "For the time being, you wait here."

He went back to Skacke.

"Drive up to the gate and wait in the car," said Martin Beck. "I'll go in alone. But be ready—we don't know how he's going to react."

Skacke pulled up in front of the house, and Martin Beck walked through the broad wrought-iron gates. The gravel path leading up from the street was bordered by rosebushes, and directly in front of the front door lay a millstone that had been broken in half to form a semicircular step. He pressed the doorbell and heard the faint sound of two chimes ringing behind the massive oak door.

The woman who answered was almost as tall as Martin Beck. She was slender, or rather, thin—dry and bony as if there was simply no flesh beneath her very pale skin. The bridge of her nose was sharp and slightly curved, her cheekbones were high and prominent, and her face was covered with light-brown freckles. Her chestnut hair, though thick and wavy, was shot with gray. As far as he could see, she was wearing no make-up. Her lips were pale and thin, and there was something bitter about the line of her mouth. She had pretty eyes, with gray-green irises under heavy lids, and she raised her arched brows and looked at him questioningly.

"I am Detective Inspector Beck," said Martin Beck. "I am looking for Mr. Sundström."

"My husband isn't feeling well and has gone to bed to rest," she said. "What is it about?"

"I'm sorry to have to bother you at this time of day, but unfortunately it is necessary. And it's quite urgent, so if he isn't too ill . . ."

"Is it about the factory?" she asked.

"No, not directly," said Martin Beck.

He always disliked this situation. He knew very little about this woman. Perhaps she was not very happy with her existence, but she probably led a calm and normal family life. In a little while she would learn that she was married to a man who had murdered his mistress.

If only the people who murdered other people didn't have families, thought Martin Beck irrationally.

"It's a matter of a few questions that I have to discuss with your husband," he said. "So if . . ."

"Is it so important it can't wait until tomorrow?" she said.

"Yes, it is that important."

She opened the door the rest of the way and Martin Beck stepped into the front hall.

"Wait here for a moment, I'll tell him."

She walked up the stairs to the second floor. She held herself very straight.

Martin Beck could hear a TV from one of the rooms on the right side of the hall. He waited.

It was almost five minutes before Clark Sundström appeared. He was wearing dark-blue flannel trousers and a Shetland sweater of the same color. The shirt beneath the sweater was also blue and buttoned at the neck. His wife followed him down the stairs, and when they both stood in front of him, Martin Beck noticed that she was a head taller than her husband.

"Go in to the girls, Sissy," said Clark Sundström.

She gave him a searching and somewhat uneasy glance, but opened the door beside the stairs. The TV sound grew louder, but she immediately closed the door behind her again.

Clark Sundström fit the descriptions given by Folke Bengtsson and Skacke, but Martin Beck was struck by the look of tired resignation around his mouth and eyes. He might possibly have had a suntan when Folke Bengtsson saw him earlier that year, but now his skin was grayish-yellow and flaccid. He looked worn. But his hands were large and sunburned with long, sinewy fingers.

"Yes?" he said. "What's this all about?"

Martin Beck saw fear in the eyes behind the glasses. He couldn't disguise that.

"You know what this is all about," said Martin Beck.

The man shook his head, but small beads of perspiration appeared at his hairline and along his upper lip.

"Sigbrit Mård," said Martin Beck. Clark Sundström turned away and took a couple of steps toward the front door and then he stopped, with his back to Martin Beck.

"Can we go out in the yard and talk? I think I need some fresh air."

"Fine," said Martin Beck and waited while Clark Sundström put on his sheepskin coat.

They went out onto the front step, and Clark Sundström began to walk slowly toward the front gate with his hands in his pockets. Halfway down the gravel path, he stopped and looked up at the sky. The stars were out. He didn't say anything. Martin Beck stopped beside him.

"We have proof that you killed her," he said. "And we've seen the apartment in Trelleborg. I have a warrant for your arrest in my pocket."

Clark Sundström stood quite still.

"Proof?" he said after a while. "How can you have proof?"

"Among other things, we found a rag that we can trace to you. Why did you kill her?"

"I had to."

His voice sounded odd. Strained.

"Are you feeling all right?" said Martin Beck.

"No."

"Wouldn't it be just as well to come in to Malmö with us, and we could talk there?"

"My wife . . ."

The sentence was interrupted by an ugly whimpering sound from the man's throat. He clawed at his heart, staggered, doubled over, and fell headlong into the rosebushes.

Martin Beck stared at him.

Benny Skacke came running through the gate and helped him turn the man over on his back.

"Coronary thrombosis," Skacke said. "I've seen it before. I'll call an ambulance."

He ran back to the car, and Martin Beck could hear him talking on the radio.

At that moment, his wife came running out into the yard with her daughters at her heels. She must have seen what had happened through the window. She pushed Martin Beck aside, kneeled down beside her unconscious husband, and told the girls to go back in the house. They obeyed, but remained standing in the doorway, staring anxiously and uncomprehendingly at their parents and the two strange men in the garden.

The ambulance arrived seven minutes later.

Benny Skacke followed it closely all the way into Malmö General Hospital, and when it came to a stop outside the emergency room, he was only a few yards behind.

Martin Beck sat in the car and watched the attendents hurry in with the stretcher. Mrs. Sundström followed it in, and the doors slammed behind them.

"Aren't you going in?" Skacke said.

"Yes," said Martin Beck. "But there isn't any rush. They'll treat him for shock and massage his heart and put him in a respirator. If he makes it that far, he could recover pretty quickly. And if he doesn't . . ."

He sat silently and stared at the closed doors. After a while, the attendents came out with the rolling stretcher, pushed it back into the ambulance, and closed the doors. Then they climbed into the front seat and drove away.

Martin Beck straightened up.

"I'd better go in and see how they're coming along."

"Shall I go with you or shall I wait here?" Skacke asked.

Martin Beck opened the car door and stepped out. He leaned down toward Skacke.

"It's possible he'll come round and the doctors will let me talk to him. It would be nice to have a tape recorder."

Skacke turned the key in the ignition switch.

"I'll go get one right away," he said.

Martin Beck nodded, and Skacke drove away.

Clark Sundström had been taken to the intensive care unit, and Martin Beck could see his wife through the glass panel in the door to the waiting room. She was standing by the window with her back to the door, very straight and still.

Martin Beck waited in the corridor. A little while later, he heard the clapping of wooden shoes, and a woman in a white coat and jeans came toward him, but she turned and disappeared through a door before he had a chance to say anything. He walked over to the

313

door. There was a sign on it reading *Duty Office*, and he knocked and opened it without waiting for an answer.

The woman was standing by a desk shuffling through a stack of case reports. She found the paper she was looking for, wrote something on it, attached it to a clipboard, and put it down on a shelf behind her. Then she looked inquiringly at Martin Beck, and he showed her his identity card and stated his business.

"I can't tell you anything yet," she said. "He's being given heart massage right now. But you can wait here if you like."

She was young, with sprightly brown eyes and dark blond hair in a braid down her back.

"I'll see to it that you're kept informed," she said and hurried out of the room.

Martin Beck walked over and read the case report on the shelf. It was not about Clark Sundström.

There was a small device like a TV set on the wall, and a bright green dot was rushing across the screen from left to right. Halfway across, it bounced up with a short, high whistle. The green dot described a constant curve, and the whistling sound recurred with monotonous regularity. Someone's heart was beating normally. Martin Beck assumed that this was not Clark Sundström's electrocardiogram.

After an uneventful quarter of an hour, Martin Beck saw Skacke drive up outside. He went out and collected the tape recorder and told Skacke to go on home. He looked a little disappointed, as if he would rather have stayed, but Martin Beck had no need for him.

At ten-thirty, the woman with the braid came back. It seemed she was the resident on duty.

Sundström had survived the crisis, had regained consciousness, and, under the circumstances, his condition was good. He had talked to his wife for a few minutes, and she had left the hospital. He was now sleeping and couldn't be disturbed.

"But come back tomorrow and we'll see," she said.

Martin Beck explained the situation, and in the end she reluctantly agreed to let him talk to Clark Sundström as soon as he woke up. She showed him to an examination room where he could wait.

The room contained a cot covered with green vinyl, a stool, and a magazine rack with three religious periodicals that had been thumbed to pieces. Martin Beck put the tape recorder on the stool, lay down on the cot, and stared at the ceiling.

He thought about Clark Sundström and his wife. She had given him the impression of being a strong woman. Psychologically strong. Or maybe that was nothing but a practiced manner, or emotional reserve. He thought about Folke Bengtsson, but not for very long. Then he thought about Rhea, and after a while he went to sleep.

When the doctor woke him, it was five-thirty in the morning, and her brown eyes were no longer so sprightly.

"He's awake now," she said. "But keep it as short as you can."

Clark Sundström was lying on his back staring toward the door. A young man in a white coat and white trousers sat on a chair at the foot of the bed biting his nails. He stood up when Martin Beck came in.

"I'll go get a cup of coffee," he said. "Push the buzzer before you go."

On a shelf over the head of the bed was a device like the one Martin Beck had seen in the Duty Office. Three thin wires of three different colors connected the apparatus to round electrodes that were attached to Clark Sundström's chest with strips of tape. The green dot registered the electrocardiogram, but the whistling sound was very faint.

"How do you feel?" said Martin Beck.

Clark Sundström plucked at the sheet.

"All right," he said. "I don't know. I don't remember what happened."

He was not wearing his glasses, and his face looked younger and softer without them.

"Do you remember me?" said Martin Beck.

"I remember your coming, and then we went out in the yard. Nothing else."

Martin Beck pulled out a low stool that was under the bed, put the tape recorder on it, and fastened the microphone to the edge of the sheet. He moved up the chair and sat down.

"Do you remember what we were talking about?" he asked.

Clark Sundström nodded.

"Sigbrit Mård," said Martin Beck. "Why did you kill her?"

The man in the bed closed his eyes for a few moments and then opened them again.

"I'm sick. I'd rather not talk about it."

"How did you get to know her?"

"You mean how did we meet?"

"Yes. Tell me."

"We met at the pastry shop where she worked. I used to go there sometimes in those days for a cup of coffee."

"When was this?"

"Three, four years ago."

"Yes? And then?"

"I saw her in town one day and asked her if she wanted a ride. She asked me if I could drive her home to Domme, because she'd just left her car at the garage. I drove her home. Later on, she told me she just made

316

up that story about the car, because she wanted to get to know me. She left her car in Trelleborg and took the bus in the next day."

"Did you go into the house when you drove her home?" asked Martin Beck.

"Yes, and we went to bed together too. That's what you wanted to know."

Clark Sundström looked at Martin Beck for a moment, then turned his head and looked out the window.

"Did you go on meeting at her place?"

"A few times, yes. But it was too risky. I was married, after all, and even if she was divorced, people gossip so much. Especially out there where she lived. So I rented a little place in Trelleborg where we could meet."

"Were you in love with her?"

Clark Sundström snorted.

"In love? No. But she sure as hell turned me on. I wanted to go to bed with her. My wife wasn't very interested any more. She never was, for that matter. I sort of felt I had the right to have a mistress. But my wife would go crazy if she found out. She'd want a divorce on the spot."

"Was Sigbrit Mård in love with you?"

"I guess she was. At first I thought she just wanted someone to go to bed with, like me, but then she started talking about how we ought to move in together."

"When did she start talking about that?"

"Last spring. Everything was going along fine. We'd meet once a week at the apartment. And then all of a sudden she starts in about how we ought to get married and how she wants to have kids. The fact that I was already married and had children didn't seem to make any difference to her. All I had to do was get a divorce, she said."

"You didn't want that?"

"Christ, no. In the first place, we've got a pretty good life, my wife and I and the kids. And in the second place, it would have been a financial catastrophe. The house we live in belongs to my wife, and the factory belongs to her too, even if I do run it. If we got divorced, I'd be penniless and out of a job. I'm fifty-two years old. I've worked like a dog for that factory. Sigbrit was crazy to think I'd leave all that for her sake. She was after money too."

Talking had put a little color back in his cheeks, and his eyes were no longer so exhausted.

"Besides, I was beginning to get tired of her," he said. "Even last winter I was trying to think of some nice way to get out of it."

The way you chose was not especially nice, thought Martin Beck.

"What happened? Did she get too troublesome?"

"She started threatening me," Sundström said. "She said she was going to talk to my wife. I had to promise her I'd mention the divorce myself, which, of course, I never meant to do. I didn't know what to do. I lay awake nights . . ."

He stopped talking and put his arm over his eyes.

"Couldn't you have told your wife . . . ?"

"No, that was out of the question. She could never accept or forgive a thing like that. She's incredibly principled about that sort of thing, and rigidly moralistic. And she's terribly afraid of what people will say too, and very careful about keeping up appearances. No, there was only . . . There wasn't any way out."

"But you finally did find a way out," said Martin Beck after a moment of silence. "Though not an especially good one."

"I worried about it until I thought I'd lose my mind.

In the end I was desperate. I just wanted to be rid of her and her nagging and her threats. Yes, I thought of a hundred different ways. And then I thought of that sex lunatic who lived next door, and I figured if I make it look like a sex murder, everyone would think it was him."

He looked at Martin Beck—a quick, fleeting glance —and there was something almost triumphant in his voice.

"And that is what you thought, isn't it?"

"Weren't you afraid that an innocent man would be convicted for something you'd done?"

"He wasn't innocent. He'd already killed one person, and they shouldn't have let him out anyway. No, I didn't worry about that."

"How did you do it?"

"I picked her up in my car as she was waiting for the bus. I knew she had her car in being serviced. Then I drove to this place I'd picked out earlier. She thought we were going to make love. We used to do that sometimes, outdoors, in the summer."

He suddenly stared at Martin Beck, and his eyes went rigid. His whole face altered. His mouth fell open, his lips tightened across his teeth, and there was a rattling in his throat. He raised his left hand, and Martin Beck took his wrist and stood up. The hand clasped his hand convulsively, and the man's eyes opened wide and stared fixedly at the spot where Martin Beck's face had been. Martin Beck glanced up and saw the bright green dot moving slowly across the screen in a straight line. The device was giving off a faint, steady whistling sound.

Martin Beck felt the hand he was holding relax, and he put it on the cover and rang the buzzer before running out into the corridor.

Within a minute, the room was full of people in white coats. Before the door closed, he saw something that looked like a tabletop being shoved in under the lifeless body.

He waited outside the door. After a while it opened, and someone handed him the tape recorder.

He opened his mouth to say something, but the man in white shook his head.

"I don't think we're going to pull him through this time," he said.

The door closed again, and Martin Beck was left standing there with his tape recorder. He rolled up the microphone cord and stuffed it into his pocket. The arrest warrant was in there already, neatly typed, folded, and unused.

Nor would he have any use for it. Forty-five minutes later, a doctor came in to him in the waiting room and informed him that they had not been able to save Clark Sundström's life. The second blood clot had entered the heart directly and stopped there.

Martin Beck went to the police building on Davidshall Square and left the tape for Per Månsson, along with instructions for closing the case.

Then he took a taxi to Anderslöv.

The fog lay thick and silver gray across the plain. Visibility was only a few yards, and to the side he could see nothing but the shoulder and the ditch, with dry clumps of yellow grass and occasional patches of snow. If he hadn't seen this countryside before in clear weather, he would have no idea what was hidden in the fog. But he had seen the plain and knew what it was like. Not flat and monotonous the way it looked from an airplane, but gently rolling, with fields of beets and hay, pastures with rows of naked, straggling willows, small whitewashed churches, and farms surrounded by enormous elms and beeches. He had also seen the sky over the plain on a clear day, as high and wide as he had otherwise seen it only above the sea, or with flying clouds that threw fleeting shadows across the bright, open landscape. But now the fog was like a wall on both sides of the road, and the journey through the gray mist had an element of timelessness and unreality.

They passed the side road to Domme, but he couldn't see the houses up on the hill.

Allwright was sitting at his desk in his office, drinking tea and glancing through a pile of stenciled notices. Timmy lay stretched out across his feet under the desk. Martin Beck sank down in the visitor's chair, and Timmy gave him his usual hearty welcome. Martin Beck pushed the dog away and wiped off his face. Allwright put the packet of papers to one side and looked at him.

"Tired?" he said.

"Yes."

"Tea?"

"Yes, thanks."

Allwright went out and came back with a porcelain mug, which he filled with tea from the pot.

"Are you going home now?" he asked.

Martin Beck nodded.

"My plane leaves in two hours," he said. "If it takes off at all in this fog."

"We'll call in an hour and find out. The fog may lift. Have you still got your room at the inn?"

"Yes," said Martin Beck. "I came directly here."

"Why don't you go lie down and get some sleep. I'll wake you when it's time to leave."

Martin Beck nodded. He was really very tired.

He packed his few things and lay down on the bed and fell asleep almost instantly. Before he went to sleep it occurred to him that he ought to call Rhea.

He woke up as Herrgott Allwright banged on the door and came into his room. He looked at the clock and discovered to his amazement that he had slept for over three hours.

"The fog's lifting," Allwright said. "They think they can take off in forty-five minutes. I didn't want to wake you up unnecessarily. But we've got to go now."

They got into the car and headed for Sturup.

"Folke's back at home," Allwright said. "I drove by Domme half an hour ago, and he was hard at work fixing his hen house."

"What will happen to Sigbrit Mård's house?" said Martin Beck. "She didn't have any relatives, did she?"

"No. There'll be an auction, I suppose. You're not thinking of moving down here, are you?"

Allwright looked at Martin Beck and laughed.

"But you can't bring National Homicide with you," he said.

The sun was beginning to break through the fog, and at the airport they were assured that the plane would take off soon. Martin Beck checked his bag and walked back out to the car with Allwright. He leaned into the back seat and scratched Timmy behind one ear. Then he clapped Allwright on the shoulder.

"Thanks for everything," he said.

"You'll be back, I hope," said Allwright. "Unofficially, I mean. I'm not going to put up with any more murders in this district. Why don't you come down on your vacation?"

"Maybe I will," said Martin Beck. "So long."

Allwright climbed into his car.

"We could go pheasant hunting," he said and winked.

Martin Beck stood and watched the red car drive away. Then he walked into the airport building and called Rhea Nielsen.

"I'll be home in a couple of hours," he said.

"Then I'll go over to your place now," she said. "And fix dinner. You'll want to eat?"

"Sure will."

"I've invented something new," she said. "Sort of a stew. And I'll pick up some wine on the way."

"Good. I've missed you."

"And I've missed you. Hurry."

A little while later he was in the air.

The plane made a wide sweep, and the plains of Skåne lay beneath him in the sunshine, while off to the south he could see the ocean, blue and sparkling. Then his view disappeared as the plane climbed into a bank of clouds and headed north.

He was on his way home.

And there was someone waiting for him.

About the Authors

Maj Sjöwall and Per Wahlöö have been called "the reigning king and queen of mystery fiction" by *The National Observer*. *Cop Killer* is the ninth in their well-known Martin Beck series, which includes the book from which the film *The Laughing Policeman* was made.

VINTAGE FICTION, POETRY, AND PLAYS

VINTAGE CRITICISM: LITERATURE, MUSIC, AND ART